BAKING ME CRAZY

DONNER BAKERY BOOK #1

KARLA SORENSEN

WWW.SMARTYPANTSROMANCE.COM

COPYRIGHT

This book is a work of fiction. Names, characters, places, rants, facts, contrivances, and incidents are either the product of the author's questionable imagination or are used factitiously. Any resemblance to actual persons, living or dead or undead, events, locales is entirely coincidental if not somewhat disturbing/concerning.

PRINT EDITION
978-1-949202-15-1

DEDICATION

To my mom, the biggest cheerleader in my life.

AUTHOR'S NOTE

Approaching the character of Joss, it was very important to both me and Penny to make sure that she was honestly written and an accurate reflection what life might be like for a young woman living with Transverse Myelitis. I could probably fill an entire chapter talking about the research that took over my life while I was working on this book, the women who inspired Joss and what she's physically capable of, and how she lives her life. I could fill another chapter talking about Brittany, the amazing young woman who offered to be my sensitivity reader for Baking Me Crazy. Because of Brittany, and our conversations, emails and online chats, I changed the reason that Joss is in a wheelchair. I could talk to you about Steph, a wonderful, kind blogger, who took the time to make sure that I was telling Joss' story in a way that respected her own journey.

Joss is a fictional individual that is directly inspired by a couple different women, and that inspiration plays out in her emotions, her personality, and her physical capabilities. And because she is an individual, it's impossible for Joss to fully encompass or represent everyone's experience. If there are errors in wording, or phrasing, those errors are mine alone, and in no way reflective of the people who shared their story with me.

I hope you love her half as much as I do.

For more information on Transverse Myelitis, please visit myelitis.org

PROLOGUE

LEVI

Five years earlier

U ntil the day I finally spoke to Jocelyn Abernathy, I never really believed in the Buchanan curse. I made it to the ripe age of eighteen years and three days old before it finally got hold of me. I'd heard my father talk about meeting my mom when he was fifteen, and how it felt like someone grabbed his heart and said, *hey, look at that one, we like that one.* My middle brother told me that when he met Sylvia—both of them sixteen—his brain short-circuited, and it took him two months to be able to make intelligible conversation with her.

As far back as my great-great-great-grandfather, it's been said that Buchanan men fall in love only once, and they fall in love—real, true love—the moment they meet the one. And once a Buchanan found The One, that was it. Nothing would come close, no one else would suffice, and you'd lay your heart out on the train tracks before walking away.

The day I met Jocelyn Abernathy, it was her hair that caught my notice first. It sprang out of the top of her head like someone shook up a box of wound-up, champagne-colored springs and then set them loose. It was so crazy, so wildly overwhelming, that her bright blue eyes and high cheekbones were a very distant second and third.

Of the players on the team I was assistant coaching, she was the fastest, had the most natural talent—her three-point shots were so beautiful, I almost cried when I watched her run drills—but she was also the quietest. It took two weeks of practice before I even got the chance to talk to her.

Every time I saw her use deft, strong movements to propel her wheelchair forward, blond curls bouncing wildly when she spun around to steal the ball during practice or when she'd ram into the side of someone else's chair to try to snag a rebound, I got this persistent tug in my head.

You know when you woke up in the middle of the night and realized you forgot to do something? It was like that. But the thing I was forgetting felt critical. Forgetting your mom's birthday. Forgetting to show up for a midterm. Forgetting to do your taxes—not that I was old enough to do my own taxes, but it was on that level.

That feeling like I hadn't done something vital was a churning in my stomach, all acid and knots, until practice on the first day of week three. Along the back of the gymnasium, part of the converted elementary school that we used as the Green Valley Community Center, I sat with my legs dangling over the edge of the wooden stage, looking at Coach's beat-up clipboard to prep for the drills he wanted to run that day.

Because the weather was still warm, and it made it easier for our players, we had the metal doors propped open with little plastic wedges. I heard her chair pop noisily over the small metal lip of the entrance when she came in.

"Abernathy, right?" I heard Earl ask from his perch at the long rectangular table. Earl and Merl, both in their nineties if they were a day, took it upon themselves to be the unofficial greeting committee for every activity held at the community center.

My head jerked up when I heard him say her last name.

She pulled her chair to a stop, twisting it as she did to face the two men. "Yes, sir."

He nodded, swiping at his forehead covered by the red hat I'd swear he'd had since the day he was born. "I knew your grandma. She was good people even though she always wore that ugly purple hat to church."

Merl leaned in, cupping a hand to his ear. "Which hat?"

"The purple one," Earl bellowed. "With the yellow bird on the front."

The two men nodded while Joss waited patiently. Or impatiently, as her fingers tapped rapidly along the top curve of her wheels.

"I can't say I've seen the hat," she said.

"It didn't come with the house?" Merl asked. "We heard she left you and your ma that house. Must have the hat in there somewhere."

"Not that I've seen. But I'll try to find it for you if you'd like."

Earl tapped the side of his red hat with a gnarled finger, chuckling hard enough to spur a coughing fit. "Sure, sure, you've got Ruby's sense of humor too."

I was far enough away that I had to strain to hear her response, but she delivered it with a slight smile on her face—her favored facial expression, as I'd learned.

"I'll have to take your word on that one. I didn't know her well, but I've heard a lot of good things about her."

Earl tsked, looking her up and down. "Shame about your legs."

I rolled my eyes because I'd heard them say it to just about every person on the team.

"Heard you got a cold," Merl said loudly, like she couldn't hear him. Everyone in the gym could hear him. "Got a cold and they just stopped working, isn't that right?"

She gave another small, tight smile. "Something like that."

It wasn't a cold, I wanted to shout. Not that I'd asked Coach. (I'd absolutely asked Coach.) Or googled her diagnoses, transverse myelitis—paralysis caused by an infection that triggers inflammation of the spinal cord—a dozen or so times in the past two weeks. (I'd googled it the night I saw her for the first time.)

Earl glanced at her over his thick glasses. "Looks like you must've been a helluva basketball player before it happened." He clucked his tongue. "Shame. A crying shame, that is."

Jocelyn laughed under her breath, snagging a basketball from the ground next to the table where they sat. It spun up on her finger like it was held by a string. "I still am, sir. It's the damnedest thing, but you don't actually need your legs to shoot perfect threes."

I barked out a laugh, and her head snapped in my direction.

She nodded at the men, then dribbled the ball next to her as she pushed toward me.

Her hair was braided tightly to her head today, and I wanted to undo it to see the curls spring out in every which direction. But as she got closer, her eyes trained on me for the first time, I stopped thinking about her hair. I didn't really think about the fact that Earl and Merl had their weathered hats bent in, watching us with unabashed interest.

All I could do was send up a fervent prayer that I wouldn't say something stupid, that I wouldn't stare, wouldn't stumble over my words, or come off like a crazy person who, after eighteen years and three days, finally believed in family curses and love at first sight.

As she came closer, it felt strange to sit up on the stage so far above her. I was no slouch at six feet one, but the raised platform kept us uncomfortably separated. I hopped off and wiped a hand down my gym shorts.

My heart stuttered once, twice, and then a third time for good measure when she continued to hold my gaze as she wheeled over the floor. She almost went past the hoop, only blinking away for a second to flick the ball up in a reverse layup that went in so smoothly the net barely moved.

The men cheered, and I smiled. Her eyes, back on me now and brighter than I realized, were center of the flame blue.

Ocean off the coast of Greece blue.

The curse is not real, the curse is not real, I chanted over and over in my head. *The curse is not real, and whether you want to admit it or not, you now currently reside in a city called Denial.*

"Saddle up, Coach," she said, tilting her pointed chin at a few extra wheelchairs lined up neatly against the stage.

"Saddle what?" were the first stunningly impressive words out of my mouth. Honestly, I was just glad I didn't croak like a bullfrog since my throat was as dry as scorched dirt.

An eyebrow over one of those bright blue eyes lifted slowly. "Yourself? I need to kick your ass in a game of one-on-one, so those old guys quit telling me how great I *must've been* every time they see me."

I blinked a few times, and she gave me a look that had me questioning whether I was imagining this entire exchange. I hoped I was because the times in my life that I'd choked talking to someone of the female gender was zero. Zero times.

And at my first opportunity to speak to this particular woman, I'd managed two words.

Saddle what?

Before I could try to redeem myself, she sighed and pushed one hand down on her right wheel, sending her gliding quickly over to where the ball landed. I blew out a quick breath and went to grab one of the spare chairs parked next to the bleachers. As per the rules, I strapped my legs together with a large, black elastic band and then rolled my neck back forth until I felt a pop at the base of my skull.

My chair was far more basic than her athletically designed one. Her wheels were thinner and wider, she had small wheels along the back for stability during play, and her backrest was only a few inches tall. While I got myself settled in the chair, she spun in tight circles, stopping and pivoting quickly to dribble the ball and flick it up to the net.

She wanted to prove something to Earl and Merl? No problem.

No really, it wasn't a problem. She was so much better than me in every single category, and not because of any attempt on my part to be chivalrous.

Without breaking a sweat, Jocelyn kicked the ever-loving shit out of me on that court. I saw her grin once—though it was gone as soon as I blinked—and it was because she hit a shot from so far past the key that I swore under my breath.

Great. The second thing I said to her was a curse word. My mother would rip my ear off.

Coach entered the gym, followed by a few of the players. They all watched from the sidelines as Jocelyn pummeled me into submission, shot after shot, until she rammed my chair hard enough that I pitched forward as she tried to snatch the ball after I bricked it off the rim.

"Oh, come on, that was a foul," I yelled out.

Jocelyn glanced over at Coach, who held his hands up. "Looked clean to me, Levi. Better hit some shots. You're embarrassing me out there."

Earl chuckled. Merl slapped his leg.

Jocelyn pursed her lips to keep from smiling, and I felt it again.

A tug. A reminder. Someone poking me in the back to get me going in the right direction.

Do something. You're not doing what you're supposed to be doing.

I held up a hand to pause the play even though there was no earthly way I could catch up to her. She stopped moving and set the ball in her lap.

"Do you give up?" she asked.

Under my breath, I laughed, running a hand through my sweat-soaked hair. "I have a strong sense of self-preservation, so yes, I concede."

Jocelyn tossed me the ball, and I caught it. "Good game."

I raised an eyebrow at her, which made her grin again. It was another quick one, just a hint of her full smile. The words were out of my mouth before I could think twice.

"Would you like to go out to dinner with me?"

Her face froze, the seemingly endless confidence I'd seen since she first came through the doors showing its first hiccup. "You wanna what?"

I breathed out a laugh, glad that no one was within earshot now. My body relaxed for the first time since she approached me. This is what I was supposed to do. "I'd love it if you'd allow me to take you out to dinner."

She crossed her arms over her chest and eyed me suspiciously.

"You don't know me. What if I'm fourteen, and you just became the pervy coach who asked out a minor?"

My head cocked to the side. "Well, then you'd have some explaining to do since you have to be sixteen in order to play."

Jocelyn puffed air out of her mouth. Not quite a laugh, but it was something. "Do you even know my name? Because I don't know yours."

Liar, I wanted to say. Coach yelled at me every practice, but I let it slide.

I held out my hand. "Levi Buchanan. Born and raised in Green Valley, just turned eighteen, future exercise science major at Maryville College, and youngest of three boys. And I'm terrible at wheelchair basketball."

Her nose wrinkled like I'd thrown dirt in her face, but she shook my hand.

"Jocelyn Abernathy, not born or raised in Green Valley, sixteen years old, I'm not terrible at wheelchair basketball, and my friends call me Joss." She tilted her head. "Or they would if I had friends."

Again, I laughed, but her face didn't change from that same mildly amused expression. My smile dropped, and I cleared my throat, not quite sure what to say to that.

The other players, sensing that our match was over, started passing drills on the opposite side of the court, with Coach yelling suggestions. Jocelyn watched them for a second, her cheeks taking on a pink tinge that I couldn't decipher because she didn't seem pleased by my offer. Surprised, maybe, but there was no excitement in her eyes and no fidgeting of her hands.

When she glanced back at me, her gaze was direct.

Tennessee summer sky over the mountains blue.

"I'm not ..." She swallowed. "I'm not in a place where I'm ready to have dinner with anyone, Levi." She gestured weakly at her lap and legs. "Even though it's been two years since I got sick and ended up ... like this, it's still ... it still takes up a lot of my head. I can't think about dinners," she said it quietly, looking far older than her sixteen years. "Or anything like that right now."

I nodded, using two mental hands to shove down the biting sense of disappointment.

Stupid Buchanan curse.

I expected that same thing prodding me forward would start railing, turning the nudge into something more persistent, but it was quiet. Waiting for what she said next.

"But," she continued, hesitation written all over her face, in her wrinkled brow, the uncomfortable smile, "finishing high school on your computer doesn't give you much of a social life. Especially when you're new in town." Her fingers curled together on her lap. "Maybe … maybe a new friend wouldn't be so bad."

It made no sense that I'd know, instantly and with complete surety, that what she'd just admitted to me was a gift. Something real and raw, hard for her to say out loud, something I definitely hadn't earned yet, but that I'd hold carefully, nonetheless.

Joss gave me a curious look when I held out my hand. Even that, the question in her eyes, had my heart doing a skip-stutter.

"Levi Buchanan," I said. "It's nice to meet you, Joss."

Then, then she gave me a *real* smile—white teeth, pink lips, tiny dimple on the right side—and I never, ever got my heart back.

CHAPTER 1

JOCELYN

"*A*rm porn" was a trendy term I wouldn't mind getting rid of. It'd gotten a little out of hand if you asked me. Don't get me wrong, I could, objectively at least, understand why you'd turn your head at a completely impossible angle to catch a glimpse of a nice bicep, the kind that looked like someone shoved a softball under a guy's skin.

It was the double standard that irritated the shit out of me. Probably no woman in Green Valley has stronger arms than I did. Without breaking a sweat, I could probably crack a walnut with my forearms.

It was the happy by-product of:

1- Being confined to a wheelchair for the past seven years, thereby relying on my arms to power all my forward motion.

2- Discovering that baking was the second greatest love of my life after my dog, Nero.

Trust me, kneading bread was a better workout than just about anything.

But no one was waxing poetic about the rippling muscles in *my* forearms.

"Careful, the steam coming out of your ears might mess up your hair," my best friend, Levi, said from behind my chair.

He sounded bored, which didn't surprise me. He'd heard this rant a time or seven.

Immediately, my right hand came up to double-check that every blond curl was in the same place that it was when I left my house.

Whew. Not a corkscrew springing out anywhere. Very *I'm ready to bake bread and muffins and cupcakes and cakes and all the delicious things.* Or at least, that was how it felt when I studied my own reflection just before Levi picked me up.

"You see the issue, though, right? I've seen women practically wreck their cars when you roll up your sleeves."

Levi laughed easily. He did everything easily, the asshole. His hand landed on my shoulder in a condescending pat that had me rolling my eyes. "Of course, I see the issue, my little feminist warrior princess."

As he spoke, I aimed my wheelchair slightly to the right when a guy walking his dog refused to concede any space. He also refused to make eye contact.

I called those people The Blinders. For the most part, people's reactions to someone in a wheelchair—especially a young someone with incredibly sexy arms—fell into two main camps.

The Blinders and The Pitiers.

The Blinders pretended they couldn't see me, which I often attributed to the fact I made them uncomfortable. *They* could walk around just fine. Staring at a young woman stuck in a metal chair might force them to come to grips with their own mortality, their health ... the things most people take for granted on a daily basis.

The man walking his dog might have looked at me if I was pre-TM Jocelyn. The fourteen-year-old me who could run like a freaking gazelle, who hopped, skipped, and jumped without a second thought until the day I couldn't anymore. Maybe he would've seen me and wondered why my hair looked like I stuck my finger in a light socket. But maybe he wouldn't have. Maybe he had blinders on for everyone around him. One of those people who did his thing, stayed in his lane, and didn't care how his presence affected those sharing space with him.

But it was just as likely that the blinders were because I was in a chair. If I'd been at my full standing height (somewhere around five feet ten), he might have shifted to give me more room with a polite smile on his face. I would've smiled back because if I was at my full standing height, it meant I could stand, and I probably would've taken that for granted too.

"Dick," Levi muttered, jogging forward so he could walk next to my chair instead of behind it.

"It's fine."

"It's not fine. He saw you. He could've moved his fat ass over six inches."

Because I couldn't reach his shoulders, given that his full standing height was around six feet one, I patted his leg condescendingly. "Aww, my little advocate warrior princess."

Levi sighed heavily because it was also not the first time, or seventh time, he'd been called that by me. He hated The Blinders. For me, it was a toss-up which was worse, depending on the day.

The Pitiers got this look in their eye that I roughly equated to, "Oh, you poor thing." They saw me in the chair and instantly made a lot of sweeping generalizations about what life must be like for me. When I took the time to think about what they saw when they looked at me, I imagined they saw a barren wasteland of not being able to have sex (false, not that anyone other than my vibrator knew that), never being able to have kids (also false, my doctor assured me), and always needing to ask for help to reach the top shelves at the grocery store (true, unfortunately).

Sometimes, The Pitiers spoke to me like I couldn't understand them. Like the chair somehow reflected a cognitive impairment as well. Only occasionally would I mess with them.

I never claimed to be a saint. Losing the function of your legs did not automatically make you a virtuous person. In fact, I'd met some real assholes who spent their lives on two wheels. Personally, I found myself somewhere in the middle. I just ... liked to keep some of my cynicism tightly wrapped unless I really trusted you.

Poor Levi.

He got the brunt of my opinions.

My mom probably would've listened if I unloaded them on her, but that never ended well.

"Who's training you?" Levi asked as we passed the entrance of the lodge. I could see the striped awning of Donner Bakery across the parking lot. Afternoon guests sat at the wrought-iron tables and chairs in front of the building, drinking sweet tea and eating whatever confections had been whipped up that day.

"I think it's Jennifer Winston, but I don't know for sure," I told him. My hands gripped the metal ring mounted just outside my wheels as I pushed down harder than necessary. He cut me a sideways look when I sped up, which I ignored because if he asked me if I was nervous, I'd ram his shins.

Hopefully, they had some cream puffs left over because ever since Levi brought me the last lemon lavender cream puff, I'd been trying desperately to recreate it at home to no avail.

"Jennifer *Donner* Winston," he corrected. "Can't forget that middle name. It's important around here."

I rolled my eyes.

"Hey, it's a woman's right to have as many names as she wants."

"I know, I know." I knew what her name was; Levi just liked to rub it in my face that I was, as he called it, Green Valley Lite. I knew people. Sort of. But even after five years of living here, I didn't know everyone by name. I didn't know their family trees or who lost their dog last week or who got pulled over after a jam session or whose daddy was in the Iron Wraiths.

"And the kitchen is fully accessible?" he asked.

"She told me it was. That's why I'm working at this location and not the one downtown."

He scoffed. "And what does *she* know about accessible kitchens?"

"Oh, probably nothing," I drawled.

"Right?" Levi shook his head. "Because unless those openings have at *least* thirty-six inches of clearance, she's gonna have issues."

Now it was my turn to cut him a look. "You gonna bring your ruler in?"

"Maybe." He patted the front of his jeans and gave me an unapologetic grin. His stupid dimples popped on either side of his perpetually smiling mouth.

Really, we were a ridiculous pair.

Made all the more apparent when a tall, skinny brunette with a giant rack almost tripped over her espadrilles at the sight of a smiling Levi. He nodded at her, and she blushed prettily.

"Oh, for the love of," I mumbled, pushing harder again just so I didn't have to watch. If he wanted to sleep with half the population of Tennessee, I didn't care, but that didn't mean I wanted to witness it either.

Witnessing it was my own fault, honestly. It would've been easy enough to turn down his offer to accompany me, but since he'd finished his master's, he got bored too frequently between job searches, and I couldn't stand the thought of him moping around his apartment.

Now I wish I'd made his ass stay home.

I could be wheeling around naked, and I wouldn't get the same number of looks from the opposite sex as Levi did just by breathing.

"Wait up." He laughed.

I stopped the chair and pivoted the wheels in his direction. His hands braced on the armrests when I folded my hands in my lap. Levi narrowed his eyes as he peered down at me. With the sun facing him, they didn't look the normal greenish hazel. They were like amber, bright and streaked with yellow. It was fitting for him. The sun always seemed to shine bright on Levi Buchanan.

So annoying.

Good thing I loved him so damn much. Not like *love* love. Brotherly love. Annoying, want to punch him in the balls from time to time, I never worry about wearing a bra around him, makeup is wasted in his presence, I don't care that I've bawled my eyes out watching *Old Yeller*, or that I got rip-roaring drunk on the fourth anniversary of getting sick, then puked all over his bathroom in front of him kind of love.

"Jealous, Abernathy?"

I'm telling you I could not have stopped the eye roll if there had been a gun to my head. "Yes. Terribly." I tried to pull my chair back, but his grip tightened. "Buchanan, if you make me late for my first shift, I'll never forgive you."

"Relax. You still have ten minutes." There was something in those sun-changed amber eyes that made me twitchy. He was about to ask me something I didn't want to be asked. "Why are you taking this job again? Didn't Sylvia say her friend would be back in like four months?"

"My classes are done for the summer, and as much as I adore you," I said, reaching up to pat his face harder than necessary, "I can't just hang out in your man cave every day. I'll go insane."

How could I explain to him that the more free time I found myself with, the more I searched for something to do. I didn't do boredom well.

Hence, the reason I started baking in the first place.

When all you did was sit (because no matter how many exercises you did or sports you participated in, you're still sitting), all you could do was sit and it got really freaking old after a while. I loved working out, something Levi and I had in common, and I was starting with a new physical therapist to continue working on my leg strength so I could have intermittent use of a walker or arm braces. Intermittent being the key word.

I'd still always spend most of my time with my ass firmly planted in the chair.

Sitting around, no pun intended, made me want to gouge my eyes out.

I barely tolerated watching TV, and only the occasional movie held my interest. Audiobooks were about the only reading I could handle.

Even now, sitting still while he searched my face for an answer made my fingers tangle together, just to give them something to do.

"I need more in my life than what I have," was all I was willing to concede at the moment. "Plus, I make a kick-ass cheesecake. I might as well make some extra cash doing it."

His soon-to-be sister-in-law was the one who told me about the opening at Donner Bakery. A friend of hers was taking an extended maternity leave, and they needed an extra set of hands.

That was something I could provide. Yes, I came with a set of wheels too, but that hadn't been an issue in my interview. Once the manager tasted my strawberry lemonade cupcake, the job was mine.

His grin was slow, but I could tell he believed me. After five years, we could read each other pretty damn well. Occasionally, it was annoying, but it was also one of the constants in my life that I genuinely didn't think I could live without.

"Fair enough." Levi released my chair, and I spun to face the bakery. His hands landed on my shoulders and squeezed before he released me. "Go get 'em."

I took a deep breath.

"And be friendly, Sonic. It won't kill ya," he added.

My hands lifted and dropped in an exasperated heap. "Now why the hell did you have to say that? I'm friendly."

His eyebrow raised slowly.

"I'm sort of friendly," I muttered. Then I pointed an accusatory finger at him. "This is why I prefer to bring Nero with me instead of you. People love dogs, and they're less likely to notice when I don't smile at them."

His chin tilted skyward as he burst out laughing. "That dog looks like he'd rip your face off on a good day. You take him places so people *won't* talk to you."

At that, I grinned a little. My four-year-old Doberman did look like he would rip someone's face off, which was why Levi told me I had to complete one full shift without him waiting for me outside the bakery.

"Sonic," he said quietly.

"I hate that nickname."

"No, you don't. There's nothing more appropriate for you than a prickly little hedgehog who wheels around like a bat out of hell."

Pointedly, I glanced at my watch.

"You're not going to be late." Levi shoved at my shoulder. "Smile at them. Ask questions. Don't assume the worst, okay?"

My tummy knotted up. His smile was softer, more understanding.

My best friend didn't have to ask me why I was so nervous. This was the thing I hated most in the world. Maybe not as much as like terrorism or global warming or patriarchal infrastructures that inherently protected sexual predators, but I hated it a lot.

It was why I was Green Valley Lite

Why I completed high school online and slid right onto college in the same way. Because of moments like this right here.

The moment when I went from Jocelyn Abernathy, the new employee showing up for her first shift, to Jocelyn Abernathy, the girl in the wheelchair. I just had to hope that whoever was waiting for me inside Donner Bakery wasn't one of The Blinders or The Pitiers. Hopefully, they'd be like Levi. Be one of those people who met me and simply saw *me*.

Those were The Unicorns.

CHAPTER 2

JOCELYN

*O*nce I cleared the door, the first thing I noticed was the smell. It was the kind of warm and sweet and comforting smell that demanded you stop, close your eyes, and let it fill your lungs. It was cinnamon bread and banana cake, Jennifer's specialty. But it was also coffee and cupcakes and warm bread and sugary confections that made my fingers curl up with excitement to get started.

A few customers looked at me from where they sat at circular tables. Their facial expressions didn't even register, which said something about how nervous I was. I moved forward, glancing behind the large glass case next to the register for any sign of Jennifer's brown hair.

A short brunette crouched behind the register, pulling a lemon-blueberry cake from the bottom row of the massive glass case with her tongue stuck between her teeth in concentration. Her cheeks were covered with freckles, and her eyes were huge in her face as she set the cake down inside a bright pink box without incident. Just as I reached the counter, I heard her let out a huge breath.

When she saw me, her face split into a massive, white-toothed, cheek-lifting smile.

"You must be Jocelyn! Oh, I'm just *tickled* to meet you."

There was actual giggling as she hustled around the counter toward me. Oh sweet merciful Lord, if she tried to hug me, this whole part-time job thing might not be worth it.

Thankfully, she stuck her hand out, and pumped mine with almost violent intensity.

"Jennifer said you'd be in at two, so I've just been counting down the minutes until you got here."

My mouth opened. Closed. Then opened again. "Am ... am I late?"

Her eyebrows, thick and dark over her equally dark eyes, bent down in a confused V. "Course not, I'm just so *excited*. You're the first person I've been able to train. We're going to be friends, Jocelyn. I can already tell."

Internally, I whimpered. Then I heard Levi's voice in my head. *Smile. Ask questions. Don't make assumptions.*

"What's your name? I didn't catch it."

Her hands clapped to either side of her round cheeks, rosy pink from the warmth in the bakery. "Heavens, I'm a mess, aren't I? I'm Joy."

"Joy," I said, the smile coming naturally in light of her comically appropriate moniker. "Nice to meet you."

That made her blush happily, turning her cheeks an even deeper shade of rose. "Let me grab someone for the register, and I'll show you the kitchen. We need to grab some more large boxes and the cinnamon roll cupcakes. We're almost out." She started back behind the counter, then stopped so fast I almost rammed into her. When she turned, she said, "Now, don't worry about your being in that wheelchair. We're all real accepting here. No one will bother you about it, and Jennifer told us we're not to make a fuss over you because you're perfectly capable of handling things on your own."

Her voice was so sincere, her eyes wide and serious, that I wanted to grab her hand and tell her to chill the hell out.

"I won't worry, Joy. But thank you for saying so anyway." I cleared my throat when she didn't start walking again. "They assured me the kitchen is fully accessible, so I should be just fine."

Joy nodded so vigorously, a chunk of hair slipped out of her ponytail. "Oh, it is, I promise. Her husband, Cletus, I'm sure you know

Cletus Winston? Of course you do." I shook my head, but she just kept on talking like I did. "He tore the whole thing apart and redid it a few years back when Jennifer needed to be in a wheelchair for a while. He knew she'd hate to be out of work." She sighed, a look so dreamy covering her face that I wanted to snap my fingers in front of her just to keep this show moving. "Isn't that so romantic? He just ... fixed all of it for her. Because he knows baking makes her happy."

I chose my words carefully. "She sounds like a very lucky woman."

More nodding. More hair spilled around her face. "She *is*. You'll probably meet her later. She said she'd try to stop in to meet you."

"Great." I pointed behind the counter. "Should we?"

"Oh, gracious, yes! Listen to me chattering away." Motioning me to follow her, we went behind the glass case, and I smiled at the crisply lined display of confections and squinted at the beautifully done chalkboard sign with the menu as we passed it.

"Joy, does that say dill pickle cupcakes?"

She giggled, glancing over her shoulder at me. "Sure does. We made them a couple of months back as a special request for someone's baby shower, and they were so good, we couldn't believe it. We only make them about once a month, but we usually sell out before noon on the days we have them in stock. I'm surprised there are any left."

My eyebrows popped up in surprise. "Okay then."

"They're delicious," she assured me. "The secret is the bourbon in the frosting."

"Huh." The opening into the kitchen was, indeed, wide enough for me, and I watched as a couple of apron-clad bakers worked efficiently around the long stainless island. They both sent me friendly smiles when Joy introduced me, no violent hand shaking this time as they were elbow deep in cupcake batter, which suited me just fine. "Will I get to do some baking today?"

Joy grinned. "Course you will. But we know you already know how to do that. We heard all about those cupcakes you brought in. We'll start you on the register for a bit, then we'll rotate back here to make one of our recipes."

My face must have been frozen into some horrible expression

19

because Joy bent closer, concern practically oozing from her pores. "Are you okay?"

The words felt like acid coming out of my mouth. "I just … I hope I do okay working at the register." My face flushed hot. "I'm not, I'm not always great with strangers."

Joy waved away my admission. "Hush, you'll do just fine. Most of them are only strangers once or twice. Soon, you'll know everyone who comes in here."

In her mind, that was that, and we started around the kitchen. She showed me where the staff kept their things, and the bins of flour, sugar, and brown sugar underneath the main island. I saw the stainless racks where all the finished items went to wait on trays, and the ovens that were pumping out lots of heat and even more delicious smells.

I smiled when she showed me the design elements and sent up a prayer to the bakery gods that I'd be able to get my hands on them soon.

The first hour flew by with little necessary from me other than to listen to Joy's happy chattering and overwhelming overshare of every square inch of the kitchen.

And this is the mixer, we got that one about two years ago. It's a lot nicer than the one we had before.

Oh, this here is the counter you can pull right out for your own workstation. Jennifer used it all the time. Isn't it amazing that Cletus made it for her? So romantic.

We store the bags of flour and sugar here. You can lift a fifty-pound bag, right? Of course, you can; just don't pay attention to a word I'm saying.

By the time we made our way back to the register, I was ready for a nap. Of course, about half of that could've been because I really, really didn't feel ready to put on my happy, friendly, non-Jocelyn customer service face. Maybe I could leach some of Joy's joy by osmosis. I kept my chair just behind her so she could show me how to work the register, and that was when her curiosity finally got the best of her.

I'd learned pretty quickly when someone was trying to figure out how to ask me about my chair, or whether the thing about to come out of their mouth was going to be completely inappropriate.

"So, how did you ..." Her voice trailed off, and she glanced quickly, guiltily down at my legs. "How did it happen?"

If Joy had been anything but sweet and sincere with me, I might have considered messing with her a little bit.

Instead, I gave her a quick smile. "I had an infection that caused inflammation in my spinal cord. The paralysis used to go higher up, past my waist, when I first got sick, but it settled lower with some steroids."

She placed a hand on her chest and gave me a sad smile. Then her eyes glossed over, and panic made my whole body freeze up like a popsicle. If she cried, right here in the middle of the bakery, I might wheel my ass out and not come back.

"And you can't feel anything at all? Like if I dropped something on your poor little feet, you wouldn't even know?" she asked, voice all whispery and trembling with emotion.

I bit down on my lip so I didn't laugh. "I'd be able to tell. Mainly because my eyes work just fine."

She blinked a few times.

"Right, sorry, I'll pull back on the inappropriate humor." I cleared my throat awkwardly.

Houston, we're losing her.

Joy sniffed, and I gave her a look.

"Joy, you promised not to make a fuss."

She blinked again, but this time, I saw her visibly pull herself together. "Right, okay. Sorry."

"You don't have to apologize." I sighed.

She nodded in answer, then waved her hands in front of her to stem the emotions literally spilling over her face. "Okay. Sorry."

I smiled. So did she.

Joy stepped back and motioned to the register. "Why don't you try the next one?"

I groaned, wheeling myself closer. "Okay, fine."

The sound of someone clearing their throat had Joy and me glancing up in tandem.

And I don't know about her, but I felt my mouth drop open a little bit.

In front of the counter, with his hands tucked into dark jeans and ridiculous ropey-muscled forearms on full display—I would've sworn it on a stack of Bibles—was the love child of Brad Pitt from *Legends of the Fall* and Chris Pratt from *Jurassic World*. And he was smiling at us like we weren't staring awkwardly.

"Afternoon," he said, voice deep and warm and caramel chocolate lava cake gooey delicious.

A sound came out of my mouth that might have been hi, but all he did was widen his smile a little bit.

Joy snapped out of her stupor first. "Afternoon. What can we get for you today?"

"You're new," he said to me.

Like directly to me. While holding eye contact and aiming words in my direction.

Joy elbowed me in my shoulder, and I swallowed. "First day, actually."

He nodded, glancing at the menu and studying it carefully. "So you won't be able to help me much with what your top recommendation is, huh?"

Joy's eyes widened at me, and I wanted to smack her. "Umm, I haven't been able to try everything just yet, no." I lifted my chin and felt really frickin' proud of myself for holding his piercing—*piercing!*—gaze. Why were his eyes so green? Why was I noticing? I never noticed this stuff. "But I hear the dill pickle cupcakes are out of this world."

He laughed, and Joy sighed dreamily.

Brad/Chris scratched the side of his face, which drew my eyes to the hard cut of his jaw. "If that's what the lady recommends, then I'll take two of those, please."

Joy nudged me again, and I clumsily punched the required buttons on the register while she pulled the cupcakes from the top shelf of the case and boxed them up for him.

"Five dollars is your total," I told him.

He handed me a ten, our fingers brushing as I reached over the counter to take it from him.

When Joy slid the box toward him, he opened it instead of taking the change I pulled out of the drawer.

"Is that a potato chip garnish?" he asked.

Joy nodded. "It is."

Brad/Chris took one cupcake out and held it up, examining it seriously. His change sat on the counter unnoticed. Then he pushed the pink box back toward me.

I stared at it, then back up at him. "You're supposed to take that with you."

Smooth, Abernathy. So very, very smooth.

He grinned, holding up his cupcake. "No, this is mine. That one is for you. I'd hate to be the only one trying this for the first time today." Then he dipped his chin. "Good luck on the rest of your first day."

My mouth dropped open as he swiped the five-dollar bill off the counter. Joy's mouth did the same thing as he tucked it into the tip jar next to the register.

"Ladies," he said and walked away whistling.

"What the f—" I said, only catching myself when I remembered that I was supposed to be a professional now. "What *was* that?"

Joy squealed quietly, doing a little shimmy. "He was flirting with you!"

"He was *not.*"

Holy shit, he was. What the hell else would you call it when a man bought you a pickle cupcake?

She laughed when I pressed my hands to my hot, hot cheeks.

Men didn't flirt with me. Basically ever. Like at all. And trying to explain that to Joy felt too much like stripping back my skin so she could see what was underneath.

"Come on," she cajoled. "Aren't you at least going to eat the cupcake?"

Since we had no customers at the moment, thank the Lord, I pulled the box toward me and considered it carefully before I lifted the lid. "Maybe later."

She sighed again but didn't push me.

"That was so romantic."

I rolled my eyes. "Okay, let's just ... go bake some cookies or something."

When she let me change the subject, I decided she wasn't all that bad.

CHAPTER 3

LEVI

From the moment I met Joss outside of Donner Bakery at the end of her shift, her dog in the truck with his scary-ass head hanging out the window, she hadn't stopped talking.

Her arms waved around and her face scrunched up as she mimicked her trainer for the day, which was all fine and good. But as she transferred herself into the passenger seat so I could put her wheelchair in the back of my truck, it was the look in her eyes that had me staring unabashedly. It was something I didn't let myself do often.

Those eyes were happy. They were excited.

Feathers on an Indigo Bunting blue.

I saw one feeding from the large feeder in the backyard at my parents' house, and the first thing the color of that little bird made me think of was Jocelyn's eyes.

"Joy sounds like a real character," I said when she finally took a breath.

Joss leaned her head back on the seat and grinned. "She is. Even sitting in my chair, she's barely four inches taller than me."

As I turned onto the road that would take us back to my place, I glanced over at her so I could drink in that grin.

That was when I noticed her clutching a pink bakery box in her lap.

"What's that?"

Her fingers tightened around the edges, and she stared down at it. "A cupcake."

"Well, what the frick, Abernathy. Be nice and share." Nero shoved his big old head between us and sniffed at the curve of her neck. She smiled and scratched under his chin. He groaned, and I had a moment of *trust me, buddy, I'd groan too if she scratched my neck.* "Besides, this is my best friend perk. Shouldn't I get perks in baked goods?"

She cut me a look. "You've been getting those perks for two years, Buchanan. Don't even pretend you didn't put on a solid ten pounds that first year I started baking." Quite pointedly, she looked at my stomach, which we both knew was covered in muscle.

"That's rude," I mumbled under my breath. I flexed my bicep. Nero licked my elbow since it was right in front of him. "Yeah, ten pounds in my left arm maybe."

The noise she made roughly translated to *you are ridiculous.* She made that sound at me a lot.

Of course, the sad truth of the matter was that I was ridiculous.

Not once in the past five years had my feelings lessened for her. I had just learned to live with them. In my junior year of undergrad, I was taking a class on brain pathology in injuries, and a man came to talk to us about how he learned to live without his right arm after it was amputated.

He told us about how, even years after he lost his arm, his brain still triggered sensations to the limb that was no longer there. The adult brain, in particular, struggled to reorganize after the loss of a limb, and given that four out of five amputees suffer from phantom pain symptoms, some of which were incredibly debilitating, it was a lesson that stuck with me.

I wasn't fool enough to think that me loving Jocelyn was on par with a man who'd lost his arm, but something about the way he talked plucked at a chord inside me. Sometimes my brain struggled to remember that we were just friends. She'd never dated, never even hinted that she wanted to. She'd never given me a longing glance. Never stared at my mouth like she wondered what it tasted like.

But my hands never, not once, stopped wanting to reach for hers.

My fingers always, always itched to dig into her crazy hair and see what the curve of her scalp felt like.

My brain knew what this relationship was, but sometimes, the signals it sent to the rest of my body didn't always match up with the truth of our situation.

We worked out together a lot, Joss and I, and when she got frustrated with the limitations of her body, I always wanted to wrap my arms around her. I wanted to pull her into the curve of my body, absorb her dissatisfaction into my skin, and carry it for her.

That was the irony when she made noises like that. She had absolutely no clue how ridiculous I really was.

The driveway at my parents' house was empty, and I breathed a quiet sigh of relief. I didn't really feel like sharing her, and my entire family was as in love with Joss as I was.

Well, not really, but it felt like it sometimes.

There was no other explanation as to why my mom and dad didn't blink when I asked them to renovate the single stall garage at the back curve of the driveway into an apartment for me. It was hard for Joss to hang out in my old bedroom because it was upstairs, and she hated for me to carry her.

Now I had a freestanding living space with absolutely nothing to impede her coming and going because, in true Buchanan-curse fashion, I'd done all the research on making it fully accessible for her.

After parking my truck, I held the door open so Nero could hop out and run into the woods lining the property while I got Joss's chair out of the back.

"Want me to take that?" I asked as I watched her struggle a little to grip the box while transferring into her chair.

"No way, you'll eat it before I'm even fully seated."

I considered that. "Depends on what's in there."

That was when her face did something weird. She blushed. All along the tops of her high, perfect cheekbones, her skin turned a delicate color I'd never witnessed.

The peonies in my mom's garden pink.

As soon as she'd settled her feet, she pivoted and wheeled toward my place. "It's a dill pickle cupcake, and it's mine."

"Gross," I breathed, jogging to catch up to her so I could open the door.

"Right?" she said on a laugh. "But I can't not try it."

"Sure, you can. You can realize it's a *dill pickle cupcake* and that you like your taste buds better than to subject them to that."

Joss was still laughing when she wheeled inside. Over her shoulder, she gave a short whistle. Nero came bounding toward us, his pink tongue hanging out of the side of his mouth. All ninety pounds of him skirted around us so he could hop up on the edge of the couch he always claimed as his.

My apartment had a small kitchenette lining one wall, which I pretty much only used to make coffee in the mornings, a light gray L-shaped couch facing the TV I'd mounted on the far wall, and my king-size bed hidden behind a half wall partition that gave me the illusion of privacy. Past that was the bathroom.

I'd chosen to forgo a table in the kitchenette because it was one more obstacle for Joss to get around, and we always ate on the couch anyway.

"You're the cleanest twenty-three-year-old man I've ever met," she said as she lifted herself out of the chair and onto the couch. Bracing her weight on her arms, she scooted back until she could pull the handle that lifted the reclining footrest. Nero stretched out, shoving his head against her thigh.

It wasn't necessary for me to look around because I knew nothing was on the floor. No piles of clothes and no shoes tossed in the general area of where I slept.

I opened my mouth to make a flippant comment, but I took a second to watch her face first. Joss probably said it without expecting a reply, so she wasn't even really looking at me. I must have been quiet long enough that she noticed. Her eyes lifted to my face.

"I'd never do anything that makes it hard for you to be here," I said. Joss blinked in surprise.

My face felt like it was heating, so I cleared my throat and walked to the fridge. "Need anything to drink?"

"Uhh, sure. What do you have?"

Surveying the contents of the fridge, I grimaced. "Water, purple Gatorade, and a beer."

Before she could answer, her phone rang. "It's Sylvia," she said before picking it up.

Mentally, I waved goodbye to my time alone with her. If Sylvia was calling, she and my brother were probably at the house, saw my car, and my brother was kind enough to not barge in on us, allowing his fiancée to call and give us a heads-up.

He knew what Joss was to me. So did my parents. I finally admitted it after I turned twenty, and they were giving me shit about how, without my cousin Grady from California still holding out as well, I'd be the first to prove five generations of Buchanan men wrong. Grady's twin, Grace, was single too, but considering she was the first Buchanan woman born in those five generations, none of us were quite sure if it worked the same.

"Hey," Joss said into the phone. She smiled and jerked her head toward the main house. I rolled my eyes, which made her smile even more. "Yeah, we're out here. I just got done at work."

On the other end of the line, Sylvia said something, then Joss hung up and tossed the phone onto the empty cushion next to her. "They're coming out."

"Of course they are," I mumbled.

"Don't be an ass. I like Sylvia." She pointed a finger at me when I flopped onto the couch on the other side of Nero. He lifted his head and looked over at me before stretching his back legs out into my space.

"I like Sylvia too," I told her, smoothing my hand over his sleekly muscled flank. He pushed his paw into my leg, his way of asking for more.

"Good, as she's about to become your sister-in-law."

29

"You never know. Connor has six weeks to change his mind. Maybe he'll back out."

Our eyes met, and she started laughing. We both knew that would never happen. I had to swallow roughly for a second because, at times like this, I felt like I was keeping a huge secret from Joss. I'd never told her about the Buchanan curse. Because if I told her that ...

There was a knock on the door before Connor walked in, trailed by his fiancée.

Nero lifted his head, and his tall, stick-straight ears and bright amber eyes trained in their direction made Connor pause. "Why does your dog always look like he wants to eat me?"

Joss scratched under Nero's chin. "This little marshmallow?"

Connor grimaced. Sylvia rolled her eyes, tucking her arm around my brother's waist.

Because it was impossible not to mess with him, I patted Nero's rump. "Smile, Nero."

He bared his big, sharp, white teeth in a terrifying doggy grin, and Connor blanched.

Joss stifled a laugh, leaning down to drop a kiss on the end of Nero's shiny black nose.

Edging around the couch like Nero might lunge at him, Connor took a seat in the recliner opposite the couch and patted his lap for Sylvia to join him. She settled in, tossing her legs over his lap and giving him a quick kiss before facing us again.

"So it went well today?" Sylvia asked Joss.

She nodded. "Yeah. My co-worker was a little ... extroverted, but she was nice. Customers were fine. I got to try one of their recipes. I'm more excited about that part than the people-ing."

We all laughed.

"My grumpy little introvert," I teased. "We're so fortunate you don't hate people-ing around us."

Joss glared at me, but it wasn't serious. "People-ing only counts as people-ing when it's someone new, or you're trying to impress them, or they're trying to get to know you or something."

We all knew what she meant. Joss was comfortable with us. We weren't strangers who were going to approach her and ask her right off the bat why she was in a wheelchair—which happened all the time —or force her into small talk that I knew was painful for her.

But what made me swallow around the sticky sand in my throat was the tossed-out reminder that she lumped me into the same category as my brother and his fiancée.

"I get it," Sylvia said, unaware that behind her, Connor gave me a sympathetic smile because he knew. I kept my eyes away from him. "This will be a big week for you then. Don't you start with your new PT tomorrow?"

My head snapped in her direction. "You're starting with a new therapist?"

She had the decency to grimace. "Did I not mention that?"

"How come? What happened to Denise?"

Joss sighed, and I felt a momentary twinge of guilt for making it sound like an inquisition.

"They have this new guy starting, and I guess working with people like me, it's kind of his specialty."

I nodded slowly. "You're still favoring your left when you're in the walker, aren't you?"

"Ugh, yes. I've been using my chair more than normal." She rubbed at her right thigh, like she could magically heal the decaying muscles there. Joss's arms and core were toned and strong, and even so many years later, I knew she still struggled with looking down at her thin legs.

"Want me to come with you to your appointment?" I asked.

From my peripheral, I could feel my brother's eyes boring a hole in my head.

"It's okay," Joss said. "You'll just glare at them if they're not doing the exercises you think I should be doing, Mr. *I have a master's in sports medicine.*"

"I didn't glare at her," I muttered. I'd absolutely glared at her. "Denise just didn't push you hard enough. You can do so much more than she asked of you."

Joss gave me a tiny smile.

31

"You guys." Sylvia sighed. "You're so cute."

My eyes snapped in her direction.

Joss scoffed. "We're friends, Sylvia."

My future sister-in-law rolled her eyes. "I know, I know, so you've said. At least tell me you'll go to our wedding with Levi. That way you get to sit at the head table and will be in all our pictures, instead of some rando girl."

Connor was trying to pinch Sylvia's side, but she swatted his hand away. Clearly, they'd had this discussion already.

Joss glanced over at me and laughed. "Yeah, right. Levi probably already has some co-ed on the hook who'll show up in a little black dress that barely covers her hooha."

"Hey," I said, only slightly affronted. "That only happened one time, and I had no idea she would flash the entire restaurant. You can't blame me for a blind date's inappropriate dress choice."

Connor and Sylvia laughed. Joss grinned in my direction, and I gave her a tiny wink.

I had no intention of taking anyone to that wedding, not unless it was her.

I just had to figure out how to ask her in a way so she knew exactly what it would mean to have her there by my side.

CHAPTER 4

JOCELYN

"*D*o you want me to drive you to work?"

I jumped in my chair, hand flying to my chest when my mom's voice came from behind me as I was pouring myself a cup of coffee.

"Sorry," she said, settling her hand on my shoulder for a brief touch as she passed behind me.

"I didn't expect you to be awake." I added some cream and stirred it into the steaming hot liquid.

She sat at the small dining room table; the same one my grandma had used when she lived in the house before she passed. It was probably the same table my mom had eaten at as a small girl, though it was hard for me to imagine it.

We hadn't brought much with us when we moved here after my grandma's lawyers informed my mom that upon her death—peaceful and in the middle of the night as she slept—my mom had inherited the house that we now lived in. A Godsend at the time when my mom was drowning, quite literally, in hospital and therapy bills after I'd gotten sick. Neither of us cared too much that the décor appeared untouched since the early nineties. It was paid off, and it was hours away from the place that now reminded us both of the immediate aftermaths of my sickness.

Working third shift labor and delivery at the Eastern Tennessee Children's Hospital, my mom had slowly chipped away at the medical debt, keeping her head down, and her eyes hyper-focused on that and only that.

Now that she could breathe again, I'd realized that for the past two years, she turned that focus to me, like she was trying to make up for the fact that I'd adjusted to life in Green Valley completely without her help.

"I probably should be sleeping," she admitted, watching me push my wheelchair with one hand as I carried my coffee mug in the other. "I could've grabbed that, you know."

"I know," I said lightly.

It had taken me a couple of years to realize that my mother defied my neatly separated little categories.

She was a Blinder. But not really. Nothing intentional or born from malice or insensitivity.

I'd realized long ago that something was ingrained in us Abernathys, something that kept our eyes down and focused on the immediate problem, and we didn't waste time dwelling on the things we couldn't change. It was why my grandma had accepted it quietly when my mom moved to Georgia just after high school. Why my mom never came to visit but didn't complain about the fact we weren't asked.

When I ended up in my wheelchair, it was much the same. Even though Mom was a damn good nurse, she couldn't protect me from a simple virus that attacked my nervous system. Complaining about it and letting it eat her alive would do no good. But she also didn't really understand my life because of her instinct to focus on what she could control.

She was also a Pitier. But not because she thought I wasn't capable of doing things.

Helping me, doing things for me when she was around, made

things easier. In her mind, at least. My insistence to do them myself did not seem easier, and it was something she'd never understood.

"Do you want me to drive you to work?"

The coffee was scalding as I took my first sip, and I hissed when I set the mug down on the table. "I've got my car. I'll be fine."

We'd taken Grandma's vehicle, since that had been left to us too, to Knoxville not long after we moved here to have it modified and the hand controls added.

"I guess I didn't need to get up, after all," she said quietly. "You've got it all under control."

I watched her stand from the table and make her way back down the hallway to her bedroom. Between us, there was no chitchat about my new job because she didn't understand why I wanted one anyway. If we'd had a different relationship, maybe I would've asked her why she became a nurse. How she decided what she wanted to do with her life and what kind of classes I should take to try to map out a course for my life when I couldn't see my future very clearly.

I might have told her about Cupcake Guy, and how I was supposed to navigate dating and guys and my chair when I'd never thought about it before.

Instead, I sat there and sipped my coffee, took a deep breath, and got ready for work.

* * *

By the time I got the bakery, it didn't take long for me to realize two things that were generally accepted as normal within those walls.

Joy was the actual happiest person in Green Valley.

And she was in love with Cletus Winston.

When I met Jennifer Winston that second day, her vivid purple eyes smiling at me as she talked about what she wanted us to bake that morning (pecan rolls and banana cake), she made a casual mention of something Cletus did for her, and Joy melted like a stick of butter.

"That's so romantic," she breathed.

Jennifer smiled sweetly, tucking a piece of brown hair behind her ear. "Replacing the brake pads on my car?"

Joy nodded, her eyes wide and serious. I rolled my lips between my teeth to keep from laughing at her.

"I don't have anyone who can do that for me," she said. "And without needing to be asked, too? He just knew it was something you needed, and he took care of it."

"Yes," Jennifer said, voice sincere, "he does recognize the importance of working brake pads in my life."

"So romantic," Joy repeated, pushing a flour-coated wooden rolling pin over the pecan roll dough until it was sufficiently smooth.

I couldn't help the chuckle that escaped under my breath. Jennifer gave me a tiny wink.

"Anyone special in your life to replace your brake pads, Jocelyn?" Jennifer asked, leaning her elbows on the counter while we worked.

Laughter burst out of me before I could stop it. "Not in the way you're talking. I have to pay someone like the rest of us."

They both giggled.

Joy nudged me with her elbow. "Oh, come on now. She had a customer buy her a cupcake yesterday just because she said she'd never tried the dill pickle, and he was ten kinds of handsome."

"He was just being nice because it was my first day," I interjected, desperate to change the subject. "The cupcake was delicious, by the way."

Jennifer and Joy shared a look, which made me roll my eyes.

"And," Joy continued, "when her shift was over, another man picked her up, and he was just as handsome as Cupcake Guy."

I scrunched my nose up. "That was just Levi."

"*Just* Levi?" Jennifer asked.

"Levi Buchanan," Joy supplied helpfully, which made Jennifer nod in recognition.

I waved a hand. "He's my best friend."

Jennifer raised an eyebrow, and I didn't like the gleam in her eyes.

"Listen, when you're sitting on the kind of throne I'm sitting on, men falling over themselves to date you is not a common occurrence.

Even if I had any desire to date, the thought of having to one, explain the chair so they're mentally prepared for it, and two, have to sit there and wait for them to ask whether I can have sex is not an evening I really look forward to."

"You're so beautiful, though," Joy said, almost sadly. "And funny. You're so funny, Joss. You should have men falling over themselves to date you."

I smiled down at my lap. The downturn in her voice was also something I was used to. It was the recognition that my being in the chair came before any other possible first impression I could make. Heidi Klum could be sitting where I was, and if you came across her at the grocery store, you'd notice her chair first. You'd judge her on that without even meaning to. I didn't hold that against anyone because before I got sick, I probably would've done the same thing.

"Thank you, Joy," I told her.

Jennifer clapped her hands. "Well, you ladies have this under control. I'll let you get back to work since I've got payroll to do. Holler if you need anything, okay?"

I nodded, giving her a grateful smile at the subject change.

We got back to work, assembling the pecan rolls, then mixing the batter for the banana cake until it was ready to go in the waiting ovens. I didn't need to do much talking because Joy took care of that for me. She told me all about her years at the bakery. That she started in high school, working Saturday mornings, and now that she was taking some business classes at the community college, she hoped one day Jennifer would make her assistant manager or something.

She knew almost every customer as they walked in, and they all greeted her by name when they saw her smiling face. A couple of minutes later, she was mid-pecan sprinkle when her hand froze.

"What?" I asked.

"He's back," she whispered excitedly.

I wiped my flour-covered hands on the front of my apron. "Who is?"

"Cupcake Guy," Joy hissed, her cheeks instantly red and flushed. "Go out there and help him!"

"No way," I said firmly. "They don't need my help up there, and you know it."

Joy's face morphed.

Gone was the sweet, ebullient young woman who'd been my co-worker for the past couple of hours.

Gone was the happiest person in the world.

In her place was determined, scheming Joy. She narrowed her eyes, and I actually sat back in my chair from the force of it.

"Mikey, can I get your help back here?" she yelled to the person who was working the register. "Joss will be right up to cover you."

I gasped. "I'm not ready to work the register by myself."

"Get up there right now, young lady."

Gawking at her for a second, I only started moving when she pointed a finger at the front. "Git," she said firmly.

"Geez, fine," I muttered, wheeling past Mikey, a sweet kid from Green Valley High School who nodded as I begrudgingly took his place behind the counter.

Brad/Chris hadn't seen me yet since he was peering behind the glass case at the daily offerings. No dill pickle and fortunately for me, there was nothing in that case that I hadn't tried yet. Casual as can be, I got behind the register and made a show of straightening the pens and the tip jar, none of which needed to be straightened. Over my shoulder, I looked into the kitchen and saw Joy peeking around the corner.

I really, really wanted to flip her my middle finger, but I was afraid I'd crush some piece of her effervescent soul if I did.

Brad/Chris straightened, and my stomach did an actual backflip when his handsome face transformed from polite interest to a pleased smile.

Oh my Lord, was this what it felt like to have a crush based on little to no information?

He could be a serial killer. He could kick puppies. Maybe he had bad breath or watched *True Housewives of Backwoods Kentucky*.

But when he smiled at me like that, I imagined all the perfect life choices he must make on a daily basis. The charities he must give all his money to. The little old lady he probably helped across the street. The healthy food he ate, and the exercise he must do to maintain that body.

It was *awful*.

My fingers twitched, and I dropped the can of pens. Mortification made my face hot at the sound of them clattering to the floor.

"Morning," he said with a smile.

"Wh-what can I get for you?"

He leaned over the counter at the mess of pens, and I caught a brief whiff of him. It wasn't strong enough to be cologne, but I caught it all the same. Just as I had the day before with the scent of the bakery, I filled my lungs with it.

"Unfortunate demise for those pens," he said casually. "And all they did was innocently sit in the jar."

A laugh bubbled up my throat, but I swallowed it down. "They sucked anyway, trust me. Donner Bakery can do better than a basic ballpoint."

His grin widened, and I saw a dimple pop to the left of his lips. Shit, now I was cataloging his facial features, for crying out loud.

"How was the cupcake?" he asked, tucking a hand into the front of his jeans. Again, his forearms were out on display for the entire world to see. A man should be careful when showing those off.

Great, now he had me swooning over his *arm porn*. I wouldn't be able to look myself in the mirror after this.

"G-good," I stammered, tucking an errant curl behind my ear. "Better than I thought it would be."

"Same. I didn't dare eat in front of you two yesterday in case I needed to spit it out."

"An unforgivable sin in the bakery world," I said gravely.

He tsked. "I never would've been able to show my face here again."

Oh my word, I was flirting with him. And he was flirting right back.

Brad/Chris glanced behind him to make sure there was no one in line, then smiled at me again. "You know, I realized after I left that I didn't catch your name."

I cleared my throat. "Joss."

Just as the realization hit me, that I introduced myself using my nickname, something I never, ever did, I heard the bell over the door ding as someone walked in.

Levi sauntered through the door, grinning widely at me. Internally, I groaned. Sure, that was perfect. My very first real attempt at flirting with a freaking hot guy who was flirting back, and my over-protective but equally handsome best friend had to walk in.

"I'm Andy," he said, oblivious to my mental freak-out.

"Nice to meet you, Andy," I said as quickly as I could before Levi got to the counter. "What can I get for you?"

Levi winked at me, that happy smile still pasted on his face. Andy must have sensed someone behind him because he looked over his shoulder. "Ah, right, I shouldn't hold up the line."

I smiled politely. "It's okay."

Andy rubbed at his jaw. "Well, since you're a seasoned employee now, is there anything you'd recommend on day two?"

Levi's eyes focused on the menu, then he glanced meaningfully down at his watch.

I gave him a level look, unable to glare without drawing attention to the fact that I knew him. And no way was I introducing Levi into this moment. Thankfully, he'd known me long enough that he needed no more from me. He held up his hands and stepped back. Yes, my shift was technically over, but his impatient ass could wait.

"No dill pickle today," I said to Andy. "But the Holy Cannoli cupcake is pretty amazing. So are the almond croissants."

He smiled, digging his wallet out of his back pocket. "The cupcake sounds perfect."

Moving carefully, so I didn't repeat the pen debacle with the baked goods, I pulled one cupcake off the tray and placed it in the container. Once the lid was closed I slid it toward him.

"Two fifty, please."

"Keep the change," Andy told me, handing me a crisp five-dollar bill.

"Thanks. Enjoy the cupcake." I dumped his change into the tip jar. He smiled before he left, nodding at Levi as he walked out.

I swear, I tried not to check out his ass, but it was an actual physical impossibility.

Andy/Brad/Chris had a phenomenal ass. He had a phenomenal everything, actually. He stood roughly around Levi's height, so I knew he was taller than six feet.

"Ahem," Levi said, and I tore my eyes away from Andy's retreating figure. "I'd like four dozen cupcakes, please."

"Too bad," I mumbled.

"Ouch. So much for your stellar customer service skills." Then he smiled. "But hey, look how friendly you were with that guy. You didn't even look like you were in pain when you smiled so politely."

I laughed. I couldn't help it. After that, I had another first. My mouth opened to tell him, to explain why that was, but then I closed it again when the words didn't want to come out comfortably, when they didn't slide out naturally. As I stared at Levi over the counter, I realized I didn't want to confide in him about this.

It felt like ... like I was doing something wrong, to tell him that a man I didn't know made my stomach do somersaults. Or that I managed to flirt without any embarrassing incident, pens aside.

Lightly, I shrugged one shoulder. "What can I say?" I told him, "I'm a pro."

"For real, though, can I get one of those pecan rolls? They look amazing."

I sniffed haughtily. "That's because I made them."

"Nice work, Sonic." I boxed it up and accepted the bills he handed me. Immediately, he opened the box and took a greedy inhale. "I hope you don't expect me to share."

Shaking my head, I backed up and turned toward the kitchen. "I'd never expect that. Hang on, let me get someone up here, I'll punch out and meet you in the front."

He nodded, mouth full of pecan roll.

"You are worse than an animal. You can't even wait to use a utensil?"

41

Levi grinned around the pastry, and I couldn't help but smile back. What an idiot.

By the time I met him out front, he was tossing the pink box into a trash can, then he turned and let Nero lick the remaining caramel off his fingers.

My boys, I thought. What would I do without them?

"Want to go play some basketball?" he asked when Nero had finished.

"Sure." He opened the door for me, and I hopped easily from my chair into the passenger seat. He picked up my chair and tossed it into the back of his truck "You just need to have me back home by two thirty. My PT appointment in Maryville is at four."

"See if they're hiring, by the way. Green Valley has a terrible hatred of any jobs for a guy with my impressive educational pedigree," he said as he got behind the wheel. "You sure you don't want me to come?"

I nodded. "Yeah, let me scope the guy out before I sic you on him. It's the least I can do."

Levi smiled proudly. "Everyone is scared of Nero, but really, they should fear me."

He puffed out his chest and I dissolved into helpless laughter. "You're ridiculous."

"Maybe I am," he agreed easily. He cut me a look as we drove away. "Work was good?"

I thought about Joy and Jennifer. Then I thought about Andy. "Yeah," I said slowly. "It was really good."

His smile was so happy, and I fought against my instinct that maybe it was strange that I didn't feel like I could tell him about Andy.

It was just new. And nothing would happen with it anyway. Or at least, that was what I told myself as we drove to the park. How very, very wrong I was.

CHAPTER 5

JOCELYN

*M*aryville Physical Therapy, a quick thirty-minute drive northwest of Green Valley, was a fairly nondescript office smack in the middle of a strip mall. It had been a couple of months since my last appointment, which was my own fault. I used the excuse of finishing up the school year and taking exams and writing papers, but the truth was that my progress was slower and harder than I wanted, which did nothing for my motivation lately.

I could still kick ass on the basketball court, and with Levi's help in the gym, my upper body strength was as good as it'd ever been. But the process of gaining enough strength to walk was frustrating. My steps weren't smooth or graceful. My legs swung out in an ungainly fashion, and I still had to hold one arm out in the air to maintain a sense of balance.

When Denise moved, and the office manager told me they'd hired someone who specialized in the exact thing I was working on, I looked forward to it with a strange sense of trepidation.

After I got sick, hope became about as dangerous as carting around a loaded gun.

I had to mourn the loss of a future I'd always taken for granted even though I still had so much to be grateful for.

Someday, they had told the fifteen-year-old Jocelyn still getting steroids pumped into her veins, if we reduce the inflammation on your spine, you might be able to use a walker on occasion.

Someday, you should be able to get pregnant, carry a child, and give birth.

Someday, you might ...

Someday, if conditions were right ...

Someday, maybe ...

There was a part of me, one I'd only confessed to Levi, that started hating that phrase. My mom never said the words out loud, but she hated watching me try to get around with my walker. The stumbling, graceless movement of my legs somehow made it worse. In her eyes, the smooth motion of my chair was preferable because hoping for more seemed like a useless exercise in frustration.

It took root like a weed and became a battle I didn't want to fight with her. Occasionally, I would work on my legs with Levi, but that wasn't part of our usual routine either. Sometimes, if my mom wasn't home, I'd put Nero in a vest with a sturdy handle along the top of his back to do some of my exercises at home. That way, if I fell, I could use him to get back onto my feet.

Wasn't that sad? I'd risk falling as long as no one was there to watch.

But the second any eyes were on me, going through the motions was my default. That was as easy as breathing.

Now that I sat parked in front of the office with a new person waiting inside for me, I took one last look at myself in the rearview mirror. Exhausted from trying to tame my batshit crazy hair, I finally tied it to the top of my head in a riotous bun.

There was one time in my life when I truly didn't care if I looked like a bag lady, and that was during PT. I wore my favorite black leggings and a baggy Green Valley High T-shirt—the one I'd stolen from Levi—that had a hole in the hem and constantly fell off my shoulder.

One did not need to put on mascara for your PT to make you

sweat and cry and push yourself past every comfortable physical and mental boundary you possessed.

I yanked the keys out of the ignition and exhaled heavily. The glass front of the office was reflective, so I had no idea if someone was in there watching me.

With a deep sigh, I opened the driver's side door. There were four to five steps from where I was sitting to the back of my car. With my right hand, I held tightly to the side of the car but left the driver's door open so it shielded me from view.

One.

Two.

My right leg swung out farther than my left, and I took a deep, steadying breath while my fingers gripped the locked door handle on the door behind mine.

Three.

Four.

I reached the back of the car and yanked open the hatch. When it was up, and I could see my chair, I took a second to close my eyes and enjoy the feeling of standing on both feet. The air felt different on my face when I was standing. But it required so much mental energy to get that feeling. Nothing about it was unconscious or second nature. Not anymore. What direction were my feet pointing? Did I have something to hold?

That stretched a mental muscle as much as it made my physical ones shake and groan in protest.

Turning slowly, I sat down in the back of the car and used both hands to pull my chair out until it bounced on the pavement.

This was one of the things I never even thought about.

Flinging my chair out, flipping the lever of the brake until I heard the click, then sliding my body from the car into the chair, I leaned back up to pull the hatch down on the car, then flipped the lever again so I could move forward once my feet were on the footplate between the two small stability wheels.

I didn't second-guess any of those motions.

Locking the car as I passed it, I got to the front door and punched the blue button that would swing the door open.

What? Yeah, I could've done it, but if I was about to have my ass kicked by the new dude, then not opening the door felt like an important conservation of my energy.

In the back corner of the office, one of the therapists was working with an elderly gentleman on some gait training. She smiled at me when I came in.

"Andrew will be right out for you, Joss!"

I waved at her and pushed myself in a quick circle while I waited. On my second rotation, my head almost snapped clean off my neck when I saw my new PT, Andrew.

Andrew. Andy. Also known as Brad/Chris. Also, also known as Cupcake Guy.

His face mirrored my shock.

"It's you," I said like a big ole dummy.

"Hey." He glanced down at the file in his hands. "Jocelyn Abernathy, huh?"

"That's ... that's me."

His broad chest was covered in a Maryville PT T-shirt, and my first terrible thought was, oh gawd, my hair looks like I stuck a key into a light socket and held on for about five seconds.

Andrew set the file down and crossed his arms over that chest. "What a small world."

My cheeks felt hot as I attempted a smile. "Sure is. Do you live in Maryville?"

He shook his head, looking far less uncomfortable than I was feeling. "I live closer to Green Valley, but I'm from here originally. Just moved back."

"Ah."

Andrew snagged a stool and pulled it in front of where I was nervously moving my chair back and forth in tight movements. His hand reached out and grabbed the front of my wheel. "I know it's not easy to start with a new PT, but you have nothing to be nervous about, okay?"

Ha. I looked like a homeless person. He was the first man to give me anything remotely related to butterflies in ... well, ever ... and now I got to do the one thing I hated in front of him, look clumsy and unsure and awkward.

Absolutely nothing to be nervous about while he sat here looking like he popped out of *GQ* for physical therapists.

"Let's start small, okay?" He let go of the wheel and hung his hands between his legs while he looked at my face. "Do you use your chair more than you should?"

I raised an eyebrow. "That's starting small? You might as well ask me to give my confession."

His face split in a smile. "Instead of Hail Marys, I'll just make you work harder."

"Great." I sighed and glanced up at the ceiling. "Yes, I use my chair more than I should. Since Denise left, I've done some work, but ..." my voice trailed off.

"Not enough," he supplied.

"Not enough." It felt like the hardest thing I could've possibly done, but I looked him straight in the eye. "I've mastered so many things since my accident, and I don't like how it makes me feel to do something poorly. I feel ... I feel like a failure. I feel clumsy."

He nodded. "Good."

"That so?" I drawled.

Andrew stood and tilted his chin toward where we'd start working. "Yeah. You're competitive. If you don't like feeling that way, then I have no doubt you'll work as hard as I ask to get you to the point where you don't feel like a failure." He stopped and leaned up against a desk. "Look, your walk may never be smooth, Joss. I won't bullshit you there. You need to re-frame the way you look at what you can accomplish."

With the side of my file, he tapped my biceps. "I see those muscles, and I can guarantee you've worked your ass off to get them, right?"

I lifted my chin. "Yes, I have."

"Good. Then let's get working on the rest of you, okay?" There was a walker about six feet behind him, and when he gave it a quick look, I knew what he wanted. "Show me what you've got, and we'll go from there."

When I started to wheel forward, he shook his head. I grumbled a really naughty word under my breath and locked my chair. He smothered his smile at my whispered expletive.

My butterflies were long gone, no matter how much he looked like Brad Pitt because I was too busy swallowing down the vain part of me that didn't want to stumble in front of this person. No one told you that your pride tasted like rotten acid going back down.

Quietly, Andrew sat back and watched my gait as I pushed up from my chair, braced my feet on the floor and made five halting, unsteady steps to the walker. I curled my hands around the handles and turned in his direction.

"Good." He walked to the other side of the room and motioned for me to follow, turning around to study my movements as I did. "Let's get to work, Miss Abernathy."

* * *

The sweat on my back was finally cooling as I drove back into Green Valley. Get to work, indeed. My legs *hurt*. And my back hurt. And my arms. The thought of going home, and how I'd never be able to talk to my mom about this without her getting that puckered expression on her face, like she'd just sucked on a lemon felt unbearable.

Are you sure that's a good idea? I'd hate for you to get your hopes up and then not have it work out. You're so good in that chair, sweetie.

I could hear the words clear as a bell. She'd said them years ago when I first told her I wanted to start working on walking sporadically. She'd never said them again, but no matter how hard I tried, I couldn't scrub them from my brain.

Without making the decision to, my car pointed itself to Levi's. When I pulled into the driveway, his big black truck wasn't there, so I parked closer to the main house. The Buchanans had put a ramp in the garage, and no, I did not take for granted how amazing it was that my best friend's family loved me so much that they modified their house to make it easier for me to be there.

After I parked and got my chair out, I pushed up the ramp in the garage and used my left hand to open the door into the mud room.

"Anyone home?"

"In here, sweetie," Mrs. Buchanan called from the kitchen. "Perfect timing."

"Yeah?"

She was at the large island, glaring at her stand mixer like it had sinned against her.

I smiled. "What's wrong?"

"The frosting is too loose, and I can't figure out why."

Leaning up so I could see what she was making, I nodded. "Mr. B's strawberry cake? I didn't miss his birthday, did I?"

Absently, she patted my shoulder. "Oh, honey, you didn't miss it. I just wanted to surprise him is all. He's been so busy at work."

I opened up the drawer to my right and grabbed a spoon, then reached over to scoop some of the frosting from the bowl. "'S'good. But do you normally put diced strawberries in the frosting? I thought you only put them between the layers."

Her eyes, the same shade as Levi's, lit with understanding. "You know, you're right. I don't normally put them in there, do I? Lord, I'm losing my mind. I think I'm going senile, Joss."

"No, you're not." I laughed. "But that would probably do it. Not much you can do about getting rid of the moisture in the berries."

With a shake of her head, she opened up the garbage and dumped the frosting. "Well, if this is any indication, I'd better practice the cake Sylvia wanted me to make for her shower,."

"What'd she ask for?"

"That wild berry tart I haven't made in about eighteen years." She waved a hand. "I suppose it hasn't been that long, but it sure feels like it."

"Mmm, I love that one. Do you need any help with the shower?"

"I think we've got it all handled, honey, but I'll let you know. My sisters are doing most of the food, and Memaw Buchanan is handling all the setup."

I gave the spoon another slow lick while I thought about their extended family, all of whom I knew. "Isn't that funny?"

"What?"

"You come from a family of all girls, and the Buchanans have always had boys, didn't they?"

She laughed. "Almost always. Mr. B's brother, you know Glenn, he and his ex-wife had the first girl in five generations. Of course, the family joke was that she was only allowed to be born a Buchanan girl because she came out with a twin brother. You remember the twins, right? Grady and Grace? It's been a few years since they visited."

"Yeah, it was Christmas about four years ago, right?"

I remembered two tawny-haired, ridiculously attractive people only a couple of years older than Levi. Grace intimidated me because she wore Daisy Dukes no matter what the weather and had a perpetual look on her face like she would beat the shit out of anyone who crossed her. Her brother was sweet, though. Reminded me a lot of Levi.

"That's right," she said. "They'll be here for the wedding."

I nodded.

She eyed me. "How's your day going, honey? Levi told me you started with a new PT today. He's out for a run with Connor, by the way. Should be back soon."

I sighed. "Yeah, I had PT."

"Come on, tell me everything."

I opened my mouth to give her a standard answer, but I got the Francine Buchanan look. The *don't you dare try to put me off right now* look.

"It sucked," I said, dropping my head into my hands. "I was so rusty, it felt like I was trying to walk on cooked noodles."

"Well now, nothing worthwhile will come from easy work, right?"

"Says the woman who can stand on her own two feet without worrying about tipping over."

She clucked her tongue. "Don't sass me. We've all got stuff that's hard for us."

I took another small bite of the frosting left on my spoon and then brought it over to the sink so I could toss it in with the rest of the dishes she had soaking. "Want me to start on these?"

"No, no, I've more of a mess to make yet. Keep talking while I work."

I went to the opposite side of the island, locked my chair, and lifted myself into one of the stools. "My new therapist is much tougher on me."

"Good. That last one was a waste."

"Okay, *Levi.*"

Mrs. B smiled prettily. "Maybe I did hear that a time or two from him. You need people in your life who are willing to push you, sweetie." She raised a perfectly manicured eyebrow as she said it.

The unspoken layer under her words was aimed at my mom, and we both knew it.

"I fell twice," I said quietly. "I've let my right leg go too much. Both of them really. And I don't have a good excuse."

She dumped a block of cream cheese into the bowl and set it to mixing. "Falling is okay every now and then, Jocelyn."

Oh great, she used my full name.

I set my chin in my hand and sighed. "But knowing it doesn't make it any easier on your way down," I said.

"Quite true." Using a spatula, she scraped along the inside of the bowl to make sure everything mixed evenly. *I love her*, I thought as I watched her. I loved this whole family. And I wish I could sit like this and talk to my own mother. Tell her that it sucked to fall in front of the cute boy who bought me a cupcake.

"You got back up, though, didn't you?" she asked.

It would have been easy to focus on what I couldn't do instead of what I could. And being able to sit in this kitchen with her made me happy. Made me feel supported and loved. The least I could do was be honest with her.

"I did."

Her eyes met mine briefly, then she handed me a spoon to try the new batch of frosting. "That's my girl."

After I swallowed, giving her a hum of approval, I fiddled with the edge of the spoon. Words started crowding my mouth, and I knew I couldn't keep this from her any more than I should've kept it from Levi.

"It was just ... someone I didn't really want to fall in front of." The embarrassment had my face hot and my body cold. How did people talk about this shit? I felt like I was being served up on a platter for someone to filet me open.

Her words came out slowly, carefully. "Isn't your PT the one person you'd be able to stumble in front of? That's what they're helping you with."

"I know. You're right."

"But ...?"

I smiled a little. Mrs. B always saw right through me. "He's ..." I paused, licking my lips and catching some frosting left in the corner of my mouth. "He's ... cute. And I met him at the bakery before I knew he was my PT, and I think he was flirting with me. And I don't know exactly how I feel about that because I think I was flirting back, and I'm terrible at this." The words came out in a rush.

The look in her eyes was surprisingly sad even as she smiled at me. Her hand came up to cup the side of my face.

"Sweet girl," she said, rubbing her thumb over my cheekbone. "You couldn't be terrible at something if you tried."

My eyes pricked hot, and I blinked quickly. "I'd be terrible at running sprints."

She laughed, unsurprised by my humor after five years, then dropped her hand back to the counter. "How did he act after he saw you today?"

My teeth worried against my bottom lip. "He was shocked but professional. No flirty vibe today, that's for sure."

Mrs. B nodded. "Well, I think you should just get to know him better. If he was flirting with you at the bakery, it means he's a man of exceptional taste."

"You're only a little biased."

She was smiling as she started dropping the frosting over the top of the strawberry cake. Just as I'd taught her, she spun the turntable that held the cake in order to smooth the frosting easier. Her eyes stayed trained on what she was doing when she spoke next. "Have you talked to Levi about this?"

Her voice sounded a little strained.

I shrugged. "Not yet. It felt ... I don't know ... awkward to bring it up."

She swallowed. "I can understand that. One of those times when you just want a woman's opinion."

"Exactly." I exhaled. "But he's my best friend, so I *should* talk to him about it, shouldn't I? Maybe he could give me guy tips. Tell me if I'm crazy for thinking Girl in the Wheelchair has a shot. No offense to the general male population, but they do have a bit of a harder time over-looking allll this," I said, waving my hand in the vicinity of my chair and legs.

Mrs. B stopped spinning the cake and took a deep breath.

"What's with the sad eyes?" I asked, suddenly uncomfortable for a reason I couldn't quite pinpoint. "I sure hope you're not starting to pity me after five years."

Immediately, she set down the spatula and came to stand in front of me. With both hands, she grabbed my face. Her hazel eyes, exactly like her son's, weren't sad. They were blazing.

"No one in this family pities you, Jocelyn Marie," she said fiercely. "I pity *anyone* who overlooks or underestimates you. Do you under-stand me?"

I nodded, inhaling shakily. This time, I didn't try to blink away the moisture pooling in my eyes. She wrapped me in a rib-crushing hug, and I exhaled into her embrace.

When she pulled away, her eyes were bright with tears too. "Good. Now, I need to get this cake done and hidden in the fridge before the boys come home and think they can eat it."

Laughing at the truth of that, I slid off the stool and back into my chair. "Okay. I think I'm going to lie down for a little bit. I'm tired."

She kissed the top of my head. "I'll tell Levi to be quiet when he gets back."

"Love you, Mrs. B," I told her as I pushed my chair back.

Damn it, and that gave her sad eyes again. "We love you too, honey. More than you know."

Her words settled sweet and heavy in my chest as I rolled out of the garage and over the driveway to Levi's apartment. In my head, I turned them over and over as I lifted my tired body out of my chair and up onto Levi's couch.

The air conditioning kicked on, and I reached back to grab his favorite blanket off the back of the couch. It smelled like him, like my best friend. Burrowing my nose in it, I took a deep breath and slowly drifted off to sleep.

CHAPTER 6

LEVI

"*I*f you think you ran that third mile faster than me, you're on drugs," I told Connor as he pulled his truck onto our street.

My brother side-eyed me. "I absolutely did."

"This is why I don't work out with you anymore. You're a pathological liar."

He was grinning. "Okay, sweet cheeks. Whatever helps you sleep at night."

My phone vibrated from the side pocket of my gym bag. I pulled it out and scrolled down until I found the email notification. "Awesome," I muttered. "Another 'your resume looks impressive, but we're looking for a candidate with more experience' reply." The third such one I'd gotten in the past three days. Tossing my phone down into the bag, I shook my head. "How the hell are you supposed to get experience if no one will give you a shot?"

Connor frowned in sympathy. "It's tough out there."

"I'm getting bored, man."

"Being J's personal chauffeur isn't cutting it for you anymore?"

The look I gave him should've shriveled up his balls, but he merely grinned back at me. "I'm spending the same amount of time with her that I do every summer."

"Mmkay."

"Shut up." I swallowed, not ready to admit out loud what I'd already started to think about in my head. "Man, what if I can't find a job around here? Green Valley doesn't have anything for me, and no one in Maryville is hiring. I've submitted to every place in Knoxville that's even close to what I want to be doing."

Connor sighed. "And if you start looking much farther ..."

I nodded. "I'm gonna have to move, and I don't want to leave her. I don't even care how pathetic that makes me sound; it's the truth."

"But you need a job, too. You've worked your ass off for the past six years. You can hardly blame yourself for not knowing she existed when you started school and picked your major."

"Picking my major is how I met her," I reminded him. "I never would've coached that team if I was in business school or something."

We pulled into the driveway, and there was her car, parked in front of the house like it belonged there.

"Have you called Hunter?" Connor asked, referring to our oldest brother who lived in Seattle.

I gave him a weird look. "What's he gonna do? He's like, a school administrator or something."

"Yeah, at that uppity rich people prep school, man. Maybe he's got some connections he can call." Connor pulled his truck in next to Joss's car, and he looked over at it meaningfully. "Isn't it worth it to check? Let's be real, sometimes pulling a few strings is the only way someone will finally give you a shot. Or maybe Samantha does," he said, mentioning our brother's wife with a pinched forehead.

We only looked at each other briefly before he started laughing. "Yeah, I know. We've talked to her like, twice ever. Maybe not Samantha. But it can't hurt to ask Hunter."

"I suppose."

"Ask Grady too," he said, referring to our cousin. "He's got that ... whatever the hell he does."

I laughed. "Don't ask me. He loses me every time he brings it up.

But it's nothing to do with sports either. Some tech thing that goes way over my head."

"Can't hurt, little brother. That's what family is for, you know." Connor slugged my shoulder as I got out of his truck, and I nodded as I got out so he could head back to his place just down the road, the house Sylvia would be moving into with him after they got married.

I glanced over at my apartment, but it looked dark, so I walked through the garage and let myself in. The kitchen was empty, as was the family room. There was no answer when I called out for my mom and Joss. Hooking my gym bag over my shoulder, I walked back to my place slowly, typing out a text to Hunter.

Me: Hey, big brother, I'm tapping out all my options here for a job, and it's not looking promising. Know anybody who might talk to an incredibly intelligent Southern boy with impeccable manners and a master's degree in sports medicine?

I hit send just before I opened the door, and through the window next to it, I saw her asleep on the couch.

As quietly as I could, I turned the knob and walked in.

Her chest rose and fell evenly, and her face was smooth as she slept deeply. She was curled on her side, my blanket covering her up to her chin. Sitting carefully on the chaise that extended out of the other side of the couch, I set my chin in my hands and watched her sleep.

In five years, I had the thought often that my life would be easier if I didn't love her. If I could look at her and not have my chest pinch painfully from the force of my tightly bound feelings. If I could be next to her and not wonder what it would feel like to tilt her mouth up to mine and kiss her smooth pink lips. It would be so much easier if I could lay awake at night and not have to wonder if I'd live with this yearning for the rest of my life.

I'd felt wild physical attraction before her—the kind of lust that only a seventeen-year-old boy could—and I wasn't a virgin. That ship sailed a solid year before I met Joss, but it wasn't something I regret. How could I have possibly known what it would feel like the day I met her? There was no way.

In the years since, I'd dated other girls. I'd kissed them, touched them, and let them touch me—sometimes spurred on by a desperation for that same spark, that same tug in my chest that Joss pulled on every time I was around her. Yet every kiss, every touch felt wrong on a soul-deep level. Not because I believed in some unattainable chaste ideal, or that experiencing other people before we found our person was wrong, but because I'd already found her.

Whatever my own soul was comprised of, that intangible thing residing in my body that made me *me* met its match the day I met Jocelyn. And trying to make someone else fit was one massive exercise in frustration.

"Stupid Buchanan curse," I whispered.

There would never be a day when I didn't wish Jocelyn would just … wake up and realize it. That one day, she'd see me differently. That she could look back on the day we met and see that I'd never wavered because the way I loved her was as constant and unyielding as the Earth rotating around the sun. Something that couldn't be stopped or prevented.

In her sleep, she shifted on her back, but her long legs remained where they were.

And I watched as Joss slowly started to wake. When she opened her eyes—the morning glories climbing up the east side of my parents' porch blue—she didn't notice me right away.

"Good morning, sunshine," I said quietly.

She smiled, stretching her arms over her head with a satisfied groan.

I wanted to see her do that every fucking morning for the rest of my life.

"That was an epic nap," she said in an adorably groggy voice. Her eyes fell shut again, her mouth curving up in a tiny smile.

"Yeah?"

Joss hummed, eyes still closed. "Can you move my legs for me? Stretch them out?"

I swallowed. My fingers curled into my palms. "Sure."

Even though I didn't need to move with such careful, slow movements—and even though she could, and probably should, do it herself—I slid my hands up the back of her calves until they were hooked under her bent knees. Turning her legs so that they were straight, I brought her feet up against my thigh. People underestimated how tall she was. I didn't get to stand next to her often, but when I did, it was so hard not to wrap my arms around her and see where her face hit.

"Where's Nero?" I asked, pulling my hands back once her legs were situated.

"Left him at home. Didn't want to scare off the new PT."

Grinning, I stood to grab a bottle of water out the fridge. "Need anything?"

"I'm good, thanks."

"How did it go? Was it a Denise 2.0, or did we actually manage an upgrade?"

Joss hated when I went to PT with her. Probably because with my degree, I was perfectly capable of helping her myself, but she wanted someone who wasn't so emotionally invested.

The irony of how little she knew of my emotional investment was not lost on me.

After draining half the water in two large swallows, I realized she hadn't answered me. When I turned, she was pulling herself up to sitting. I smiled at the absolute mess that was her hair. Half was still up in a bun while half fell around her face and shoulders.

"I like what you've got going on there," I said, lifting my chin at her head.

She patted her hair and groaned. As she went about fixing it, she sighed. "Yeah, figures that I look like absolute shit today."

"You don't look like shit," I said instantly. Joss raised an eyebrow at my tone but didn't comment. "Besides, since when do you care how you look at PT?"

Hair fixed and somewhat tamed, Joss looked me square in the eye, and blurted, "I'm having date feelings, and it's weird, and I don't know what to do about it."

I froze with the bottle halfway to my mouth. Where it was buried in my chest, protected by skin and muscles and bones, my heart turned over in an unhealthy, chugging motion. Biological impossibility aside, that was what it felt like.

Words sprang up on my tongue, and I breathed through them, taking my time to set down the water bottle before I joined her on the couch again.

Was this ... was this it?

Her face didn't look dewy or glowy or suddenly transformed with *I'm in love with my best friend* feelings.

"Date feelings are good," I said carefully. Her eyes were watching my face so intently that I felt sweat break out on the back of my neck. "I've always enjoyed them."

The second she rolled her eyes, I knew I screwed up.

"That's not what I meant," I stammered.

Joss flopped back and stared up at the ceiling. "Of course you enjoy them. All you have to do is breathe, and every single woman under the age of eighty-two in Green Valley looks at you like you just cured cancer."

I breathed out a laugh, spearing a hand through my hair. The irony, the irony, the mind-bending irony of what she just said. Yeah, except for the *one* single woman who I wanted to look at me like that.

I felt like Joss just tossed me ass first into a minefield. Blindfolded.

One wrong move and *kablooey*.

In her lap, she was wringing her fingers together, one of her nervous tells. I sighed, leaning forward to lay my hand on hers. Finally, she dropped her chin and looked at me again. She looked miserable.

Okay. *Time to be what she needs*, I told myself. Not time to be what I want.

I got up from the couch and went to the cupboard next to the fridge. On the middle shelf, I always kept an emergency stash of her favorite snacks. She smiled when I tossed the bag of Twizzlers onto her lap.

Once I was back on the couch, my legs stretched out next to hers so that we were facing each other, I jerked my chin. "Talk to me."

I could do this. Joss pulled out a piece of licorice and chewed on the end, those beautiful eyes unfocused.

I could do this. For her.

"I've never had date feelings before," she said. "Until this week."

"Never?" I asked carefully.

She shook her head.

"And"—I swallowed—"and you are now?"

She nodded, her eyes pinched shut now. "It's complicated, though."

"H-how so?"

Joss opened her eyes, face scrunched up in misery. "It's my new PT."

"Oh shit," I whispered unthinkingly.

She dropped her face into her hands. "I know," she wailed. "It's awful."

Was

it

ever.

As much as I wanted to launch off the couch and pace the room to untangle my tangled, racing thoughts, she needed me more because she was so clearly uncomfortable.

"Sonic."

Her hands still covered her face. I smiled a little, reaching forward to pull them away. Her cheeks were flaming pink.

"Why is it awful?"

"I-I met him before today." My confusion must have been evident on my face because she exhaled heavily. "At the bakery. He came in twice before I had any idea he was my new PT."

"He was stalking you?" I roared.

Her mouth fell open at my reaction. "Whoa, psycho, dial it back about ten notches, okay? He didn't know who I was either."

My shoulders deflated a little bit, but man, my heart was one rough beat away from bursting out of my chest. "Sorry."

I didn't sound sorry. I sounded insane. With Herculean effort, I schooled my expression.

"Remember when you came in at the end of my shift today?" When I nodded, she scrunched up her nose. "Well, you were standing right behind him in line. That was him."

I hadn't paid much attention to who was in front of me. The only thing I could remember was that he was tall, about my height, and he'd left her money for a tip.

Shit. He was a nice guy.

"I remember," I admitted. "Not that I paid much attention to him."

"Can't blame you," she said evenly. "It's not like you'd expect to see someone flirting with me."

I gave her a long look, which she returned with one eyebrow arched up. "That's not what I said, and it's not what I was thinking."

Now it was Joss's turn to deflate. "I know. This is all so, I don't know, foreign."

It was impossible not to shake my head at the thought that no one had ever flirted with Joss. "This doesn't make sense, Sonic. There's no way this has never happened to you before."

"Gimme a break," she said, sounding as tired as she had when she first woke up. "Don't play that game where you act like my chair doesn't matter, or that the world should be blind to its existence. It doesn't work that way, and you know it."

It would be so easy to rise to the bait and argue with her about what I saw when I looked at her; that I *did* think people were stupid if they looked at her and only saw the cold lump of metal and plastic that happened to help her get around.

"I know it doesn't."

Joss stared down at her lap, then glanced briefly at her chair, locked into place next to the couch.

Foreign was a good word for this whole damn exchange. Maybe I didn't notice her chair anymore. But I was an idiot in a whole different way because, up until this moment, I damn well took for granted that this hadn't come up before.

It was only a matter of time before someone looked at her and saw what I'd seen five years ago. As I sat and watched her, I knew that I'd been a lucky asshole that it took this long. But it wasn't lucky for her. She deserved to have men seeing her, noticing her, being interested in her. I just ... wanted her to end up with me outside of all that.

Choosing my next words carefully, I took a deep breath.

"It doesn't make sense because you are an incredibly smart, funny, beautiful woman, Joss, no matter where you sit. It doesn't make sense to me that there are men out there who could possibly not see that."

She didn't want to look at me. Joss kept her eyes trained down at her lap, and she sniffed.

"You know," she said after a long moment, "your mom made me cry today too."

"That bitch."

Joss laughed, finally looking up at me. It had been a long time since I'd seen her cry, and I forgot what it did to the color of her eyes. It deepened the blue and made the black of her lashes darker.

"It's never bothered me that I didn't have date feelings or that I didn't know what it felt like to have someone flirting with me." She swallowed roughly. "But today, in PT, with him acting perfectly professional, I fell twice. Hard. And I hated how embarrassed it made me when I had to pull myself up."

I had to breathe through my almost violent desire to check her body for bruises. To run my hands over her legs to soothe whatever hurt might be left over and pull her in my arms because I knew how much she hated falling in front of people. Even now, she didn't like walking in front of me.

"Date feelings suck, Levi."

"They don't always suck," I said quietly, keeping my eyes on her face.

Joss blew out a slow breath. "I'll get over it."

"It's not always that simple, you know?"

Her teeth flashed white behind her pink lips when she smiled. "Oh, yeah? You seemed to get over what's-her-name from Maryville pretty easily."

I played dumb. I'd only dated one girl from Maryville in the past two years, and I liked that Joss was paying attention. "What's her name?"

She gave me a look. "The crazy one."

"Ahh, yes. Mallory."

Joss rolled her eyes. "She was one step away from stealing a lock of your hair."

"That she was." I grinned at her. "Okay, yes, those date feelings are simple to get over."

With a groan, Joss sat up and pulled the blanket off her legs, lifting them so that she could reach for her chair.

"Heading home?" I asked pointlessly.

"Yeah. My mom is sleeping all day because she has to work tonight, and Nero probably needs to be let out."

I wished I hadn't gone for such a long run so I'd been back earlier. Normally, I didn't get this desperate edge when she left. Maybe it was the topic. Maybe it was the tall, muscular, probably stupidly handsome, generous tipper who was giving my best friend date feelings that had me jittery to see her leave.

"Want me to go get him? I can bring him back here if you want to hang out longer."

She braced her hands on her chair and slid over, flipping the locks and sending me a quick smile. "No, it's okay. Thanks, though."

I walked her out, following behind her chair as she headed across the driveway.

"I work tomorrow morning," she said as she hopped into the driver's seat. I took the chair and put it in the back hatch of her car.

"Sweet. I'll come by for another pecan roll."

Joss shook her head and smiled at me.

I didn't breathe normally for at least two minutes after she pulled out and drove home. That shit should've just earned me an Oscar nom because inside, my body was freaking the hell out.

I needed to talk to Connor. Now.

CHAPTER 7

LEVI

*C*onnor and Sylvia were definitely not expecting me. When I burst through the door without knocking, she shrieked, burrowing her face in Connor's chest where they were tangled on the couch.

Everyone was dressed, so I ignored the dirty look he gave me.

"You need to fix this door," I said, hooking a thumb over my shoulder. My skin was tight and jittery, my mind racing and my heart thrashing in my chest. "It's why Joss can never come over. Her chair bumps on one side, and it's embarrassing for her."

My brother got up off his fiancée and sighed heavily. "Levi, can we talk about this later?"

"No," I yelled. "Do you ever wonder why she's only hanging out at my place? She can't just go anywhere she wants, Connor."

Sylvia's face was full of sympathy, and though my brother's was tight with annoyance, he grimaced when I finished my little rant.

"We'll replace the door soon, Levi," she said, setting an arm on my brother's back. "As soon as we get home from our honeymoon, okay?"

Jamming my hands in my hair, I paced into their kitchen, then opened the fridge and slammed it shut.

"What's up, little brother?"

The fridge was still empty of whatever the hell I was looking for when I opened the door again. I didn't even know what I was looking for.

"She's got date feelings."

My proclamation, which I spit out like it was coated in vinegar, was met with silence.

Turning toward them, I held my arms out. "She's got date feelings. For the first time ever. And they are definitely not aimed at me."

Sylvia punched a fist in the air. "I freaking *knew* it. I knew you liked her."

Connor shrugged when my face went blank with shock.

"She didn't know?" I asked incredulously.

He shook his head. "Didn't think it was my place to tell her."

She punched him in general area of his kidneys, and he yelped. "*You* knew? How long has he liked her?"

The dining room chair behind me made for a good resting place as I sat heavily in it. Connor was still rubbing at his side when understanding dawned in Sylvia's face.

"It's always been her, hasn't it?"

I rubbed at the back of my neck.

She clucked her tongue and crossed her arms over her chest. "And here I thought you escaped the curse. But you just did a good job of hiding it, you little sneak."

"I definitely didn't escape it."

Her eyes narrowed on her fiancée. "You've known the whole time?"

"Not the whole time," he hedged. Sylvia went to punch him again, but he blocked it. "Okay fine, yes, he told us, and we've known for about ninety percent of their friendship."

She gasped. "Seriously? Wait, who's us?"

"My parents," I answered since my kidneys were safe. "Honestly, Syl, I thought you knew because of how often you dropped really not-subtle clues."

"I wasn't trying to be subtle."

"No shit," I muttered.

Connor turned and pointed at her. "That's why I didn't tell you. If you knew he's been in love with her for five years, you would've been relentless, woman."

"Don't you 'woman' me," she warned, eyes turning glacial.

"Okay, we're getting off track," I interjected. "Everyone is caught up, I'm pathetic, and now I'm probably too late because she's having date feelings for her new physical therapist."

"Oh shit," Connor said.

Sylvia grimaced.

"Yeah." I rolled my neck until it popped a few times. "I managed to listen to her tell me about how he flirted with her the first time they met, and then she flirted back, and how she thinks she's awful at this."

"He flirted with a new client?" Sylvia hissed. "That's got to be some breach of ethical conduct. Let's report his ass."

"Calm down," I said. "They met at the bakery first. Neither of them realized she was his new client."

She deflated. "Oh."

Doing my best robot impression, I told them everything Joss told me. And at Sylvia's request, I told her about the moment I knew—how the moment she aimed that smile at me, I was a fucking goner.

Her hands were resting on her chest when I got to the end of my little story when Joss said she'd like to have a friend.

"Oh, Levi," she whispered. "For five years?"

"I know, it's ridiculous." I shook my head. "I'm ridiculous."

"No, you're not," she said. "Because you really do think of her as your best friend, don't you?"

"Of course I do," I answered instantly. "I wouldn't be able to fake a friendship this long."

Connor shifted on the couch and gave his fiancée a quick look. "Don't punch me again, but it's a little ridiculous."

"Thanks," I said.

"How do you figure?" Sylvia asked.

He turned so he was looking at her. "Imagine if, when we met, you had shot me down instead of agreeing to go out with me. I never asked you again. I never even hinted that I felt more for you than the passing interest that someone feels when they ask for a first date without knowing the person at all."

Sylvia pushed her tongue into the side of her cheek but didn't answer. I closed my eyes, not really interested in seeing any more of her nonverbals.

Connor kept going. "So imagine five years go by. Would you ever fathom that I still feel the way I did when we were sixteen?"

Sylvia didn't answer right away, and as much as I didn't want to, I opened my eyes to watch her. But I knew what she'd say.

After giving me an apologetic look, she shook her head. "Probably not."

"Thanks for telling me this now," I said to Connor.

"Would you have listened? Would you have attempted anything with her without the clearest of signals that she was ready for more?"

I looked away, and that was answer enough for him.

"Listen, no one doubts the sincerity of your feelings. We all love her, we all consider her a part of the family, but you need to pull your head out of your ass and start trying."

Sylvia's eyes widened. "Especially if she's got a hot guy who's helping her learn how to *walk*." She sucked in a quick breath between gritted teeth. "That's some wicked competition right there."

"She already knows how to walk, Syl. Let's not get dramatic. He's just helping her with some exercises to build up her strength."

Sylvia held up her hands. "Fine. Let's diminish his role if it makes us all feel better."

Connor gave her a chiding look.

"What?" she asked. "He came here for honest advice, right?"

"I did," I agreed. "Because apparently, my big brother has sat back thinking I'm ridiculous and didn't bother to tell me."

"Would you have listened?" he asked again.

"Okay," Sylvia said, holding up a hand to silence him. "Here's the deal. You just need to start courting her."

I gave her a blank look. "Right."

"If she's having 'date feelings,' then do date things with her. Don't just hang out at your place like you always do. Let her know you're thinking of her."

"I'm always thinking of her," I said under my breath.

Her face went all soft and happy. "I can give you ideas until I'm blue in the face, but Levi, you know her better than anyone. At the end of the day, a woman wants someone who sees her. Who understands her, respects her, and treats her as though she's valued and important and cherished."

I already felt all those things for Joss; they were tightly wound around the core of who I was. Inextricable and inflexible.

Sylvia sat forward and took a deep breath. "Don't get mad at me for asking this, okay?"

I exhaled a laugh. "Hit me."

"We all know you're one of the best advocates she has, outside of herself, but are you holding yourself back because she's in that chair?"

The breath left my lungs in a rush. Connor dropped his head but didn't say anything.

"What the hell, Sylvia?" I asked, standing slowly. "Are you seriously asking if I treat her differently because of what happened to her?"

My voice sounded sharp to my own ears, but to her credit, she never flinched. Sylvia lifted her chin.

"What I'm asking is if you tread more carefully in regard to her emotions because of it, yes. Do you tiptoe around how she feels because of it? If she stood on her feet all day, would you have taken another shot six months later? A year?"

Anger and defensiveness swirled dangerously in my head, and I could feel Connor watching me carefully. He wasn't arguing with her, but he didn't agree with her either.

I paced into the kitchen and braced my hands on their counter, my head dropping down as I took a few deep breaths.

"I can't answer that," I said, words coming up like I'd yanked them from my throat with a rusty hook. "Because you're asking me to imagine a world that doesn't exist."

Sylvia's brow furrowed at my response.

"I'm not mad at you for asking, but Joss has to view the world differently because of where she sits. That's her viewpoint. Her chair, her legs are a part of her reality. Just like I can't look at the world from yours or Connor's viewpoint, I can only look at it from mine. She is not just a small part of my reality, Sylvia; she's the most important part of it." I straightened and met her gaze head-on. "So yes, I took her situation into consideration when I made my decisions, and maybe that makes me ridiculous, but I wouldn't change anything. I don't regret a single day of the past five years because for those five years, she's been my favorite person in the world to spend time with."

I didn't even realize Sylvia was crying until she swiped a hand over her cheek.

She sniffed. Connor smiled softly, rubbing the top of her leg.

"Okay," she said in a watery voice.

"Okay?" I huffed out laugh. "Just okay?"

Sylvia got off the couch and walked toward me, wrapping me in a tight hug when I turned to face her. "She's really lucky to have you, Levi."

I set my chin on her head and smiled. "I've always thought so."

Connor rolled his eyes, and Sylvia laughed.

After she pulled away from me, Sylvia grabbed a tissue from the box on their counter and noisily blew her nose.

"You have to ask her to the wedding, Levi."

"I know," I said wearily. "But that feels like a cop-out for a first date option."

She nodded in agreement. "Then start small. Do sweet things for her that you know she'll like. Tell her when you think she looks beautiful. If she's feeling these date feelings for this PT guy, as you say, then you can make her feel date feelings for you. Mark my words." Her eyes swept me from head to toe. "She already likes your personality, and you're not horrible to look at."

"Gee, thanks," I said dryly.

Connor choked on a laugh.

"I'm telling you," Sylvia added. "This will be easier than you think."

"Making my best friend for the past five years fall in love with me?" I raised my eyebrows. "Yeah, I'm sure it'll be a piece of cake."

CHAPTER 8

JOCELYN

"I think we need to tell Jennifer," Joy said, wringing her hands together, face pinched with uncharacteristic worry.

"I promise, he's fine. He won't bother anyone." I pinched the fondant together at the end, then placed the rolled end into the buttercream, one perfect little green leaf sticking out from underneath the blossom I'd made for the top of the cupcake.

"But we've had complaints," Joy whispered.

I lifted my eyes to her. "You mean the *one* woman who asked why there was a dog outside?"

She nodded vigorously.

"Is that a complaint or a comment?"

Joy froze, eyes darting toward the entrance. Just to the right of the door, Nero had chosen his spot, and he was currently fast asleep underneath one of the wrought iron tables. "I suppose it's a comment."

I set another finished cupcake on the tray and looked up at her. "I promise, if one single customer comes in and says he shouldn't be there, I'll have Levi come pick him up and take him home."

Her eyes lit up. "Really?"

"Yeah," I answered.

"And he'd just do that for you?"

"Levi?"

She nodded vigorously.

"You know him? I mean, beyond seeing him pick me up the other day."

Joy gave me a look like I was crazy. "I was a freshman when he was a senior. He's ... we all know the Buchanans. Of course, I know him."

"Ahh." Right. One of those moments when my 'sore thumb' status in Green Valley was ever so apparent.

"He's so handsome," she told me as if I didn't look at that face every single damn day.

I shrugged. "He's all right."

Joy's offended gasp made me burst out laughing. Her face looked like I'd just told her that her cupcakes tasted like dirt.

"Jocelyn?" Mikey asked, head poking around the corner into the kitchen. "Can you come out here?"

Joy was muttering about Levi when I wheeled past her. "Just all right," I heard her say under her breath.

I was still grinning when I made my way behind the counter. Mikey was talking to a woman who was ninety, if she was a day, and holding the sides of a walker like it was the only thing keeping her standing.

Swallowing roughly, I tried to imagine being out in public in my walker. My chair kept me moving smoothly and quickly, I could pivot and spin, hop a curb with relative ease, and pop a wheelie if I felt so moved.

Oh, but pride was a bitter pill to swallow, wasn't it?

The fifteen-year-old me trying to get used to my chair never would've imagined that I'd use it as a safety net.

"What's up, Mikey?"

He nodded at the customer who peered over her thick-lensed glasses at me. For a few seconds, she stared at the wheels on my chair, then back up to my face.

"She had a question."

I blinked in confusion. "Okay." Giving her a polite smile, I turned my chair a bit so I was facing her more fully. "How can I help you, ma'am?"

"There's a wild dog sitting outside." Her voice was shaky, but her eyes were unflinching. The skin around them was wrinkled and translucent, spotted with age.

"Oh, that's my dog. He just ... likes to stay with me as much as possible, but it's a health code violation to have him inside the bakery."

From the back of her throat, she made a small harrumph sound. "He looks scary."

I smiled at her. "He's very sweet, I promise."

"What's his name?"

"Nero," I answered.

She glanced over her glasses at me. "After the Roman emperor who burned people alive?"

Mikey cleared his throat to cover a laugh.

"Yes?"

"Don't you know your own dog's name?" she asked.

"Yes," I repeated. "I just liked the sound of it. It sounded ... tough."

"Huh." She looked at my chair again. "You need him for help getting around?"

Like he knew we were talking about him, Nero stood and stretched his back legs, then plopped down in a sitting position and stared over his shoulder at me.

"Not technically, but sometimes I hook up his leash and harness to my chair, and he pulls me up some of the foothills when I take him out for exercise."

Her eyes narrowed. "Fine. I'll take a banana cake."

At her strange non sequitur, I blinked. "Umm. Okay."

"I'll go box one up," Mikey said.

"Make sure it was made today," she called after him. "I don't want one that's been sitting around for a couple of days."

I bit down on my smile as I told her the total. Very carefully, she counted out exact change from her metallic purple coin purse. It matched the chain on her glasses.

"I had a dog," she said as I was putting her money in the drawer.

"What was his name?"

"Her name was Daffodil." She tucked her coin purse back into an embroidered pocket hooked around the side of her walker. "She was a Shih Tzu."

"Those are very cute dogs," I told her.

Her iron eyes looked over the rim of her glasses again. "Meanest bitch of a dog I've ever met in my life. She bit everyone who tried to pet her."

"Oh," I said dumbly. "I'm sorry?"

"She's dead now, so it's fine."

Where was Mikey with that damn cake? I cleared my throat. If anyone wondered why I hated small talk, it was moments exactly like this one. She was staring straight at my chair.

"You're Ruby's granddaughter, aren't you?"

"I am." I eyed her curiously. "You knew her?"

If someone could roll their eyes without moving a single muscle, she just managed it. I felt her eye roll like she'd shoved it down my throat. "I'm old, aren't I? All us old people know each other here."

I swear, if Mikey didn't show up soon, I'd walk back and get the banana cake myself if it would make this go faster.

"I've heard she wore a purple hat to church," I said lamely.

She puckered her lips like someone shoved a lemon in her mouth. "Shame that she and your momma never spoke much. A woman shouldn't have lost out on a relationship with her only grandchild."

Right. There was no way I was touching that statement.

"You been in that thing long?" she asked, lifting her chin at my chair.

"Uhh, about seven years."

"Hmm. How come?"

I kept my face as straight as possible. "It's a really comfortable seat."

She narrowed her eyes, but then a tiny smile curled her thin, pale lips.

Mikey appeared with the box, and she beckoned him to come around the corner with a curl of one bony hand. With wide eyes, he walked it around to her so he could set it on the seat of her walker.

"You're funny, young lady," she told me.

"Oh, don't tell her that," a voice said from behind her.

I hadn't even noticed Levi walk in, and he was standing to the side, holding a flat box in his hands. He was grinning at me, tawny hair in desperate need of a haircut and a deep dimple carved into his cheek.

"Why not?" she snapped.

"It'll go straight to her head, and then she'll never answer people nicely when they ask her things."

"What's your name, boy?" she asked. "I recognize your face. You look like your daddy."

"Levi Buchanan, ma'am." He held out his hand, and she took it. "It's a pleasure to meet you."

"You're too charming for your own good, Levi Buchanan."

He nodded seriously. "Just charming enough to keep me out of trouble."

She barked out a laugh. All I could do was roll my eyes. He winked at me.

"Now," Levi drawled, "you haven't told me who I have the pleasure of speaking with. That's not very Southern of you."

"Only my gentleman callers get to use my first name," she said. Levi's mouth fell open, and I slapped a hand over my lips to keep the laugh in. "You can call me Miss Barton."

He snapped his mouth shut. "Well, Miss Barton, I hope to see you around."

She looked over her shoulder at me. "This your man? He's cheeky."

Before I could answer, Levi inclined his head toward the door. "Oh, I come in a close second to the dog out there. But I'm okay with that."

All I could do was shake my head. Something on his face today, a glint in his eye made me smile.

"Enjoy the banana cake, Miss Barton," I told her as she walked past Levi. When she paused to pat Nero's head just outside the door, I laughed. "Man, I hope I'm like that when I'm her age."

Levi nodded, his eyes still watching Miss Barton shuffle away from the entrance of the bakery. "I can picture it far too easily."

I crossed my arms over my chest, trying to catch a glimpse of what he had in the box. "I didn't know you were coming in."

"Can't I ever try to surprise you?"

Before I could answer, Joy came from the kitchen, wiping her hands on the apron covering the front of her body. "Hey Joss, everything okay out here?" Her eyes snagged on Levi, a pretty pink blush covering her round cheeks, and she smiled widely. "Oh, how sweet! You came in to say hi."

"I sure did. You must be Joy."

If her smile got any bigger, she'd split her face wide open. "I am! Oh, I just love working with Jocelyn. She's wonderful."

I rubbed at my forehead and shot daggers at Levi with my eyes, which he ignored. "She *is* wonderful." He tilted his head down to the box that he held in his hands. "That's why I figured I'd bring her these."

Narrowing my eyes at him, I leaned up in my chair. "What's in there?"

He set the box down, and I noticed he was having a hard time holding eye contact. In two neat rows were small brown paper bags, the crisply folded edges of each bag held down by different colors of tape. In black marker, the bags were labeled with different names.

Almond

Wheat

Cake

00

Pastry

Spelt

Rye

Buckwheat

Barley

Rice

Oat

"Oh," Joy breathed out as I stared into the box like a giant dummy. "*Flours*. They're kinds of flour."

My eyes snapped up to him. "You brought me flours?"

His hazel eyes were bright, but before he could answer me, Joy sighed loudly. "That is *so* romantic."

I burst out laughing. "Oh my word, Levi, you didn't."

He smiled. "You told me once that buying flowers were a waste of money because all they did was suck up water and then die two days later."

"I did say that," I said around my helpless giggles. "But-but you totally ripped this off from that movie, you cheater."

His face blanched. "You've seen it?"

"What movie?" Joy asked, still staring raptly at the box of flour.

I shook my head, still grinning at Levi. "I can't even remember the name of the actor, but he's an IRS guy. She's a baker. It's good, you should watch it." Clucking my tongue, I gave Levi a mock-disappointed look. "Was this a test of my movie knowledge or something? You're the one who made me watch it a couple of years ago."

"I did?" He scratched the side of his face. "Huh."

I rolled my eyes and grabbed the box so I could set it on my lap and head back into the kitchen. "Oh, how quickly they forget. I'll be off work in an hour if you want to wait."

"I'll wait," he told me.

"Thank you for the flours," I said over my shoulder.

He answered in a weary tone. "You're welcome."

Joy was smiling at Levi like he'd dropped off a check for a million dollars. "I still think it's romantic."

"Thanks, Joy." He sighed. "Do you know how far I had to drive for the spelt flour?"

"*So* romantic," she repeated.

I was still laughing as I went back to my cupcakes. But every time my eyes caught on the box containing the neatly folded brown paper, I smiled.

CHAPTER 9

JOCELYN

The night before my next PT session, I promised myself that I'd draw the line at a quick swipe of mascara. The reflection of the girl staring back at me from the rearview mirror of my car the next morning all but called me a big fat liar.

My hair was tamed in two neat braids that met at the base of my skull. The shirt I wore was a deep bluish-purple color that made my eyes look "freaky blue," according to Levi, the one time I wore it to the gym. Freaky blue eyes or not, I liked how my arms looked underneath the cap sleeves. I stuck with my black leggings because there was no hiding how skinny my legs were, no matter what I wore.

This time when I arrived, I didn't hide behind the open car door. I stood and took a deep breath, inhaling the warm mountain air, which promised to turn into a hot June day in no time.

Five steps, and I had the back of the car open. When I sat down, I was proud of myself for not letting the butterflies overwhelm me. The other thing I promised myself last night as I laid in bed and stared at the ceiling was that I going to woman up and ask the man to Connor and Sylvia's wedding.

Not right away or anything, because the truth was that I knew very little about Andrew. It simplified things in my head to think of him by the name he went by at PT. Cupcake Guy was no longer in the building as soon as he realized I was his client.

What was it with the bakery anyway? It like, shot out some weird Jocelyn pheromones or something. First Andrew buying me the cupcake, then Levi showing up with his ridiculous box of flours. He'd waited for me the day before as promised, after taking Nero to the park and running some of his energy out. There was no more mention of the box, or the movie, and when he asked if I wanted to take Nero on a hike down one of my favorite paths, I agreed.

For some reason, once I was inside those walls, I was a different person. And I needed to figure out how to bring that person out of the Donner Bakery kitchen.

As I wheeled up to the door, I could feel someone's eyes on me, so instead of hitting the button, I yanked the door open with my left hand and pivoted my chair so that I was able to hold the door open for myself.

Andrew was behind the main desk, smiling at something in his hand.

"Good morning," he said without looking up.

"Morning."

The office was empty, which was a little unusual for the morning. His smile was friendly when he aimed it at me. "Ready to work?"

"I guess so."

He hooked a thumb over one broad shoulder, and I saw a long ramp set at an angle up against the wall. "You'll love this."

I scrunched my nose at it. "I almost don't dare ask."

Andrew laughed when he set the clipboard down and came around the corner. "We need to start building your glute and quad strength. You have more muscle atrophy than I'd like to see at this point."

My cheeks were hot when I looked back at the ramp. "Yeah, it's just … easier to use my chair."

He nodded like he expected my answer. Just as he had the last time, he snagged a stool and sat on it. Now he was eye level with me, and I couldn't tear my gaze away from the veins mapping the top of his hands and arms.

Very nice vein action.

"What'd you like to do before you got sick?" he asked.

"Walk," I said dryly, which made him laugh. Then I groaned. "You probably want a real answer, huh?"

"That's a real answer, but yes."

"I was a runner. A basketball player. Volleyball in the summers. I didn't spend much time just sitting around, that's for sure." I waved a hand over my legs. "So *this* was an interesting transition to get used to."

He looked pointedly at my arms. "It's obvious you still don't like to just sit around."

"No," I said feelingly. "I don't."

Andrew crossed one of his legs over the other and pinned me with a serious look. "So tell me why you're not taking care of your legs too. You clearly spend time in the gym."

Okay. These weren't date feelings. These were 'how 'bout you stop interrogating me' feelings. Suddenly, I missed Denise.

No, that was a lie.

I heard Levi's voice in my head, saying I needed someone to push me. And I thought of the times over the past few months when he'd asked if I wanted to go with him to the gym, and I'd said no.

Trying to think about how to answer him in a way that made sense, I shook my head for a moment. "I'm a bit of a perfectionist," I started. "And I'll never walk smoothly again. I will always look clumsy when I do it. A little ungainly. Everyone around me will hold their breath because they'll be afraid that one wrong foot placement will have me down on the pavement. I hate that feeling. I've gotten used to the way people look at me while I'm in this chair." I shook my head and swallowed audibly. "And that was hard enough. This feels like a much bigger mountain to climb, for some reason."

It was the most honest I'd been with anyone about this outside of Levi. Andrew leaned forward and held my eyes. "You aren't wrong about any of that, Jocelyn. They will watch you that way because they love you, not because they don't believe in your ability to do it."

I blinked away, staring at the ramp like it had morphed into every symbolic thing I hated about this situation.

"Come on," he said, standing from the stool. "Let's go climb up that mountain. Literally."

"What do you mean?" I followed him over, locking my chair into place when he stopped at the base of the ramp.

"You're going to crawl up this ramp."

I huffed out a disbelieving laugh. "Oh goody, for a second I thought you'd really make me embarrass myself."

He smiled. "Come on. Up you go, Abernathy."

And that asshole really did make me crawl.

Underneath the patient instructions, calm encouragement, and educational pedigree that assured me he knew what he was doing, Andrew had my legs absolutely burning with the effort it took to stay balanced. I'd go up the ramp an inch at a time, my progress slow and frustrating. And that was nothing compared to when I had to go backward.

Occasionally, he'd lay a hand on my back or hip to move one of my legs with a gentle correction and suggestion of how to position my body. Every time he did it, I felt the spread of his fingers over my skin and breathed a little faster.

They weren't sexual touches. He never lingered. The touches were brief, they had a purpose, and I wanted to cry at how they made me feel.

It was embarrassing enough to have to literally crawl on my hands and knees in front of this person, but every time he touched me, I desperately wished I could transform those touches into something else. Something more.

I got to the bottom of the ramp, sweat pooling underneath my shirt and the backs of my legs quivering from the effort of what I was doing, when he asked me to lift my right arm.

"There you go, straight out from the shoulder." He set his hand over my shoulder, and I closed my eyes.

His hands felt all wrong.

This wasn't how I imagined it, and I wanted it to feel how I imagined it. I wanted strong touches, fingers brushing over my skin with a different purpose in a way that lingered and luxuriated. No one had ever luxuriated over *anything* of mine.

"Come on, keep your focus," he said, taking his hand off my shoulder when I wobbled.

"Easy for you to say," I mumbled. "You're not on all fours like a freaking dog."

He chuckled. "Okay, drop your hand. I'll help you over."

Once I'd braced my hand on the ramp again, I hung my head and took a few deep breaths. "I hate this ramp."

"Most people do," he agreed easily. "But it'll get easier if you start doing more leg exercises like leg presses and hamstring curls. There are so many things you can do at the gym, Joss."

I glanced over at him. "I know."

"Then why aren't you doing them?"

His question held no censure. Not an ounce of accusation. Hidden beneath the layers of professional curiosity, I heard the steel behind it.

"You sound like my best friend," I gave, instead of an answer. "He always wants me to work out with him."

Andrew nodded. "You should." He lifted an eyebrow. "And not just your upper body. Pretty sure you could take me in an arm wrestling match."

I laughed because his arms were about three times the size of mine, so we both knew the likelihood of that happening was slim.

"I'm serious, Jocelyn. If your friends want to help, you should let them."

With a smile, I gave him a tiny salute. "Yes, sir."

He held out a hand, and I took it so I could lower myself more easily onto one hip. Once I was sitting, he moved back, and I turned my legs so that my knees were up. My feet, clad in my bright white Adidas sneakers, stared uselessly back up at me.

"My shoes always stay perfectly clean," I said without even realizing the thought had popped in my head.

83

"I'm sure they do." He leaned down to grab an exercise band, which I curled my lip at. I hated those things too. "I had a client last year, eighty years old, and she refused to wear anything but high heels except for her PT visits, because why wouldn't she? She didn't have to worry about falling over since she couldn't actually walk in them."

I laughed. "Good point. I still go for sneakers because that's all I wore. Before," I added needlessly.

"Nothing wrong with that." He twirled the band in a circle. "Come on, I'll let you off the hook early. You did good work today."

Exhaling heavily, I smiled before using the bars installed on either side of the ramp to hoist myself up. Thankfully, my chair was close because holy shit, my legs were sore.

"I hate to say this, Andrew, but I will probably wake up tomorrow cursing your name."

His laughter echoed through the empty office. "I can accept that."

I wheeled myself back out to the car with plans to be back the next week at the same time. With the chair tossed in the back, it took all my strength to focus on taking strong, even steps back to my seat after the work I'd done on that evil effing ramp. Despite that, despite the labor I'd done, I sat in the driver's seat and stared out the windshield, a current still humming unchecked under my skin.

Unspent energy that had nothing to do with the physical efforts he'd just put me through, and it needed to go somewhere.

I dug my phone out of my backpack and pulled up Levi's number, tapping out a quick text before I started my car. Maybe I wasn't supposed to just work my upper body, but I wanted something that made me feel strong. Something that I control and master and dominate.

Me: Meet me at the gym in 30 minutes?

He answered immediately.

. . .

Levi: The actual gym or the house?

I dropped my head and considered the options. The Buchanans had a pretty epic home gym, and since it would just be just Levi and me, there would be no watching eyes and no judgment. *But no smoothies either*, I thought with a pout.

Sighing, I knew which one would win.

Me: The house. But you owe me a smoothie since your commute is a thirty second walk.

Levi: Your wish is my command.

After I finished picking out the perfect eye roll GIF, I threw the car into reverse and started in the direction of Green Valley.

CHAPTER 10

LEVI

"*I*diot, idiot, idiot," I whispered under my breath, though the sound of the blender drowned it out. As soon as I got her text, I almost fell over as I stripped out of my regular clothes and into mesh shorts. For a ridiculous amount of time, I stood in front of the drawer that held all my gym shirts, most with the sleeves long ago ripped off.

Without fail, I wore one of those shirts when working out.

Would she notice if I didn't? It wasn't as if we were at the actual gym, where I'd look like a giant douchebag for strutting around in only shorts. Yeah, I worked my ass off on my body, and I was proud of it, not just as a by-product of an education built around studying the muscles and ligaments and pieces that crafted the body into a flawless working machine, but because working out was an *excellent* outlet for unspent sexual frustration.

Just once, I wanted to know what would happen if she came through the door and saw me like this. If her eyes lingered on me the way I tried to keep mine from lingering on her.

When she wasn't looking, I'd study the curve of her neck and the slope of her shoulder. The way she danced in her chair when the music was on and she thought no one was looking. The graceful length of her fingers, and the shift of muscles in her arms when she moved.

There were so many small, seemingly insignificant parts of Jocelyn that I had memorized. She'd spent all morning with PT guy. Did he see the same things? Did she?

Was she looking at his neck and hands and arms and the way he smiled in the same way I looked at her?

My hands tightened on the lid of the blender when I thought about it.

I was shaking the appliance a bit too hard after it stuttered on a chunk of ice when she came up behind me, pinching my side.

"Son of a bitch," I yelled, jumping backward and yanking the top off the blender as I did. Blueberry-banana shake exploded everywhere.

Joss was bent at the waist, laughing as I punched the button to turn off the blender. Her peals of laughter might have been more infectious had my face not been coated in cold-ass purple liquid.

"Oh my gosh, Levi." She giggled, wiping a tiny speck off her cheek. "You should see yourself right now."

The only other place she had a spot was on her arm, which she lifted and licked off. My eyes narrowed at the flash of her pink tongue.

The cold liquid dripped down the front of my chest, and I swiped at it with a towel, glaring about as effectively as I could when my face was covered in goop. "You think this is funny?"

In answer, she pulled out her phone and snapped a picture. "There. My new lock screen."

Slowly, methodically, I mopped up as much as I could with the dish towel, then turned to her with a grin. "Is that so?"

She lowered her phone. "Don't you dare."

"What?" I asked, eyes wide. "This is your smoothie. I'd hate to keep it from you."

Joss started pushing her chair backward. "Levi Robert Buchanan," she warned as I advanced on her.

The speed with which she was able to pivot her chair always

88

impressed me, but I was also ready for it. I leaped forward as she made the corner around the island and grabbed the back of her chair with one hand, which made her squeal.

Hunching over her for maximum surface coverage, I wiped the towel across her face and neck.

When her face was just as blueberry-banana soaked as mine, and I was laughing as breathlessly as she was, I finally took pity on her and straightened.

Joss turned her chair, wrapping one arm around her waist like she'd be able to contain the graceless sounds coming out of her mouth.

I never wanted them to stop.

With a smile so wide and bright, I couldn't even be sad about how she'd pinched her eyes shut and hid that perfect shade of blue from my view.

"It's so cold," she shrieked. Wiping at her cheeks, she only succeeded in spreading it farther up her face and into her pulled-back hair.

When I could breathe a bit more easily, I yanked off some paper towel, ran it under the faucet to get it wet and then crouched in front of her.

As I carefully wiped off her face, she was still grinning, but I felt my smile melt away.

There were so few opportunities for me to touch her like this. My thumb tilted her chin to the side so I could wipe off her cheek, the bottom curve of her delicate jawline. Underneath that one finger, her skin was soft and warm.

The tips of her lashes had purple on them.

"Close your eyes," I told her.

She complied, a smile still curling her lips. It was a full three seconds before I could move to do anything. I wanted to lean forward and capture those lips with mine, see if they were cold and sticky and sweet. I wanted her hands to dig into my hair and grab hold, her eyes to meet mine and flash with heat before I slid my tongue against hers and found out what her mouth tasted like.

I took a deep breath and wiped the damp paper towel over her closed eyelids to clean them off as gently I could with slightly shaking hands.

"By all means," she muttered, "take your time. I love having a smoothie facial."

Just because it would piss her off, and because I had no foolish intentions of wasting this opportunity, I slowed my movements even further, dragging the towel down the straight, proud line of her nose and over the arch of her cheekbone.

Some remained along the edge of her mouth, and I stared at it for three awkward chugs of my heart.

Buh—duh-boom.

Buh—duh-boom.

Buh—duh-boom.

Lowering the hand that held the paper towel, I used the edge of my thumb and dragged it slowly along the bottom edge of her lip until the purple was gone.

Her eyes snapped open, and her breathing picked up when I put my thumb into my mouth and sucked the tart liquid off.

"Delicious," I said quietly.

After a quick and sharp inhale, she narrowed her eyes in confusion. Then she blinked. "Sorry I scared you."

And just like that, the moment was over. I could see it in the smoothing of her face.

I stood and tossed the paper towel into the trash. "No, you're not."

"You're right," she said around another grin. "I'm totally not. That was the highlight of my week." Her hands waved in the direction of my face and hair. "You've still got a little ... everywhere."

Sighing, I grabbed more paper towel and wet it in the sink. "I'm sure I do."

"I didn't think you'd actually make me a smoothie."

Lifting my eyebrow as best as I could while trying to scrub the drying liquid out of it, I gave her a look.

Joss held up her hands. "Okay, fine, I figured you'd make me one. I just didn't think you'd jump like a bobcat was standing behind you."

"Oh no," I drawled, "not a bobcat. Just a sneaky little hedgehog."

She smirked. "You might as well go take a shower."

"Another shower," I clarified with a mock glare, which made her chuckle. I glanced down at my chest, the shirt I decided to don at the last moment splattered with the mess. With one hand, I yanked at my T-shirt behind my head and tore it off.

Joss was looking at her phone when the shirt cleared my head, but the tops of her cheeks had reddened. Disrobing in front of each other wasn't exactly our norm.

"What about you?" I asked her.

Her eyes trekked up the front of my chest slowly, but her face was blank when it met mine. "What about me what?"

"Do you need a shower?"

The sides of her lips twitched. "Do you happen to have a shower chair just lying around in case of emergency?"

Embarrassment had my face heating. Of all the accommodations I'd made for Joss so she could be in our home easily, showering was not one of the things I'd had to think about. But it made sense that she wouldn't be able to hold herself steady long enough to shower.

"Ahh, no, I don't."

Briefly, I wondered if my parents would think it strange if I ripped out my current shower and put it in a brand new one just for her.

Nope. Probably not.

They'd probably rejoice if Joss and I finally got to the "shower stage" of our relationship.

"And unless you're going to help me out of the bathtub, I think I'd rather just splash some water on my face if you don't mind."

The woman was officially killing me. I didn't even have a bathtub in my apartment, but holy shit could I imagine her in one if I did.

Thoughts of Joss and showers and baths were not a good combination with mesh gym shorts. I turned to face the sink. Fast.

With rough movements and while reciting the Pledge of Allegiance in my head, I cleaned any remaining smoothie residue from my neck, face and hands while I fought to control my burgeoning hard-on.

Joss was quiet, and I could feel her watching me.

"What is it?" I asked, not meeting her eyes.

"Who says I'm thinking something?"

The look I gave her over my shoulder while I washed my hands was quick and loaded. "Who do you think you're dealing with here?"

Her eyes rolled, a facial expression I was so familiar with, I smiled.

"Do you ever wonder why I don't work my legs more when you and I work out together?"

My hands slowed under the water, which was getting colder by the second. Probably good for me to douse any part of my body in cold water, but her words had an equal ardor-dousing effect. I'd noticed it, especially over the past year and a half. Number one, she didn't take me up on my offer to work out as much as she used to, and number two, she'd become really skilled at deflecting my offers to work on her legs and focused on her upper body instead.

Before answering, I took my time turning the water off and drying my hands, using the damp towel to make sure my face was clean.

"I've wondered," I said, leaning my hip against the island and facing her with my arms crossed over my chest. "But I think I know why, if that's really what you're asking."

Not that I'd obsessed over it, but I knew she'd had a PT appointment before she texted me.

Which meant she saw PT guy.

Which meant something happened.

Because Joss was overthinking that something.

Just as she was currently overthinking whether she wanted to ask me what my opinions were on why—despite mastering so many challenges in her life—I thought she was pulling back on the one area that common sense would assume she'd want the most.

"What happened at PT?" I asked when she still didn't open her mouth.

Her eyes never left my face. "I had to crawl like a dog."

Anger had me straightening from the counter, my fingers curling into tight fists at my sides. "He made you do *what?*"

When her lips twitched, I sank back against the counter and gave her a deadpan look. Oh sure, it was *so fun* to ignite the jealous instincts of your best friend—the man who would jump in front of a Mack truck for you—who possibly felt a smidge overprotective of you because he'd loved you for five years even though you didn't know it.

"Not that your overreaction isn't fun, but it was just a little embarrassing, you know?" She shrugged one shoulder. "It's like he's determined to shine the world's brightest spotlight on every single place that I'm the weakest." Before I could point out that her legs would always be the area she'd be the weakest, she held up a hand. "Shut up, you know what I mean."

"I do." I scratched the side of my face. "So what's with the crawling?"

"Ugh. It was this ramp going up to the wall, and I had to crawl forward and backward, then do different balance exercises. Almost like inverted planks."

The wheels in my head instantly started churning. The small gym in my parents' house had spots where I could easily build something similar. "Probably lit your glutes on fire, huh?"

She laughed, but I could hear the embarrassed edge to it. "They were shaking so badly after just a few reps. I could hardly walk back to my seat after putting my chair in the back of my car."

Carefully, I watched her face as I asked my next question. "And you still wanted to work out more afterward?"

That had her eyes flashing.

Heart of a peacock feather blue.

"You think I can't handle more?"

I held up my hands. "I may not be the quickest guy in town, but I'm not stupid, Sonic. Telling you that you can't *anything* is the fastest route to getting my balls punched."

Her eyes lowered to the area of which I spoke, then narrowed thoughtfully, which made me want to cup myself just to be safe.

"Hey now, I wasn't giving out suggestions," I said, which made her eyes snap up and a smile stretch over her face. "I'm just wondering, is all. When I have a tough workout, the last thing I want to do is head back to the gym."

Joss swallowed and stared past me for a couple of seconds. Maybe it was the sudden rise in date feelings that had me overanalyzing everything, but it seemed like I saw her questioning what came out of her mouth more and more. Had she always done that? Or did I just not notice?

When she finally answered, her voice was quiet, and her eyes never met mine. "I needed to put the rest of this ... energy somewhere."

I nodded slowly. It was easy enough for me to read between the lines. Something that made her feel strong. Something that would allow her to push against the barriers that she could flatten, not ones that would make her stagger back.

"I hear you."

Finally, finally, her eyes drifted over to mine. "You do?"

I leaned down and braced my hands on her armrests. Joss held her breath, her gaze flitting down the front of my body.

"Think you can do more pull-ups than me, Abernathy?"

Those eyes narrowed again. But the spark of challenge, oh man, it did beautiful things to her.

"In what world do you think I can't?"

I smirked, straightening to my full height.

"Can't you put a shirt on?" she snapped.

"I am capable of doing so, yes."

Did I move my hands to my hips on purpose?

Yes.

Did I flex my abs to see if she'd so much as move her eyes a single inch?

Hell yes. I wasn't stupid.

But Jocelyn Marie Abernathy was as stubborn as the day was long, so all she did was shake her head.

With a sigh, I dumped the messy blender into the sink and did a quick swipe of the countertops so that my mom wouldn't tan my hide when she got home.

"Good thing I came over."

"Yeah? Why's that?" I tossed the dirty towel into the sink next to the blender.

"Looks like you've been slacking on your abs. You might want to do some crunches while we're in there."

Slowly, I turned my head to glare at her, and she was already backing her chair up with a grin. She pivoted and turned toward the direction of the gym when I took off, grabbing the back of her chair and tipping her backward until her hair was almost touching the ground.

She shrieked, holding tight onto the arms of her chair as I held her captive. Her breaths came in helpless gulps between laughter. "Put me down, asshole."

Because I couldn't help myself, I held her there for another second before she lifted her fist in a warning.

"Not fair," I told her as I set her to rights.

Joss smacked me in the stomach before she pushed forward. "Life isn't fair, Buchanan. Get over it."

I watched her turn the corner before I dropped my face into my hands with a groan.

"Get over it, she says," I muttered.

Yeah, because it was that easy.

CHAPTER 11

JOCELYN

It didn't take long until I was convinced that somewhere inside my body, a writhing, pulsing mess of hormones had been uncapped. Whatever thing caused a person to start noticing things they'd never noticed before was officially unleashed.

Just as he always did, Levi held my feet steady while I did crunches, then Russian twists until my core muscles were shaking. He used only one hand while the other scrolled through his Instagram feed.

Every time I levered my upper body back up, I caught myself noticing the vein that twisted around the top of his forearm and over the generous curve of his bicep. After the smoothie incident, he'd decided to forgo a shirt, and I felt ... weird about it.

Because I didn't usually spend much time cataloging muscles. On anyone.

Levi wasn't covered in bulky, gym rat muscles.

Everything was tight and wiry and densely packed, stretched like a snare drum and as precise as the stick hitting the surface.

And when did his six-pack become so ... perfectly defined? Each compact square underneath his skin had neat lines delineating them. There was a V exactly where a V should be on a man.

Because of course there was.

As I grunted through another twist, I damn well knew I didn't have the same cut of muscle on my own midsection. I could probably do a thousand stupid twists every day, and I wouldn't be able to replicate it.

I had abs, faint, toned ones that absolutely no one saw because I wasn't exactly rolling down Main Street in a bikini.

"You should start one of these," he said, giving me quick glance.

"Start one what?"

He turned his phone screen to face me, and I caught a quick glimpse of one of the fitness accounts he followed.

I blew a raspberry as I heaved myself back up and twisted my clasped hands back and forth. "No, thank you."

"Why not? You're like, inspirational and shit."

My back hit the floor with a thud when I started chuckling. "Thanks."

"Done?" he asked.

When I nodded, he let go of my feet and held out his hands. From where I lay on the floor, I stared up at him, breathing heavily for a few seconds. We both knew I didn't need Levi's help to get up. I could turn over onto my hip and hoist myself into my locked chair. I could brace both hands on the armrests and pull myself to standing.

"I've got it," I told him once I caught my breath.

His eyes never strayed from my face as he towered over me. "Okay," he said after a beat. "What's next?"

With one hand hooked under my knees, I turned my legs to the side and sat up. I scooted toward my chair and stared up at it.

It didn't happen often anymore because this had been my reality for so many years, but for a moment, I was swamped with the overwhelming thought that I'd never been able to just ... stand easily. I couldn't brace a foot on the ground, push a hand down on my knee, and straighten my body to all five feet ten inches.

If I closed my eyes, I could remember quite clearly what it felt like. Which was precisely why I didn't close my eyes, because it was a train of thought I tried not to indulge in. It gained me nothing. It served no purpose other than to spur self-pity and discontent.

Maybe that got uncapped inside me too—the unfortunate and unforeseen by-product of these spilled hormones racing and tumbling through my body. Having Andrew lay gentle, caring, instructional hands on me earlier, right in the midst of something that made me weak and frail, pissed me off.

I didn't want to feel anger or resentment for his role in my life, that his hands moved over me like that of a practitioner helping a patient because I'd deal with the rest of my life. Andrew, Denise, my doctor—it didn't matter who the hands belonged to, at the end of the day, I'd always have people in my life whose sole purpose was to treat me for the things I lacked.

The sudden course of anger needed to get out, out, out. I wanted it gone. I didn't want to follow where it might lead me.

"Sonic?" Levi asked.

I blinked, unaware that I'd been staring through my chair for the past few seconds. Unthinking, I held my hands to him. "I think I want to do some chin-ups."

His brow wrinkled for a second because I rarely asked for help. Strong hands gripped mine, his calloused fingers wrapping completely around my palms. He pulled me up, and instead of helping me into my chair, Levi all but forced me to stand.

I managed to steady my feet with only one clumsy shuffle forward, but steady myself I did.

"I forget how tall you are sometimes," he said quietly, his eyes holding mine.

Smiling a little, I pulled my hands slowly from his sure grasp. "Now I can't punch you in the balls as easily."

His grin spread, and I couldn't help but notice how his face transformed when he smiled. The skin by his eyes wrinkled in a way that shouldn't have been attractive but was. That dimple in his cheek was deep, and just to piss him off, I poked at it with my finger.

"Put that away, Buchanan. Your unfair height advantage is no laughing matter."

He backed up, trying to smother his grin, and failing miserably.

"Come on, Sonic. Show me what you've got," he said, jerking his chin in the direction of the chin-up bar mounted up on the far wall, about ten feet away from where we stood. He braced his hands on his hips and started tapping his foot.

I stuck my tongue out at him, which made him laugh. Those ten feet felt like twenty as I stared, no walker in front of me, even though the safety of my chair was directly behind me.

"Don't help unless I start falling," I told him.

His jaw was tight, but he nodded.

Levi had seen me walk, probably more than anyone else, but I still hated doing it in front of him. In front of anyone. And, ultimately, that was my problem. Working through the pride issues that still haunted me seven years later felt like something I'd struggle with for the rest of my life. It was why The Pitiers, on the whole, bothered me more than The Blinders.

With my arms out like a little kid crossing a balance beam, I swung my right foot forward, then my left, using that upper body I'd worked so hard on to give myself the proper momentum forward.

Levi walked beside me, within arm's reach, and out of the corner of my eye, I saw him physically stop himself from reaching out to me when I almost pitched too far to the right. I favored that side, and when I was underneath the chin-up bar, that leg caused my arm to shoot out to the wall in order to stop myself from falling forward.

His voice was rough when he spoke. "See? Inspirational and shit."

"Ha." I caught my breath and looked over my shoulder at him. "I look like an airplane about to land."

"You do not."

I rolled my eyes because I knew what I looked like. "You won't win this one, Buchanan. Come on, boost me up."

Levi came up behind me when I lifted my hand toward the bar. His hands, big and capable, gripped my sides with a strength that had the air shooting out of my lungs. His fingers curled around my hip bones, and when he exhaled, it ruffled the curls that escaped down the back of my neck.

"You are fucking amazing, Jocelyn, airplane arms and all."

My eyelids fluttered shut, and I was so, so glad I wasn't facing him.

I didn't want to see what was on his face as he said it, and I didn't want him to see what was on mine.

He'd helped me hundreds of times—more than I could count—and not once, not for even a fraction of a second had I thought about his fingers when they covered any surface of my body.

If this was because of Andrew, then I was officially in a fight with him, because what I didn't need in my life was something that made me catalog how the skin covering my bones changed when my best friend touched it.

With no more effort than breathing, Levi hoisted me up, and my hands grabbed the bar, fingers curled in the direction of my face. Levi stepped back. My hips felt cold and bare.

"Thank you," I whispered, staring straight at the wall. "Can you bring my chair over?"

Without a word, he did. And like normal, once my chair was locked into place, he made deft movements with his hands, wrapping a thick, Velcro band around my knees to keep them together, to hold my legs steady.

I took a deep breath and pulled myself up, relishing the way my muscles curled and bunched.

Again, and again, and again, and again, and again, I pulled myself up.

My arms and shoulders ignited after only a couple of reps. With each shift, I felt the fire spread into different places.

My back. My abs. My obliques.

I blew out a hiss of air as I did another rep and then lowered myself back to hanging, arms shaking visibly.

Levi stayed quiet behind me, but I felt his eyes on me.

A bead of sweat rolled down the side of my face, and I breathed in and out.

"Done?" he asked.

"One more," I said, dropping my chin and adjusting my fingers.

Inch by excruciating inch, I pulled myself up one more time until my chin cleared the metal bar. With my teeth clenched together, I struggled not to drop down too quickly.

When my arms were fully extended, I nodded over my shoulder.

Levi held my waist this time, not my hips, and even through the layer of my shirt, the heat of his hands was instant.

My brain jumbled as he helped me down until I could sit back into my chair. Like someone punched the fast-forward button on a VHS tape, and I was struggling to stop in the place that I wanted.

When he held out a towel, I took it gratefully, wiping it over my face as I struggled to catch my breath.

"Thanks," I told him.

"You okay?"

Surprised at the seriousness of his tone, I looked up at him. "Yeah, why?"

"That was three more than you usually do."

"It was?"

Levi nodded, searching my face.

I handed the towel back and unlocked my chair. "Maybe I'm still in a weird mood from PT. I should probably go home and let Nero out. He's probably pissed at me for leaving him at home."

"Why didn't you take him?"

Under my breath, I laughed. "Taking Nero to PT is about the same as taking you."

He adopted a mock-hurt expression. "Gee, thanks."

"You know what I mean. Your sole purpose is to intimidate."

"But unlike your marshmallow of a dog, I'd actually hurt someone." He waved a hand in front of his face. "Behind this pretty face is the soul of a killer."

I rolled my eyes, giving his leg a condescending pat before I backed my chair up. "Okay, Cujo."

"You work tomorrow?" he asked as he followed me through the kitchen.

"Until noon. Why?"

Levi was quiet as I went down the ramp in the garage and out onto the driveway. I unlocked the car and opened the driver's side door. "Do you mind?" I asked.

He shook his head, taking the chair to the back after I boosted myself into the car.

"Speaking of work, when are you going to start contributing to society?"

His smile was easy, but there was a tightness behind his eyes. "I've got an interview in a couple of days, actually."

"That's great," I exclaimed, shoving at his shoulder. "Why the hell didn't you tell me?"

Levi shrugged. "I'm sure nothing will come from it. It's a phone interview, and I think they're indulging me because it's a connection through Hunter."

I nodded. "Ahh. The elusive oldest brother who hates Green Valley and never comes home."

"He doesn't hate Green Valley," he hedged. "I don't think. I know his wife does, though, so they never really come home."

"It's weird that you have this whole other sibling who I don't know."

His hand tapped the roof of my car. "Bothers you, doesn't it?"

"What's the interview for? I thought you couldn't find anything around here."

A truck rumbled down the street, and he squinted in the direction of the sound. "It's definitely been harder than I thought."

"I'd be going out of my *mind* by now if I were you."

Levi huffed out a laugh. "Yeah, most days I definitely feel like I'm going crazy."

The words, the lack of eye contact, the way he held his body had me searching for the hidden meaning in what he'd just said.

"Is that so?"

"Only most days," he said when he finally looked back at me.

"I still think you could start your own place here or in Maryville. Even Knoxville. It's not that far."

His eyes searched mine steadily. "Is that what you would do? Start a business if you couldn't find the job you want?"

I looked back just as steadily. "I don't know, smartass, considering I still have no freaking clue what I even *want* to do."

"There's nothing wrong with that," he told me for the eight hundredth time since I started my classes.

"I know, I know. But it's still easier to tell you how to fix your life than try to figure out my own." I swept my arm out toward him. "Hence me planning your imaginary business that you're going to start."

"Would you finally be one of my clients if I did?"

"No way. Conflict of interest much?" I smiled. "Besides, I'd argue with you too much when you told me what to do. I'd drive you insane."

He braced his hands on the doorframe and studied my face with a slight grin. "You say that like you don't already drive me insane."

"Good point," I said thoughtfully. "Let me know if you want to do something after I'm done tomorrow."

He shut the car door for me and nodded. "Will do."

As I drove away, my skin still humming and twitching the same way it did when I left PT, I realized he didn't answer my question about the interview. Their street disappeared in my rearview, and I told myself I'd ask him about it tomorrow.

CHAPTER 12

LEVI

*H*ave you ever accidentally popped the seam on one of those refrigerated tubes of cinnamon rolls? If you pressed too hard or even just peeled the wrapping off, you risked releasing the pressure. Once that happened, you had no choice, no way to undo what you'd just done.

It was the worst, most accurate analogy I could think of for what was happening once I'd realized I had to start trying to get Joss to see me as something other than her best friend.

There was no way for me to undo it.

Bringing her a box of flours was ... ill-advised, considering I'd forgotten that we'd once watched that movie together. So what if some clever scriptwriter thought of it first? But the look on her face, even after she realized it wasn't precisely my idea, made the whole thing worth it.

It made her happy. Made her smile. But that was still not what made me feel like I was driving a runaway train.

Working out with her was.

In the five years of being friends with her—being friends with her while also being in love with her—I'd never felt the tension between us like I had in the gym today.

I wanted to lick the sweat off her collarbone. Prowl over top of her and take her mouth with mine while gripping her hips for an entirely different reason.

And even if it had only been for a split second, I saw how still she became before I lifted her up, when my hands were on her. Joss was holding her body so tightly, with such control, because something had popped open, air hissing from a split seam, and there was nothing I could do to undo it, even if I'd wanted to.

It would have been so easy to lean forward and touch my lips to the back of her neck, to wrap my arms around her and bury my nose in her hair and inhale her like an addict would a neatly tapped line of drugs.

Which was why it was so ironic that I now couldn't figure out what to do next. For as much as Joss gave me shit about my ease with women, she was the puzzle I couldn't figure out how to put together. The edges were connected, the majority of the picture clear and assembled and snapped in place, but you needed the missing pieces to see the full picture. Without them, you couldn't quite figure out what it was.

Did I think I was the best man for her? Hell yes.

In a very masculine and non-pathetic way, I'd love her for the rest of my life, no matter whether she ever realized it or not. The Buchanan men had never done it any other way.

The story was told that when my Great-Great-Grandmother Kathleen died of pneumonia at the age of thirty-two, leaving my great-great-grandfather a widower with two sons, he never once thought of remarrying. His heart was done for long ago, it was said. It met its match, found the one that changed his life, and he never regretted the years he spent alone because he had twelve years with the person he loved.

It was as good as gospel in my immediate family. Anyone who met my parents viewed them as the holy grail of partnerships.

Maybe that was stupid. My dad's brother, Uncle Glenn, thought the entire thing was "twice-baked bullshit," which was why my cousins, Grady and Grace, thought we were insane for buying the stories.

Easy for them to say. They'd never felt their heart leave their body at the mere presence of the right person.

Joss still had that effect on me, five years later.

When she worked the next day, we texted but didn't see each other.

And as I sat, staring at the blank computer screen since I'd closed out the window I'd used for my video interview—something that I'd thought it was only a favor from my oldest brother, but now it felt like a real opportunity, one I'd be a complete idiot to turn down if they offered it to me—I knew I'd have to find a way to stick those opened cinnamon rolls in a hot oven.

Groaning at the stupid, stupid comparison, I dropped my head on my desk and banged my forehead against the hard surface a few times.

When Hunter called favor, he *called in a favor*.

I have a family at my school that would probably talk to you, he'd said in a text. *Let me see if they'll look at your resume.*

That family owned an NFL team in Seattle. The wife was the owner. Of a *professional football team*. The professional football team that won the freaking Super Bowl the previous year. Her husband was the retired quarterback. And I'd spent an hour chatting with their head trainer because the daughter of the owner was a student at my brother's school.

It was a dream come true. Working with athletes of that caliber had my mind racing and my heart thudding in my chest at an uncomfortable pace, like someone had replaced that simple organ with a bass drum mallet and was hammering away at the insides of my rib cage.

And if they offered me a job, I'd be a fool to say no. An absolute, utter fool.

But the only thing I could think was how wrong it felt to even consider living across the country from Joss. The idea made my stomach curl with acid. Might as well chop my arm off and leave it back in Tennessee.

How did I explain this to her in a way that would make sense that I'd want her to come with me if it happened? The trainer, Brian, all but promised me that they'd want to fly me out to Seattle for a final interview.

I rubbed at the aching spot in my chest when I imagined trying to tell her.

Yesterday, she sent me a picture from the kitchen at Donner Bakery, her nose flecked with flour and an annoyed expression on her face when a batch of pastry dough cracked open during baking. She was holding her middle finger up to one of the offending baked goods.

Joss: Asshole pate a choux didn't bake up right. Joy can't figure out how I learned so many swear words during my young life, and I had to try to explain how spending my impressionable teen years with the Buchanans gave me the vocabulary of a drunken pirate.

Me: That's cute. You say that like you weren't the one to prove to me how many times someone could use the word 'fuck' in the span of sixty seconds. You made my ears curl in on themselves.

I scrolled past my response to the picture and stared at her face, a strange combination of helplessness and desperation making me twitchy and uncomfortable. Was it as simple as sitting down her with, holding her hands with mine, and admitting that I loved her?

"Yeah, right," I muttered, shoving back from the desk after I slammed my laptop shut. Roughly, I unbuttoned the dress shirt I'd put on for the interview and tossed it onto my bed. I flopped back and scrolled through our texts, randomly stopping at the pictures she'd sent me.

When that felt like nothing but an exercise in frustration, I dropped my phone and stared at the ceiling. Joss had come over after her PT because she felt restless and in need of an outlet for the type of energy that made her feel good and strong and competent.

She was always good and strong and competent in my eyes, but that didn't mean it felt the same way in her head. I'd long ago noticed how she favored the activities that made her feel strong after something poked at the places she felt were her weakest.

I sat up, an idea floating up like a bubble.

It was one of the hottest days we'd had all summer, so I knew exactly what she and I could do that afternoon. Something that I just might be able to capture some of that snapping tension from the gym.

Five minutes later, I hung up my phone with a grin on my face and sent Joss a text.

Me: You're done with work, right?

Joss: I am. Just got back from taking Nero for a walk. It's stupid hot outside.
Joss: What do you have in mind?

Me: I'll pick you up in twenty minutes. Wear your bathing suit and leave the beast at home.

The GIF she sent me of a woman staring suspiciously at the camera made me laugh. This was either completely genius, or it would explode messily in my face. But at this point, I was willing to risk it. I'd probably risk anything as long as it got me Joss. Maybe that should have scared me, but as I pulled on my swim trunks, I knew it didn't.

The only thing I was really scared of was living a life without her in it.

* * *

"Oh great," she mumbled from behind me. "Now we can add breaking and entering to the list of horrible ideas you've had."

Over my shoulder, I gave her a pointed look. "It's not B and E if you've got the code to the lockbox, Sonic."

"Whose house is this?"

"Someone who loves my dad and said we could use their pool while they're out of town this weekend." I glanced to the side of the garage and told her to wait in the driveway while I checked the backyard, so she could decide whether she wanted to go through the house or the yard.

The sprawling home, one that my dad had been trying to sell for about four months, sat along the winding Tennessee River in Maryville. Our drive out there, farther than I remembered, consisted of Joss singing off-key to country music and me quietly obsessing over what the hell I was trying to accomplish with this little outing.

We could've gone swimming somewhere in Green Valley, but I wanted time with just her. I didn't want to worry about who we might see, or who might be jotting down the comings and goings in order to satisfy the local gossip wheel.

As I jogged down the slope of the side yard, I knew she'd be able to navigate that in her chair just fine because of the pitch of the grass. I shaded my eyes with my hand, grimacing at the flight of stairs going up to the pool. The view would be worth it once we were up there.

The hills of green were a gentle rise and fall, leading down to the tree-lined river, which hooked in curves and angles through the valley. The sun's rays reflected off the water's surface in a way that made me squint. I only took another moment or two to look at it before I ran back up to the driveway, only to stop in my tracks when I saw Joss maneuvering her chair down the grass. I shook my head, smiling at the way she'd mastered this. I'd seen it before when we were on trails around Green Valley.

The best way I could describe it was that she took the slope in one long wheelie. She knew how to lean back just enough to suspend her small front wheels in the air, the larger wheels held all her weight, and she released them in a slow, steady grip of her hands on either side.

From where I stood, hands on hips and a smile on my face, I saw the pink of her tongue pinched between her teeth in concentration.

By the time she made it to where I was, her cheeks were flushed, and her eyes were bright.

I leaned down to stop her with my hands on the armrests.

Joss grinned up at me. "I'm wheelie impressive, huh?"

It took every shred of self-control not to lean down and kiss the hell out of her right there.

"Yeah," I said with a smile.

If anything was plastered on my face that gave away what I was feeling or the way my body was drawn to hers, then she either didn't see it, or she was really good at pretending she didn't.

Joss grimaced when she looked over my shoulder and saw the stairs. "Whoops. Guess I should've been patient, huh?"

"And act completely against your character? What fun is that?"

She flicked my arm.

"*Ouch.*"

"That did not hurt." Her eyes met mine briefly. "Around to the front, or do I get a piggyback ride up the stairs?"

"That's up to you," I told her.

My vote was easy to cast, but when it came to matters like this, I'd never, ever make the decision for her. Joss' ability to get around as normally as possible was a huge source of pride for her.

She shrugged. "Might as well stay in the back. Hard to say what's inside the house."

I kept pace alongside her while she pushed through the blessedly short grass. If it had been overgrown, getting through it would be an even bigger pain in the ass than it was for her.

Our bag of towels was hooked over one of my shoulders, and I dropped it at the bottom of the white stairs.

Joss snapped her fingers. "Turn around, pack mule."

"Why you gotta bring donkeys into this? They've never done anything to you," I said as I turned around. Her chair locked into place, and I heard her stand. I swallowed heavily when her hand touched my back and slid around to the skin over my heart. Joss clasped her hands over my chest, and I closed my eyes, desperately committing the feel of her body to memory.

I squatted down, sliding my hands back until they were under her thighs. Boosting her up onto my back was easy, as was hooking my hands into place behind her knees so that they were flush against my sides.

Joss rested her chin on my shoulder. "I really should make you carry me more often."

My laughter was strained but not from her weight. "Yeah?"

No, any strain I was feeling wasn't because of her weight, I thought as I took the first step. It was all of it. I got such fleeting glimpses, touches, moments with her that even came close to what I wanted, so this felt like an embarrassment of riches.

It was the way she smelled, warmed by the sun.

It was the tickle of her hair against the side of my face.

It was her breasts pressed against my back.

It was the way she trusted me like this.

"Yeah," she said, slicing neatly into my ruminations before I could get carried away. "It's like you're my servant. I enjoy the way it makes me feel."

"You know, if someone told me five years ago that you'd thrive on humiliating me ..."

She smacked my chest. "You'd still be here with me."

I couldn't help but sigh. "You're right. I would."

Large teak loungers topped with bright red cushions surrounded the pool. Carefully, I lowered Joss's legs until she could stand next to one of them, using the back of the chair as a hand rest.

While I turned the metal crank to pull the pool cover back, I saw Joss slide her black skirt off her hips until she could step carefully out of it.

As the water revealed itself, one foot at a time, the custom tile, a dark royal blue, lining the edge looked like a punch of summer brightness against the drab brown of the deck. Just as I did every single time I saw a color that even remotely approached her eyes, I tagged it onto my list.

Pool tile on a summer day blue.

Once the cover was in place, I stripped off my shirt, slid my feet out of my flip-flops, and took a running leap into the pool, tucking my legs up under my arms for maximum impact.

The water was the perfect temperature, bracing and painful for a moment until I surfaced in a rush and felt the heat of the sun on my face. I slicked my hair back and grinned over at Joss, who was glaring at how much water I'd splashed on her.

She was sitting on the foot of the chaise only a short distance away from the edge of the pool. With two hands, she pulled her tank top over her head and tossed it behind her.

I sank under the water, eyes pinched shut, because her simple blue swimsuit shouldn't have given me such a visceral reaction, but damn if there was anything I could do about it. Suddenly, I wished that I was swimming in ice cubes.

When I resurfaced, she'd lowered herself to the deck and slid herself across until her legs were in the water. I'd expected her to sink into the pool right away, but she leaned back on her hands and angled her face to the sun. Her hair was twisted up into a messy knot, curls poking out haphazardly as they caught the light.

Now that her eyes were closed, I took a greedy look at her. No, nothing about her held the artifice of trying to entice or seduce. There wasn't a single inch of her coated in gloss or the manufactured sheen of someone trying to push or tuck or highlight.

The sexiness that I saw in her was just her.

If the simple V of her swimsuit gave me a teasing glimpse of cleavage, the twist of the fabric on the side made me notice the curve of her waist, or the color somehow made her skin glow golden, it wasn't intentional.

"Are you swimming or not?" I asked; my voice rougher, deeper, and lower than I intended.

Before Joss, I never thought someone could roll their eyes with their eyes shut, but believe me, it was possible. But she got in, and I saw the way her eyes went soft and gooey, the way her shoulders relaxed and her chin lifted when she started gliding through the water.

In the water, she could walk easily and confidently and smoothly. To keep myself from staring at her with a giant dopey smile, I dove under, swimming around her and tweaking her side as I passed behind her. When I came up for air, she was ready, shoving her hand forward and catching me in the face.

Water went up my nose, which had her cackling.

I narrowed my eyes at her, and she held up her hands. "Come on, we're even now. Let's play nice."

"Fine." I pointed a finger. "Though we're hardly even. I had water up my nose, Sonic."

As she threw her head back and laughed, I knew that an afternoon in the pool was exactly what the doctor ordered.

She floated on her back and let the sun kiss her face. I swam lazy laps around her. We talked about the bakery, what recipe she wanted to try next, and the funny way Joy seemed to be very much in love with Cletus Winston.

With the chill vibe we had going, the two topics that I actively avoided was PT guy and my interview.

Occasionally, like now, she'd hoist herself up onto the edge to let her suit dry off. The water beaded on her skin, drying quickly in the hot sun.

Which was good because then I couldn't spend too much time thinking about how I wanted to lick it off her.

Whatever tension had been present in the gym was nowhere to be found, but I couldn't figure out whether I was disappointed by that or not. Here was the confusing thing about my feelings for her: I wanted to be with her, but I couldn't imagine losing my best friend either.

The current state of our friendship was one of the most certain, unwavering things in my life.

If Joss experienced the proverbial light bulb moment, if the blinders fell off and she suddenly looked over at me with giant red hearts for eyes, how much of that friendship would disappear?

As I did another lap, pushing myself a little bit faster and a little bit harder, I had to recognize that it was one of the biggest reasons I'd kept myself clipped to a self-imposed leash. My arms churned furiously through the water as it sliced over my body.

I'd never thought of it that way. My own ridiculousness, the one I'd readily admit to even if my brother had been reticent to point it out, was fueled by a fear of how our friendship might change.

I was cursed. But she wasn't.

What if I was the first person in five generations of Buchanan to fall in love with someone who wouldn't love me back?

When my fingers touched the edge of the pool, I turned and pushed off with my feet for another lap.

Harder this time, and faster by just a smidge.

I was probably nearing the midway point of the pool when her hand touched me. I stopped, shaking the water out of my hair as I caught my breath.

"Okay, Michael Phelps." Her eyes searched my face. "What's chasing you in that head of yours?"

My chest heaved, and her gaze flickered down to it briefly. "Nothing," I lied.

You.

It's always you, and I have no fucking clue how to tell you that.

My mouth opened to say something, anything, but no words came. A drop of water slipped down her face and disappeared into the line of her neck. I reached out to wipe it away even though it was gone. Joss swallowed but didn't move.

"Are you sure?" she whispered. "I feel like … like that's how I must have looked when I was doing chin-ups the other day."

I smiled a little, breaking my gaze away from hers.

It was an accurate comparison. Standing behind her that day, she had the furious movements of someone trying to chase demons away by sheer force of will. Instead of stepping in, even when I saw her back and arm muscles shaking underneath her skin, I let her go until she couldn't go anymore.

Joss shifted forward in the water. If I wanted, it would take very little effort on my part to slide my hands around her hips, up her back, to cup her neck with my hand, and angle my face to hers.

But if she pushed me away, if she recoiled, I didn't know that I'd ever recover from that. Worse, if she laughed me off or acted disgusted, it would be too much after so many years of waiting to know what she tasted like, or how our lips fit together.

Pulling in a deep breath, I sank underneath the water so I could take a second to regroup. Nothing on her face made me think she had anything other than swimming on her mind. No bright blinking sign that said, "Kiss me, you moron."

Tipping my head back as I came back up, I slicked my hair back with both hands. When I opened my eyes, she was closer again. Just slightly. Whether it was her or me that moved, I couldn't tell, not with the way the water slipped and slid around us.

"You didn't really answer me," she said, eyes daring me to look away from her. Her lashes were spiky and dark, and this close, I could see the light smattering of freckles spread over her nose and high cheekbones.

"Nothing is chasing me," I told her honestly. I swallowed. "But sometimes, it feels like it'll always be the opposite."

Her eyebrows bent in a V. "You chasing something?"

My hand, under the water, moved forward until it brushed against her hand, but I held her eyes steady with mine. "Always."

Joss's finger shook slightly as she moved it under mine, curling the edge around mine. Her chest heaved as she inhaled. "Wh-what are you chasing?"

I had to close my eyes, and the water pulsed against my chest when she took a step closer.

If she came much closer, she'd feel me against her stomach, because I was so turned on I could hardly speak. Hell, if she looked down, she'd know.

"Talk to me," she pleaded.

In the breath before I opened my eyes, I felt her hand spread over my face, her thumb brushing slightly against a drop of water on my cheek.

"Jocelyn," I said, opening my eyes, which landed unerringly on her sweet, sweet mouth. It wasn't smiling now.

"Uh-oh," she replied, her tone teasing even if her face didn't show it. "The only time you use my full name is when I'm in trouble."

I pressed my hand over hers on my face, mainly because I didn't want her to pull away. Not yet.

I'd chased a lot of things in my life, but without a doubt, she was the most important. The thing I wanted more than any of the other things I could've possibly achieved. How did I tell her that in a way that didn't sound completely terrifying?

"You're not in trouble," I promised.

Those lips curled up slightly. "Okay."

Risking the chance, because she was close and the mood felt right, I pulled her palm off my face and brought it to my mouth and pressed a kiss against her warm skin.

She sucked in a surprised breath when my lips lingered just slightly. Her fingers curled up in reaction, but she didn't yank her hand from my grasp.

Her skin was salty from the heat, warm from the sun, and against my mouth, it felt like perfection. Slowly, she pulled it back when I was done.

We froze there, her and I, waiting for the other person to make the next move.

Then Joss blinked.

Moment over. I had to fight not to blow out a harsh puff of air as she glided backward into the water.

"I'm getting a little hungry," she said as she reached the edge of the pool. "Any snacks in that bag of yours?"

"Uh, yeah." I swiped a hand over my face. "There are some chips at the bottom. And those gas station brownies that you pretend to hate but really love."

Her responding groan of happiness had me chuckling.

117

"You're the best," she told me, grinning over her shoulder before she hoisted herself out of the pool.

Normally, I loved it when she said that.

So why did it suddenly feel like it wasn't enough?

Because you can never go back, the insidious thought whispered in the back of my head. I hated that voice. But I knew it wasn't wrong, and that was the scariest part of all.

CHAPTER 13

JOCELYN

"You imagined things."

If any voices lived in my head, they were not answering me. Nobody to tell me that, in the pool, I'd almost kissed my best friend.

"It was all in your head, Jocelyn," I tried again.

Nero raised his head from his massive paws and tilted it to the side. His ears, standing like sentinels on either side of his head, twitched restlessly when I groaned. My torture was enough that he stood from where he lay next to my chair and stretched his back, raising his rump into the air.

Absently, I ran my hand along his sleek back when he set his muzzle on my lap.

"Can't you tell me that I imagined things?" I asked him.

Nero whined, pushing his face into my hand when I scratched the top of his snout.

"No, I know you can't."

We were out on the deck in my backyard where I was supposed to be throwing the ball to him. It was cooler today, a sweet breeze coming off the mountains and dropping the temps to something more manageable.

Yesterday hadn't been manageable. It had been hot.

Too hot, I thought miserably, then dropped my head into my hand.

Since when did I spend a quiet ride with Levi, rinse off in the shower, then lay on my bed dissecting every single frame, like I was threading film through an old-school camera?

I saw it all, each little picture building up to me watching him swim, approaching him in the pool because something about his actions didn't look like him.

It was this alternate version of my smiling friend, the one who floated (no pun intended) through life with annoying ease. There had been an edge to him, something sharp and new, but not unpleasant.

When I hit the part where my hand cupped his face, then I became the one on edge. The one who noticed the hard line of his jaw. The fact that his lower lip was fuller than his top lip. That his lashes, wet and spiky, were tipped in gold. The line that bisected his ab muscles into tiny, tight squares underneath his skin. The line of hair that disappeared underneath the water.

That Joss, the one who laid in her bed thinking about it, was twitchy and restless. Unfulfilled. Left wanting something that I wasn't sure I could think too deeply about. Not yet.

"Nero," I said, smiling when he lifted his head and stared at me. "I think I'm going crazy."

He shook his head, snuffing out air, which made me laugh.

"It's the only explanation," I continued. "It was probably stupid to think that I could be friends with someone who looks like Levi and not imagine him naked at some point. Which I'm not doing," I rushed. "Or ... I don't know."

My dog, who was completely used to hearing me ramble as all good dogs are accustomed to from their owners, sat patiently and kept those golden eyes trained on me.

"It's probably just repressed sexual tension. Not like, between him and I, per se." I tapped my hand on my armrest as I tugged on the most convenient thread currently unraveling in my brain. "But in me, you know? Like my faucet was broken, and no water was coming out of the pipes. But boom, you put in a new valve, and all of a sudden, you've got a flooded bathroom."

I grimaced because it wasn't the most flattering view of myself. But it felt true. Or it felt better than any line of thinking that had me wanting to feel up Levi, of all people. That would be most inconvenient.

When Harry Met Sally ... but on two wheels.

He'd have to calmly explain to me that men and women could never truly be friends because the desire to sleep with the other person would always undermine the relationship. And if I ever lost him ...

The thought, just allowing a moment of contemplating it, had my rib cage squeezing too tight and my heart thudding uncomfortably.

No, even that was too mild. It almost doubled me over in stomach gripping, cold sweat inducing, clammy hand fear.

"What I need is another outlet."

Nero tilted his head.

"You get what I'm saying." In my lap, his tennis ball sat between my legs, so I picked it up and tossed it up into the air to get his attention. Scampering to his feet, he turned in a few excited circles. I pulled my arm back and heaved it across the grass.

As he sprinted across the yard, I knew that was the answer. It didn't matter who was throwing the ball to him, Nero would get his energy out, that first important burst to calm pent-up energy churning through his big body.

And considering that was what started this mess, seeing Brad/Chris/Cupcake Guy/Andrew, I knew I had to circle back around to him.

"It's his fault, anyway," I told Nero when he dropped the slobbery ball in my lap. "Isn't it, my big boy?"

He barked, and I grinned, throwing the ball for him again.

I glanced at my watch. I had to be at PT in an hour, then go from there to a shift at the bakery.

One more toss to Nero, and I then went inside to touch up my makeup and change into clothes that would be appropriate for therapy and a few hours at work. As I was leaning over to tie the laces on my white Adidas, I caught a glimpse of Connor and Sylvia's wedding invitation.

I set it back on the top of my dresser and stared in the mirror.

For as different as I felt on the inside, it was strange that it didn't reflect anywhere else. Shouldn't there be a sign above my head?

Beware of the twenty-one-year-old virgin with repressed sexual feelings. Explosion imminent. Touch with extreme caution.

May spontaneously combust with prolonged eye contact and cupcake purchasing and/or casual swimming sessions.

"You are pathetic," I told myself, backing my chair up before I could fall down the rabbit hole of why this was happening now.

But I wasn't pathetic. That was the decision I came to as I drove out to Maryville.

Lots of people waited to have sex. Twenty-one was a perfectly respectable age for one to maintain their V-card. And it wasn't like I didn't have good reasons.

1- I lived in a small town.

2- Most people watched me wheel by and probably assumed that I had to pee in a bag, let alone have perfectly functioning lady parts.

They functioned, okay? They functioned *just fine*. I'd explored on my own, so I knew that everything ... worked, so to speak.

I pulled into the parking spot at PT and tried desperately not to think about last night, and how when lying in bed and staring at the ceiling, my hand had slid slowly down my stomach, under the edge of my sleep shorts, where I toyed with the lace band of my underwear.

It stayed there for just a second or two, but the moment that my eyes closed, and I saw drips of pool water sliding down a golden-skinned chest, I snatched it out of my shorts and turned on my side, giving my pillow a good punch or two before attempting to sleep.

I was definitely not pathetic as I went inside and watched Andrew finish up with a client. He winked at me, and I forced myself to dissect his appearance in the same way I'd dissected Levi's.

Long legs, broad shoulders, really good freaking hair. Handsome smile, bright eyes, and a straight, proud nose.

He didn't move with the same grace as Levi. And without Levi's dimple, the smile wasn't quite as potent.

Levi's hair was lighter, longer, and it curled up at the edges. Plus, Andrew's jaw was clean-shaven, but Levi was always in need of a razor.

"Oh shit," I said out loud, slapping a hand against my forehead. "Get out of my head, you ass."

Andrew's head popped up, and the hunched over little old lady he was helping glared at me.

"Not you," I explained weakly. "Sorry."

He was smiling as he finished up with her, and by the time he walked over to me, I was one giant ball of mortification.

My cheeks probably looked like someone had shoved a red traffic light under my skin.

"Hi." I smiled a little, except it felt like a grimace.

Andrew set his hands on his narrow hips, which I would not be comparing to Levi's, and grinned down at me.

"Rough day already?" He glanced at the clock on the wall. "It's not even noon."

I exhaled heavily. "Let's not talk about it."

He shrugged. "No problem. You ready to work today?"

"I better not be on that stupid ramp again."

As he laughed, sparkling white teeth showing behind his lips, I made a decision.

No more comparison. Because that inferred that one was better than the other, or that there was a right or wrong choice.

I was a very not-pathetic twenty-one-year-old virgin with sexual needs and a decent rack. So what if I got around on two wheels instead of two legs?

"Would you like to come to a wedding with me?" I blurted out.

Andrew's head came back in surprise, and he breathed out a laugh, rubbing at the back of his neck as he took a seat in one of the chairs by me.

Well, he didn't immediately say no. That was good. But he wasn't exactly tripping over his acceptance either.

He sat forward, hanging his hands between his legs as he regarded me. "Whose wedding is it?"

"Oh, umm, my best friend's older brother. I've known the bride and groom for like, five years, so I guess they're my friends too now since I've known them for just as long as I've known Levi."

Okay, rambling rambler, zip it. I rolled my lips between my teeth and waited while he tried to smother a smile.

But in his eyes, I saw his answer because they were disappointed. There was regret there. If I thought my cheeks were hot before, that was nothing compared to how they felt now.

"I wish I could," he said gently.

"Right. There's probably some client/therapist rule you can't break. Next thing you know, you'd be burning the ramp at my request, and I'm sure they can't have that happen."

OMG shut up, Joss, I thought furiously.

"There's no rule set in stone about that," Andrew said, smiling again. I hope that wasn't supposed to make me feel better, because knowing there wasn't a rule meant that it was me. It was all me. I trained my eyes on my lap and fought valiantly against the tidal wave of embarrassment. But he kept talking. "Honestly, if you'd asked me that day when I first met you in the bakery, I would've said yes in a heartbeat."

My eyes lifted. "You would've?"

"Yeah." He shrugged one shoulder. "I don't buy cupcakes for just everyone, you know."

I nodded slowly. "But ..."

Andrew breathed out heavily. "I did set aside what I thought about you when I found out you were my client because even though there's no rule, I do think it makes things trickier once you cross that line. And this is a new job for me."

I waved a hand at him. "Yeah, no worries. I totally get it."

"That's not why I'm saying no, though," he interjected.

"It was my crawling technique last week, wasn't it?"

Andrew chuckled. "No. I, umm, I started dating someone recently. And I like her. I think she'd have a hard time understanding why I'm going to a wedding with a funny, beautiful woman when I just asked her to be my girlfriend."

"Oh," I whispered. My face was hot now for a different reason. Fiery inferno hot. It was amazing how you could be a fairly confident person, live a life like I did, being the center of attention for something out of my control, and get ridiculously flustered when someone told you that you were a funny, beautiful woman. "I'm glad you're saying no," I told him.

"You are?"

I nodded. "Because that means you're a good guy. I'd hate to realize that my asshole radar was broken."

He was still laughing as he stood. "Any man you go with will be lucky, Joss. I hope you ask someone else."

"Ha. My list of options is pretty epically long."

Andrew adopted a mock-hurt expression. "So I'm not special? Ouch."

"I'll tell you anything you want to hear as long as I don't have to do the same thing as last week."

He nudged my shoulder as he headed back by the equipment. "Come on. We'll see how far your flattery gets you."

Before I turned my chair and followed him, I closed my eyes and fought against the feeling that I never should have asked. I should've left this stone unturned because now I knew I was simply too late for Andrew to be an outlet for whatever crazy bullshit was making me feel like this.

There was literally no one else who even remotely held my interest.

No one else—the voice I'd been waiting to hear argue with me all damn day whispered—*except Levi.*

CHAPTER 14

JOCELYN

*T*hwack.

"Stupid men."

Thwack. Roll. Roll. Turn.

Thwack. Thwack.

My hand gripped the handles of the rolling pin so tightly, I wouldn't have been shocked if my bones burst through the skin.

"Stupid men who flirt and make you think things and go crazy and then start dating someone else."

Thwack. Thwack.

"Stupid men who help you work out and make you smoothies and look hot when you're swimming."

"Joss?" Joy asked cautiously.

I gave the dough one more unnecessary hit before I turned to her. "Yeah?"

Her wide eyes took in my face, which was actually sweating a bit from the mini-therapy session.

"Let's just ... back away from the bread dough, okay?"

"Right." I looked down at it, beat the hell up and rolled way too thin.

"Are you ... are you okay?" Her already big eyes took up about half her face as she watched me carefully set down the offending pin.

What a bitch I was, I thought glumly. I'd been at work for over an hour, and I hadn't spoken two words to anyone, heading straight back to the kitchen to work on bread and mini berry pastries for the case. Jennifer had given me a concerned look when she caught sight of my face but wisely gave me space. Her eyes, man, they freaked me out. Joy had tried to talk to me. Tried. I'd been about receptive as a concrete wall.

No wonder Levi called me Sonic. When my prickles were up, they were *up*, and God help anyone who tried to approach.

So even though I didn't want to answer Joy's question about whether I was okay, I took a deep breath and closed my eyes.

"I asked someone out today. And he said no."

"Ohhhh," she breathed. "I'm sorry, Joss. He's stupid."

I smiled a little bit. "He's not stupid, just unavailable."

She nodded earnestly. "I understand unrequited love."

"Yeah?"

"Yeah." She sighed.

I wiped my hands on my apron and eyed her expression. "So no boyfriend for you?"

She leaned up against the large stainless steel island, facing me. "Nope."

"Me neither."

"No girlfriend, either," she continued. "Not even a dog or a cat."

Nero's dopey face popped into my head. It was nice to have someone to cuddle with at night, even if he got around on four paws and ate his own shit from time to time.

"It's depressing, actually."

I grimaced. "Sorry. I shouldn't have brought it up."

Behind Joy, Jenn's husband Cletus came in, giving me charming, wide smile in greeting. He was a giant grizzly of a man, barrel-chested with a full beard covering his handsome face.

If my sweet co-worker understood unrequited love, it was probably because of this guy. I tried to elbow her, but I missed because I wasn't looking.

Joy was off in her own head, staring straight ahead at the large trays of finished cupcakes. "I really need to replace my vibrator now that I'm thinking about it."

My eyes widened, my mouth fell open, and Cletus froze midstride with a horrified expression on his face.

"I, uhh," he said haltingly, "I'll go now. Just ... just trying to find Jenn."

Joy gasped and whirled around, her hand clasping the front of her apron. "Oh Lordamercy, did I say that out loud?"

His bright red face clashed with the shade of his hair, and I had to bite my lips not to burst out laughing. Thankfully, his legs were long because it only took him a few strides to exit the kitchen, a proverbial cloud of dust in his wake.

I dissolved into laughter when the door swung shut, and Joy covered her face with her hands.

"I really said that in front of him, didn't I?"

"Yes."

She groaned. "I'll never be able to face him again, Joss."

Suddenly, my morning didn't seem all that bad, so I laid a hand on her arm. "Hey, don't worry about it. Seriously. You're a grown ass woman, and if you want to talk about your vibrators in public, you go right ahead."

To my absolute horror, her eyes were full of tears when she dropped her hands.

"Oh Joy, please don't cry."

"I'm not crying," she said as she started crying.

"Shit," I whispered under my breath. I locked my wheels and pushed myself up to standing so I could shuffle forward and wrap my arms around her.

"Oh, merciful Lord in heaven, you can walk!" she shrieked, jumping sideways, almost knocking me over in the process.

"Would you calm down so I can hug you?" I snapped once I'd

gotten my balance. *Sorry, Doctor, I didn't mean to fall over and break my leg. I was trying to awkwardly comfort a co-worker who started crying.*

Joy flung herself at me, and I breathed out a laugh, patting her back with one hand while I braced myself on the counter with the other, just in case.

"You're so tall." She sniffed.

Pat, pat.

"I am."

Sniff, sniff. "I'm sorry I almost knocked you over."

I sighed. "It's okay. I did kind of spring that on you."

Joy pulled away from my hella awkward hug, wiping her face. "So you can walk?"

"Not exactly." After lowering myself back into my seat, I leaned down to straighten my feet on the footrest. "I'm working on building my leg strength, but I still don't really have much feeling from just above my knees down to my feet. So with a walker or arm braces, I can walk. On my own, I can only manage about fifteen feet right now before I need help with my balance."

"That's amazing, Joss," Joy said, eyes dry and clear, full of more than a touch of admiration. That always made me feel twitchy, and I'd never wanted to delve into why. As if I should be handed a trophy because my body did something I had no control over. I didn't feel like there was anything about me worth admiring, other than that I was living, like everyone else.

We all had shit we dealt with—things that made life hard some-times—and mine was just simply more visible to the naked eye because I sat in it every single day. I think that was what made it seem bigger to people. Because you couldn't not be aware of it.

If Joy was lonely or depressed, she'd be able to hide that.

Someone who was anxious, stressed, or whatever it might be could paste a smile on their face, and even the people closest to them might not understand the challenges they faced every day.

My challenges were different; they involved narrow doorways and more of a workout to get dressed, skinnier legs than I would've preferred to have, and looks of pity or active ignorance.

"I think you're amazing too, Joy," I told her. She could tell I meant it, based on the shy smile covering her round, happy face. "Your parents picked a good name for you."

"Isn't that funny? I could've been the grumpiest person on the planet, but it's like they knew. I'd much rather be happy and make people happy than dwell on the awful things. Because dwelling on them doesn't make them go away."

"Aren't you insightful today?"

Joy laughed. "I guess."

I glanced at the wasted dough on the island. "I'll start over on the bread. Sorry about that."

She waved it off. "No worries. Listen, if you don't feel like sticking around, we're pretty slow today. I think because the weather is so nice, people are out enjoying it instead of loading up on sugary treats."

"What idiots," Levi said from the doorway of the kitchen.

Joy beamed at him. "Hi, Levi!"

"Good afternoon, ladies." He gave me a look. "I think you should take her advice and leave early."

"You really don't mind?" I asked Joy.

"Not at all. Besides, I think you're a danger to the well-being of the rolling pins if you stay for another two hours."

I rolled my eyes. "Ha, ha. Okay, thanks, Joy."

Levi waited patiently while I took off my apron and washed my hands.

We left through the front door, Joy sending us off with a beaming smile as Levi swept his arm in front of him to let me through the door first.

"So romantic." I heard her sigh.

I was still shaking my head when he jogged to catch up to me.

"What was with the rolling pin comment?" he asked.

I pushed down hard to be able to keep his pace. "Nothing."

He gave me an epic side-eye, but I didn't answer.

We passed two women who couldn't have been much older than me, and they both smiled widely at Levi, complete with hair flounce and obvious arching of the chest area.

Nope, I couldn't answer Levi. That man had probably never been turned down in his entire life, so there was no way I was going to lay out my pathetic attempt with Andrew during the one time I'd ever asked someone out.

"Your brain is working awfully hard over there," he said casually.

"What was your first date like?" I heard myself ask, not even aware that I was going to ask it until the words were out. Suddenly, I wanted to know.

"Geez, like, *very* first?"

He thought for so long that my annoyance popped up like a damn jack-in-the-box. Because clearly, he'd been on so many dates over the years that his tiny, pea-sized male brain couldn't filter through them all?

My hand shoved down hard again, gripping the circle outside the wheel so tight that my fingers almost got caught in the spokes. Great. Now I was making rookie mistakes.

"Yeah, first-first date, where you have no clue what you're doing and everything feels huge and important." Or so I imagined. "You know what? Never mind."

My pace was slightly faster than his, but he caught up with a couple of quick steps. "Hold up, Sonic, what's this about?"

"Nothing," I snapped. A curl fell out of my ponytail, and I shoved it ruthlessly behind my ear. "Never mind."

"Stop." He laughed. "Just give me a second, okay? It's not like I think about my first date often. I'm old, and my memory sucks."

I stopped, giving him a look over my shoulder. "You're hardly senile. You're twenty-three."

Levi sighed, propping his hands on his hips. "I was sixteen, and I asked Katie Sue Wright to the movies. She was in my algebra class, and I thought she was the prettiest girl in school. I picked her up, bought her popcorn, and she tried to shove her hands down my pants before the previews ended."

My nose scrunched up. "Seriously?"

"We hadn't even kissed yet." He set a hand on his chest. "I was traumatized."

I snorted. "Yeah, right. I'm sure you put up a valiant fight."

"Considering a young family was sitting right next to us, yeah, I politely yanked her hand out of my Calvin Kleins and told her that it wasn't the place to make a man out of me."

This time, I laughed because I could imagine his horrified expression pretty well. That was only a couple of years before he and I would've met. He seemed so smooth back then, so sure of himself.

Just like that, the proverbial bomb went off over my stupid, senile head.

I blinked. Levi *had* been turned down. *I* turned him down.

Holy mother effing shit, I'd turned down Levi Buchanan once upon a time. The fact that he'd asked me, that *he* could've been my first date, a full five years earlier, knocked the breath from me.

"What?" he asked.

"Nothing," I answered in an absentminded tone. "Just thinking about something I'd forgotten."

Back then, I'd told him I wasn't in the right head space to date, and I hadn't been. It took a solid eighteen months after sitting in my chair for the first time to stop thinking about things like catheters and bed sores and needing to be turned when I slept and learning how to navigate the world. About how to exit buildings with no ramps or elevators. About how to pay attention to the parts of my body that I couldn't feel but still needed to be taken care of. There was no way I would've been a good dinner date back then. It made sense that I said no, at the time. And it brought me his friendship, which I could never, ever do without.

But looking up at him now, I felt irrationally furious with myself.

All this self-pity about Andrew, when he had a perfectly justifiable reason to say no to me, was ridiculous. Here I was, so wrapped up in what hadn't worked out at my request that I'd forgotten about the things I'd turned down. The opportunities I'd been given and had passed up.

"What about you?" Levi asked.

"What?" There was a fire in my belly, stoked higher and higher the more I thought about it.

He started walking, and I followed. "Your first date."

Immediately, I stopped again, gaping up at him. "Give me a break."

Levi turned to me. "What?"

Maybe I didn't have flames shooting out of my eyeballs because he gave no indication he could see the bright anger making my skin melt.

"You *know* I've never been on a date, you insensitive ass," I snapped. And okay, Levi was apparently my new scapegoat for my internalized anger that I couldn't unload on myself. "And apparently, I never will because men are stupid."

His mouth fell open.

I crossed my arms over my chest and looked away. If there was a list of most irrational creatures on God's green earth, I just took the top spot. But I could no more calm myself down than I could cap an erupting volcano with my bare hands. Oh no, the lava was a-spewing, falling out of my mouth with a hiss and spit and a scratch.

"Jocelyn Marie Abernathy," he said calmly.

I closed my eyes. "Shut up, Levi. I know how I sound right now."

He got closer; I could hear him. His hands landed on my armrests, and I pinched my eyes shut tighter, blocking out even the slightest glimpse of him as the sun beat down on us.

"Look at me, Sonic."

"No."

Then he did the worst possible thing he could've done. Gently, so very, very gently, he ran the edge of his thumb over the arch of my eyebrow where my forehead was probably wrinkled from the effort to keep my eyes shut. If he'd commanded, I could've ignored. If he'd pounded away at my defenses with a hammer or chisel, I would've been able to mute him.

But the gentleness slipped through the hairline crack in my anger like a fog, and I couldn't stop it. He did it again, a slow swipe over my eyebrow and along my hairline, and I felt my face relax with every centimeter of skin that he touched.

When my eyelids lifted, a devastatingly handsome smile split his face.

"What?" I asked suspiciously.

He crouched down so we were eye level, and I hated how that made the backs of my eyes burn. "I'd love to take you out to dinner tomorrow night if you're available."

"What?" I whispered.

My heart flip-flopped as he searched my eyes.

"You heard me."

Cocky ass. My thoughts must have stamped across my face because he tipped his head back and laughed.

"Do you have plans tomorrow night?" he asked.

I pushed my tongue against the inside of my cheek while I studied his face. "No."

"Good. You get dressed up, I'll pick you up at six, and I'll take you out for a nice dinner." His tone brooked no arguments.

I swallowed and found myself nodding. "Okay."

He stood, clapping his hands. "Good."

"Good," I repeated dumbly.

"Wipe that look off your face, Sonic." He started strolling, his hands tucked into his front pockets. "It'll be great."

I was still locked in place as I watched him walk toward his truck.

"What the *hell* just happened?" I whispered when I knew he couldn't hear me.

CHAPTER 15

JOCELYN

"What are you going to wear?"

My mom sat on the edge of my bed, twisting my hair into a complicated knot of tiny braids and curls anchored at the base of my skull. Normally, there wasn't much to be done with my hair, but when I told her Levi was taking me out to dinner, my "practice first date" so to speak, she threw herself into it in a way that had me side-eyeing her all damn day.

Since I couldn't move my head, I'd been staring at my closet for the past fifteen minutes while she worked.

"Maybe the blue V-neck. The silk one with the flowy sleeves, and my nice dark jeans."

"Jeans on a first date." She clucked her tongue. "Fix it, Jesus."

Her Southern belle came out swinging when she was confused. I winced when she tugged on a chunk of hair with a misplaced bobby pin.

"Ow."

"Sorry," she mumbled. "Goodness, no wonder you never do your hair. I can hardly see what I'm doing in all these curls."

Ahh, there was the first minor sideswipe of the day. We'd made it all day, which was pretty good for us.

I didn't answer because I was determined to stay in a good mood until I was out the door with Levi. There was no way I would let her ruin this for me.

"I don't want to wear a dress," I said, directing us back to the clothing situation.

Behind me, she was quiet, because she knew why I didn't want to wear a dress.

"Your legs aren't that skinny. I think it would be fine." Another bobby pin stabbed me, and I hissed in a breath. "Besides, it's just Levi. He doesn't care what your legs look like."

I'd once heard someone say *Be the thermostat, not the thermometer.* Set the bar for your reaction instead of allowing outside circumstances to tell you what the temp was.

Today, I'd be the fucking thermostat if it killed me.

It wasn't even that she was wrong because I knew Levi didn't judge my chicken legs. It was that she couldn't understand that it was about what was in my head and not what anyone else thought.

"There," she said, standing up from the bed. "Looks good. Want me to help you get dressed?"

"No, thanks."

Her sigh was heavy, like I'd managed to offend her because I didn't accept her offer, and hoo boy, I let that slide in one ear and riiiiight out of the other.

"I manage just fine every day, Mom. I have for years."

"Just trying to make things easier on you, Jocelyn," she said, words crisp and cold. "It's my job. I can't really turn it off."

I didn't say anything until she was facing me. Nero sat up, his head moving back and forth between her and me. A small whine came out as if he knew she was upsetting me, and it made him uncomfortable.

"I know, Mom." What I wanted to say was that her babying me, treating me like I wasn't capable, only made things hard in the long run. But that would only trigger the same conversation we'd had forty-seven thousand times in the past seven years. "Thank you for offering."

Oh, look at that! I didn't even choke on the words. I was the best freaking thermostat ever.

She nodded, not meeting my eyes. "I'd try that black shirt. The one with the lace sleeves and the boat neck. Lots of mascara. It'll make your eyes pop."

My smile was tentative. "Good idea."

It was a good date shirt.

She smiled back and left me to finish getting ready.

I almost wish she'd stayed, so she could watch me. That was the thing she didn't realize. The system I had down, the way I shifted from chair to bed to pull up my pants, or how easily I could reach the things I needed in my closet, it was something I didn't even have to think about anymore.

I leaned toward the mirror, mouth open because who could put on mascara without their mouth open, and I made a few choppy swipes on my lashes. Then a few more.

It was so rare for me to wear makeup that even the thick black coat of liquid over a tiny row of curled hair made me stare at my reflection.

The inky black shirt with delicate lace stretched across my chest left my collarbones exposed because of how my hair was braided back off my face.

I felt like I was watching someone else as I swept a little blush over my cheekbones and then did one more coat of mascara after the first had dried. My mom was right. My eyes popped bright in my face, even if my nerves were obvious.

All day, I'd convinced myself that this was a pity date. That he was merely being kind to his friend and letting me have this experience without the pressure that would come from sitting across from a stranger. It was Levi. Anything I'd felt in my head between Levi and me over the past week was just that ... in my head.

As I leaned down and lifted my foot so I could push it into the nude kitten heels that I never wore, I took a brief, selfish moment and imagined that it wasn't a pity date. That I was making all this effort for a man who would pick me up, tell me I looked beautiful, and feel the same fluttery, flittery things hopping around in my stomach. By the time I had the other foot in the other shoe, and I slid the soles of the heels carefully back onto my footplate, making sure that my ankles were straight, I let the moment go.

"That's enough," I whispered to myself as I sat up and stared at my reflection.

I heard my mom talking to someone, and Nero perked up at the sound of Levi's deep voice, whining immediately to be let out of my bedroom. His entire backside was wiggling as I leaned past him to pull the door open. He was off like a shot, which made me laugh.

My dog couldn't pretend this someone was new either.

I came down the hallway, a strange something curling up in the base of my tummy. Apparently, my traitorous body hadn't gotten the memo that fluttery, flitteries needed to go away because when I came around the corner and saw him crouched on the ground, scratching the sides of Nero's neck, they exploded dangerously, sweeping up my chest in a hot rush.

Levi's eyes landed on me, and he stood slowly.

I might have laughed at the fact that he was, to my mom's horror, wearing dark jeans with his bright blue dress shirt with the sleeves rolled up his forearms, but I was too busy watching my best friend look at me like he'd never seen me. His golden eyes were bright and happy, his hair styled neatly and jaw shaved clean.

"You look ..." He shook his head slowly. "Jocelyn, you look beautiful."

Words. I needed words, but someone had tossed a bucket of sand in my mouth, and it took me a second to unstick my tongue. "Thanks."

His eyes twinkled, and I shook my head because that ass could see right through me. He knew I was nervous; he knew I was struggling to figure out how the hell I was supposed to act.

"Shall we?"

I nodded, grabbing my purse off the end table by the front door. As I passed Nero, I scratched him on the top of the head.

My mom poked her head out of the kitchen. "Have fun. Don't be out too late."

In my head, I rolled my eyes because I was twenty-one, not sixteen, and she'd never once worried about how late I was out, especially since she'd be leaving for the hospital soon anyway. Levi smiled at her, dimple deep and ridiculous, and even my mom wasn't immune.

"Of course not, Mrs. Abernathy."

Levi followed me out the front door, chuckling as soon it closed behind him.

Normally, I would've joined in. But I still felt like the ground under me was unsteady, shifting slightly with each inch I covered.

"Hey," he said, resting his arm on my shoulder so that I had to stop.

"What?" I asked, only meeting his eyes for a second before I looked away again.

Levi crouched down in front of me and didn't speak until I finally caved and met his gaze straight-on.

"It's just you and me," he said. "Okay?"

"Okay," I answered quietly. How was he so sure about this? How did this not feel ... strange to him?

"We've eaten together hundreds of times."

"Not at a nice restaurant," I countered.

"How do you know we're going somewhere nice? Maybe I'm taking you to the Pink Pony."

My eyes narrowed when he grinned at me.

"I'm kidding."

"I know," I said evenly, but I wanted to laugh because *this*, this alone, helped settle me. This was us. Him and me.

"We're going to the steakhouse."

Moment over.

It was a date restaurant. Dim lighting. Fancy things on the menu. Food that had dollar amounts next to them that made me want to shrivel up when I imagined Levi opening the bill at the end of our meal.

Levi stood and opened the passenger door of his truck for me, then held out his hand.

For a second, I stared at it because this wasn't normal. This was date Levi I was seeing. The scenario I let myself think of was unrolling right in front of my eyes. To him, I looked beautiful. And there was door opening. Maybe there'd be candles.

I swallowed and slid my hand into his. There was no smile on his face as I locked my chair and used my free hand to brace myself on the armrest. There was no humor making his eyes light up as I stood and straightened.

"I did tell you that you looked beautiful, right?" he asked, his thumb running over my knuckles.

When the hell did that become a spot on the body that made me want to rub my thighs together?

"You did," I choked out.

He smiled slowly, leaning down until he was close enough that I could smell a sharp burst of mint on his breath. "Then I guess I'm telling you twice."

Thoroughly flustered, I blinked away from the minty fresh breath and sharp jawline, taking the step necessary so I could grab the handle on the door and pull myself into the passenger seat. Just as I started to lift myself, Levi curled his big hand around my waist and helped. He didn't pull it off until I was seated, and his heavy gaze was burning a freaking hole in the side of my face, but I kept my eyes forward as I fumbled with the seat belt.

I heard a small sigh as he shut the door and put my wheelchair in the bed of his truck. He hopped into the driver's seat and gave me a quick flash of a grin before he reached behind the seats and pulled out a bouquet wrapped in the telltale green florist paper.

Before he handed it to me, my mom's car backed out the garage, and she gave us a tiny wave when she drove past.

When the sound of her car faded down our driveway, Levi turned and handed me the bouquet. But the feel of it was all wrong as my hands took it.

"These are definitely not flowers," I said as I set it in my lap.

He jerked his chin. "Open it."

I gave him a curious look, which made him roll his eyes. I laughed under my breath and found the seam in the green, crinkly paper. When I peeled it back, I burst out laughing, because it was a bouquet made entirely of Twizzlers. They were beautiful and bright red, tied together in the middle with a perfectly tied white bow covered in blood red hearts.

First flours. Now my favorite candy.

How was I looking at him? I wondered as I stared into his face from across the bench of his truck. Only a man who truly knew me would give me the things he'd given me. No other first date would ever be able to do exactly the right thing to make me smile or set me at ease.

For a second, I had the most irrational feeling of sadness.

It was so unexpected that I felt myself tear up as I slowly pulled one of the individually wrapped stems from the middle of the bouquet. Levi was watching me quietly, but I knew he wouldn't be able to see the moisture in my eyes because of the angle of my head. I blinked furiously before handing him one.

"Pre-dinner treat?" he asked.

"Why not?" My voice sounded normal, not like I was one sweet gesture away from bursting into ugly, messy, didn't make any sense tears. Good frickin' thing I was doing this with him first because if it was someone I didn't trust, someone I didn't really know, I'd scare them off for sure if I started sobbing five minutes into a first date.

He took a bite while I pulled one out for myself.

Instead of eating it, though, I stared at him chewing.

"These are terrible," he said around the candy. "So much excellent candy in this world, and this is the one you choose."

"I don't judge you for liking candy hearts. Talk about a waste of sugar," I replied. He shook his head, and when he turned the key in the ignition, the truck started up with a roar.

"They're iconic."

"I'll remember that when one of them snaps your molar in half."

My hand gripped the edge of the seat as that unsteady feeling came back to me even though we hadn't started moving.

A simple conversation about candy had me reeling, and I felt crazy because of it.

Every single time Levi ate Twizzlers, he told me they were terrible. But he still always stocked them for me, simply because he knew I loved them.

When he knew I was going to get my period, he bought two bags.

When I was going in for a big doctor's appointment, he brought one over to me.

Because he was my best friend.

My best friend, who was taking me out for an expensive steak dinner where crisp white tablecloths covered the tables and the silverware was shiny and expensive. Each table would definitely have candles, providing soft and romantic lighting in the restaurant. I'd sit on one side, staring over at the man who knew what kind of tampons I used, how much I hated peas, and how avocados make me sick to my stomach because I'd puked one up in his bathroom after he made guacamole.

Twice, he'd told me I looked beautiful, and he'd shaved his handsome face, put on a nice shirt, and picked me up so that I wouldn't feel like the pathetic girl who'd never been on a first date.

That unsteady feeling was in my head because I couldn't reconcile these two versions of the man I knew so well.

It was like I was trying to combine a color picture with one in black and white, but it was supposed to be one seamless shot.

In the pool, I stared at his chest and wanted to bite it.

At his place, he made me watch the same movies over and over because he knew I was too lazy to pick something else.

When we got to the restaurant, I knew he'd pulled the truck into a parking spot toward the back of the lot because he knew I hated using the handicap spot when I was out with him.

And because I was a terrible, thoughtless person—who didn't know how to deal with big scary emotions like the ones threatening to make my eyeballs leak all over and who didn't know how to package them neatly and label them in a way that my brain and heart could filter them better—the words spilled out before I could even process what I was saying.

"So if this is my first real date, am I supposed to pretend you're someone else?"

I never would have said it, thought it, or even contemplated it if I'd been with anyone other than Levi. And when he froze, when he puffed out air like I'd just punched him in the stomach, I knew with unerring certainty how badly I'd just screwed up.

CHAPTER 16

LEVI

here was no hiding my reaction to her words, just like she couldn't stop the horrified widening of her eyes or the way she covered her mouth as soon as she saw me.

"I-I didn't mean it like that," she said on a rush.

There weren't words for how I felt. For how she'd just made me feel. I swiped a hand over my mouth and breathed in and out through my nose.

Because I knew her, rationally I could understand there was no ill intention behind what she'd said. No malice. But intention only went so far when the person you loved said something that made it feel like they took a baseball bat to your lungs. Then ran you over with a car for good measure.

My first instinct was to make her feel better by laughing it off. My second instinct, stronger and darker, was to get in her face until she had no choice but to see. See why I was doing this, and why I wanted to be here with her more than any place I could possibly be.

I dropped my hand and gave her a quick look.

"Levi," she whispered. "I'm so sorry. I didn't mean to say that."

"What did you mean to say?" I asked quietly. This time, I wouldn't overlook it. This time, I wouldn't swallow down my pride so she didn't feel bad for saying something shitty.

Joss took a deep breath and knit her fingers together in her lap. For a second, she stared down at them, then lifted her eyes up to mine.

"I don't know how I feel." She blinked, shook her head a couple of times. "Right now. On this ... date or whatever. I don't know how to feel about the fact that it's *you*. And you know me better than anyone, Levi."

My hands ached to touch her, to cup her face and pull her into my arms because she looked so miserable as she said it.

"Why do you say that like it's a bad thing?" I asked.

When she didn't answer my earnestly spoken question, I turned and faced her. One arm stretched along the back of the seat, the other hung on the top of the wheel, and between us, the stretch of the seat bench seemed like it was a mile long.

Joss was breathing fast, her lips closed and tight with tension. She was so beautiful, even with the bright sheen of fear and uncertainty surrounding her. Big feelings had always been terrifying to Joss, so her inability to answer right away didn't surprise me. It didn't even really scare me.

I drummed fingers on the steering wheel and took a deep breath. "Because the way I see it, Sonic, there's no way in the world it can be a bad thing." I kept my voice easy, my tone steady, and my body casual and loose. "The worst part of going on a date with someone new is that you have no idea if it's going to be the longest two hours of your life, or if you'll walk out of that dinner feeling like you met the person you're going to marry."

Her eyes watched me, guarded and wary.

Evening sky over the edge of the Smoky Mountains blue.

In that wariness, I knew that this was my moment. Her fear, strange as it might have seemed, was exactly what I needed to feel like I could take a step, just one single step over the clearly defined line of our friendship.

If she'd fallen into our normal rhythms, if she'd acted like herself right away, I might not have felt so certain about what I needed to do.

"So I'll tell you, Jocelyn Marie, I'll tell you exactly why there couldn't be a thing better in the world than the fact that you know me as well as you do and I know you in the same way."

Her throat, elegant and graceful, worked in a visible swallow, but she stayed silent.

"Because you know that when I say something to you, it's the truth, even if it's hard to hear. Even if it scares the hell out of you, you know that I'd rather rip my tongue out than tell you something that's a lie."

She blinked, and her jaw worked back and forth.

I licked my lips and lifted my hand from the back of the seat. Framing her face were a few curls, the ones that escaped the confines of whatever she'd done to it. I touched one, and she held herself so still that I almost smiled. The hair was soft, and the way it coiled around itself made me want to pull it straight just to watch it spring back into place.

Her chest lifted on a sharp inhale while I stared at the one curl.

"Do you know what the first thing was that I noticed about you?" I asked.

Joss shook her head slowly, one short back and forth motion as she held herself in place. Okay, I guess I'd be narrating this one solo.

"It was your hair." I slid my thumb and forefinger along the curl and stretched it gently, smiling when it bounced back. "I remember, like it happened yesterday, seeing you come into the gym that first day. It looked like your hair was exploding from the top of your head."

She exhaled a laugh. That little puff of air had my shoulders relaxing.

"It was your eyes next," I continued. I moved my thumb from her hair to the soft patch of skin underneath the edge of her lower lashes. "I've never, not in my entire life, been as intimidated as I was when you spoke to me the first time and turned those eyes right on me."

"Seriously?" she whispered.

I gave her a self-deprecating smile. "Seriously. Don't you remember the ass-kicking you gave me?"

"Maybe." But her smile, bright and sweet and fast, told me she remembered.

"I was stumbling over my words, couldn't even think of what I wanted to say because I couldn't stop staring. You were so fast, so graceful, so confident, I felt like I had a brick tied to my tongue for all the good it did me."

Joss shifted on the bench, lifting herself up a couple of inches so she could angle her legs toward me. "I don't remember you sounding awkward."

I swallowed. "I asked you out to dinner when we were done playing."

She nodded, her eyes turning sad. "And I said no."

I nodded back. "Do you remember what you said next?"

Her chin tipped up, and she inhaled slowly. "I said I could use a friend, though."

My thumb moved from the skin around her eyes, traced the sculpted edge of her high cheekbone, then touched the soft downy lobe of her ear, which made her shiver. She was so soft everywhere.

"Being your friend has been the greatest part of my life," I told her. "And even though I very much wanted to take you out for dinner just like this one, I don't regret a single day of the past five years because you know me in a way that no one else ever has."

"N-not even your family?" she stuttered when my thumb followed the edge of her jaw. I slid closer, thank God for bench seats.

"No one." Finally, I reached the edge of her mouth, those pink lips that were open as she breathed unsteadily. The line along her bottom lip was full and soft as I touched it. "Your mouth, that was next."

Her eyes fluttered shut. "Wh-what?"

I leaned in further, and the soft exhalation from her mouth hit mine. I pulled it into my lungs.

"I noticed your mouth next. Even now, this mouth makes me insane. When you smile, it's like a weapon."

Those eyes snapped open.

I traced the upper lip now, the sweet V of the cupid's bow. The tip of Joss's tongue darted out to lick her lips, but she caught the pad of my thumb as she did it.

My hand moved to cup the side of her face, and slowly, slowly, slowly, she tilted her head more fully into my palm.

That was my sign, the one I was waiting for. I wet my lips, her eyes tracking each movement. I dipped my chin and lightly, so lightly touched my lips to hers.

Click.

A puzzle piece. A lock. A key fitting into place, the one, singular, unique place it was meant for.

I brushed my lips back and forth slowly, memorizing the satin of her lips as she exhaled shakily, her hands sliding up my forearms to grip my wrists.

Joss tilted her head to the side for a new angle, and I touched my tongue gently to the seam of her lips. Immediately, she opened, and the sweet touch of her tongue against mine had me groaning deep from within my chest. This was my drug. This was the bright shot into my veins that had me flying.

I sipped at her lower lip, and she made a sound, a plea for more when she shifted again, tightening her grip on my wrists.

My hands were shaking as I held her face, then tilted my own to kiss her more deeply, sweeping my tongue against hers harder than before. There was so much pent-up energy coursing through my body I had to fight, claw, and snarl at the impulse to pull her onto my lap and kiss her as deep, wet, hard as I'd imagined so many times. To feel her skin under my hands. To know what her weight would feel like in my arms.

Joss released my wrists and wrapped her arms around my neck, her breasts pressing against my chest as we leaned into each other. She held me so tightly and kissed me with such delightful, unpracticed intensity, like she was a champagne bottle that had finally been uncorked.

"Joss," I whispered into her neck, kissing her underneath her jaw.

At the sound of my voice, muffled by her skin, she stilled, carefully pulling back so she could look at my face. Her hair was a mess, probably because of my fingers digging into it, and her lips were pink and puffy, her cheeks flushed, eyes bright.

"Whoa," she whispered, touching the tips of her fingers to her mouth.

I dropped my forehead to hers and exhaled, which sounded unsteady even to my own ears. Smoothing my hands up and down her back, I simply breathed her in, something clean and sweet and her.

"Pretty much."

Joss lifted her head and stared at me, her eyes were curious and careful. "You really wanted to kiss me that badly?"

I spoke on a laugh. "Yeah. I've wanted to kiss you that badly since the day I met you."

Her face fell. "You're joking."

"Why would I joke about that?" I asked.

"You've ... you ... for five years?" She gasped. "There's no way."

My eyebrows popped up. "Trust me, I'm not lying to gain brownie points right now."

She shook her head. "Levi, you're my best friend," she said, like it was all the explanation necessary.

Something dark and huge opened in my stomach. The worst-case scenario I always worried about, like a weed sprouting up between us. "I know. And you're mine. Those things are not mutually exclusive, Joss."

She laughed unsteadily and pushed backward on the seat, adding space between us. "Come on, be serious."

"I am being serious." My voice was firm because I wanted her to know how real and true this was for me, but inside, inside, I felt the cold brush of panic at her reaction.

If there was one thing I knew about her, knew about this woman who I loved so desperately, it was that she could burrow into her safety net and mute the feelings that would only serve to make her feel worse. Her kiss told me everything I needed to know, that she felt exactly what I wanted her to feel, but I knew how capable her brain was at shutting off the feelings that scared her.

With a flick of her wrist, she'd slide the lock into place, and that had my brain whirring furiously at how I should handle this.

Her breathing picked up again, quick and panicky and furiously paced. "There's no way," she said again. "There's no way you've been sitting back for five years. There's no way you'd want to deal with what this would do to your life."

As she said it, she looked down at her legs, then back up again. I damn well knew what she meant, and given how well she knew me, it was a bullshit excuse.

It was the most convenient thing she could grasp at, and that alone stoked the tiny flames of frustration inside me.

I leaned in until we were practically nose to nose. "Ask me, Joss."

She pinched her eyes shut. "I'm scared to."

All the times I worried about not pushing too hard, Sylvia's question about whether I tiptoed around her feelings because of what happened to her, they all thundered ominously in my head, and I knew, I knew this was no time to back down.

"*Ask me* how long I've felt like this," I pleaded, my hands itching to pull her into my arms again.

"I can't," she whispered and frantically fumbled for the door handle behind her.

CHAPTER 17

JOCELYN

*I*f I stopped to think about what I was doing, I would've moved more slowly. Been more thoughtful about my foot placement, or the fact that I was wearing heels.

"Jocelyn," he called out when I gripped the handle on the roof of his truck and swung my legs over.

Out. I had to get out.

I couldn't ask, because if I asked, I'd know. And if I knew, it might make me think back on the five years through a lens that all of this was a giant, huge fake.

Levi was already opening his door when I slid down the seat, which was what made me look over my shoulder at him. I didn't pay attention to where my foot was landing until my ankle slipped to the side, and my other foot caught on the step up into the truck.

I cried out, my hand gripping the handle as tight as I could manage as my legs slid out from under me. My other hand came up to grasp blindly at the door handle.

"*Shit,* Joss, hang on," he yelled as he sprinted around the truck to me.

I felt awkward and weak and pathetic, my legs dangling helplessly, twisted up like a pretzel. And I felt irrational. Manipulated. Lied to. Like everything we'd been through was fake. Contrived.

Even though I tried to breathe myself out of the tight, snapping squeeze of panic wrapping around my lungs, I couldn't.

I felt his hands on my back, and I tensed up.

"Don't," I snapped. "Please don't help me right now."

My forehead pressed against my forearm, and any tears I'd held back before hit my cheeks with hot strikes, little lashes of the most acute embarrassment. My hands tightened, and I pulled up as hard as my arms could manage in their awkward placement.

With a quick glance down at my legs, I straightened them as well as I could, quads and glutes shaking. I heard the bounce of wheels hit the ground, and my chair appeared behind me. Silently, Levi clicked the locks into place.

I took a deep breath and lifted my head, trying to ignore the wetness on my cheeks. When I felt like my feet were straight and my ankles steady, I dropped the hand on the handle and brought it down to my chair.

Relief almost had me falling backward because if this entire thing had ended with me literally curled up on the ground, I'd never, ever be able to face Levi again.

My other hand gripped the armrest, and I lowered my body into the chair. I was shaking when I set my feet onto the footplate.

He'd stayed silent the entire time, and out of the corner of my eye, I saw that he had one hand covering his mouth and the other propped on his hip.

I couldn't bear it. My own reaction, not even factoring in what happened after, had me sinking my face into my hands so I could just … hide for a second.

Kissing Levi. Oh, my heart could hardly think about it without triggering a fresh wave of tears.

"Joss," he pleaded. "Talk to me."

I took a second, quick swipe of my fingers under my eyes to clear the tears before I unlocked my chair.

Stay, stay, stay, a voice screamed in my head. I felt jittery and frantic, the desire to flee so overwhelming that my body couldn't even risk listening to my head.

"I-I can't be out in my driveway for this."

Okay, that made about zero sense, and even as it came out of my mouth, I heard the screaming illogic of it.

But where that desire came from, I damn well knew. If this was the one sliver of control I could regain over this situation, then I'd lift my chin and go back into the house like it made all the sense in the world.

Levi breathed in and out, loud and frustrated, but he came after me, closing the passenger side door when I was clear of it. His quiet was almost as frustrating as if he was pestering me with questions or demanding I stay and talk to him.

The quiet was patience.

The quiet was persistence.

The quiet was constancy. Humility. A composure that one of us was severely lacking.

The quiet was absolutely fucking terrifying.

I felt my nose tingle as I got to the top of the ramp and dug my keys out of my purse. My hand was shaking so hard that I could hardly fit it into the lock.

Levi gently took the keys from my hand and slipped the key in. I stared straight ahead, but I could see the tension tight in his jaw.

Nero greeted us happily, and his massive, wiggling body brought a tiny smile to my face as I scratched his head.

"Back up, Nero," Levi said, and my dog complied instantly. I pushed forward until I was by the couch. Levi closed the door, locking it behind him.

Nero's excitement faded instantly because he could sense the tension in me. His snout shoved underneath my hands, and he lifted up, whining loudly. "It's okay, bud," I whispered. "I'm okay."

Levi stood by the couch, hands still on his hips. "Want me to put him outside?"

My hand trembled over the ridge at the back of Nero's skull. He felt like a suit of armor I desperately wanted to wrap around me, but I nodded.

Levi whistled, and Nero hesitated for a moment, licking my hand furiously before I told him to go. He bounded toward the slider, which opened and closed immediately.

Before Levi joined me in the room, I stared at the couch, trying to decide if I would feel more comfortable there, but the decision was made for me when he came back in, long sure strides in my direction. Levi sat on the couch directly in front of me, where I'd have no choice but to look at his face.

I couldn't read it. Couldn't decipher it. The face I would've sworn, just one short hour ago, held no secrets from me, suddenly felt unfamiliar.

"Talk to me," he begged quietly, firmly. Now I could see something I recognized in the set of his jaw. The flames in his eyes trained on me with no wavering, no indecision. I wouldn't be able to run away from this today; I wouldn't be able to hide from what he was handing me with both hands. "Tell me what scares you, Sonic."

My eyes watered until his face got blurry and unfocused.

"Please. I'll make it go away if you just tell me."

I inhaled shakily, not trying to stop the tears. "I-I feel like if I ask you how long you've felt this way, I'll look at our whole friendship differently. Like, like it wasn't real if I know the truth."

"No," he said immediately, leaning toward me and clasping my hands in his while shaking his head. "No, Joss. It was real. You know me better than anyone in this entire world, and you know I'd never put up with someone this long if I didn't mean it. Whether I wanted to kiss you or not is completely irrelevant."

My laugh was watery. I wiped at my face until Levi took pity, leaned over to the end table, and plucked a tissue out of the box. His eyes were soft, so understanding, that I couldn't hold them for very long.

Because he knew.

The thought that someone might have been manipulating me—that showing anyone the sides of me that I kept tucked behind the thickest pieces of metal could've somehow been used against me—was the first thing that would have me come out swinging.

Levi, of anyone on this earth, knew what the softest, most vulnerable part of my underbelly looked like. And now it felt like he could wield that knowledge against me. Hold it in his hand like a sword or aim it like a gun.

So yes, he knew me. I knew him. But not really as well as I'd thought. That had my head lifting and my hands retracting slowly out from under his. Gently, so it didn't seem like a rejection.

It wasn't rejection—it was protection.

"So it was like, an experiment or something? Kissing me?" I asked quietly. *Please, let it be an experiment.*

His jaw flexed as he stared at me. "No."

I shook my head.

"You don't believe me?" he asked, voice raising a touch. Frustration was clear in his tone, the set of his eyes, and the way he held his hands. "You think I'd *lie* to you about this? When have I ever lied to you, Joss?"

"I don't know, Levi. That's my point. You keep saying I know you best of everyone, but that's obviously not true!"

"Give me a break. That doesn't mean you were some game to win or challenge to conquer. It just means that I have feelings and have had feelings that go a hell of a lot further than the desire to kiss you. And because I'm being honest with you at a time that finally feels right, you think I'm a liar."

And that had *my* voice raising, the little hairs lifting on the back of my neck as they did when I felt an irrational need to defend myself. "I *think* you can't possibly have wanted to date me this entire time, Levi. I think maybe everything in your life has come so easily to you that I've felt like some weird challenge you had to overcome because there's no freaking way you want to take all this on in your life. Not really."

His mouth dropped open, and he leaned forward. "Take on all of this ..." he repeated slowly, head shaking.

I shifted in my seat, face hot and heart pounding, hands shaking and the desire to flee so strong that I almost unlocked my chair just to back away from the way he was looking at me. "You know what I mean. You can date anybody, and you have. All the single women in Green Valley under the age of forty would fall prostrate if you looked in their direction."

"Good for them," he said. "I'm not interested. You tell me one person I've dated seriously in the past five years. One."

"I—" My mouth snapped shut, and I looked over his shoulder at the wall. Because I couldn't.

"Exactly. You can't name anyone beyond a couple of dates because I didn't *want* to date anyone other than you, but you weren't ready. You never saw me that way, and the moment I felt something change …" He leaned in again, staring down at my lips when he did. "The exact moment I knew you were feeling something different, I knew it was time to redefine."

"Redefine?"

"Us," he said simply. "Redefine the way we spend all our time together. Redefine being best friends who can now make out whenever the hell we feel like it. That I can hold your hand. Take you out. Feed you grapes or Twizzlers or cupcakes or whatever the hell you want to be fed. Sleep in a bed with you."

The flames under my skin roared to a dangerous level. It felt too big for my skin, too much for my mortal flesh and bones to contain, to withstand any longer.

"And you're going to turn me at night? Make sure I have blankets between my knees so I don't get sores? Deal with the fact I haven't gotten a solid night's sleep in seven years? You're going to stand by when people look at me the way they do? Be rude when they meet me? Assume I'm helpless?"

His face was implacable. "Hell yes, I'll deal with it. It's not about *dealing* with it, Joss, it's your truth, and I know what the reality of your life looks like."

I laughed under my breath, and it helped cool the flames, inch by inch, beat by beat, until I felt like I could breathe again.

"No, you don't," I told him. "You know parts of it. And you know the parts that you've seen. But you're not ready for this. This isn't what you want."

Even as the words came out, I knew how unfair they were. Everything I'd heard from him, and everything he hadn't said yet, but what I could see in his eyes, I wanted to hide from. In my head, the words were a bulletproof vest, unbreakable and unyielding.

Levi breathed in and out, his eyes trained firmly on my face. He then ripped that vest apart like it was cardboard.

"Bullshit," he whispered.

"What?"

He slid forward on the couch and grabbed the wheels on my chair so I couldn't move, his face inches away from mine. Air slid harsh and fast from my nose as I struggled to breathe.

"I call bullshit. My best friend is not a coward, and right now, you're acting like one. You're using this flimsy piece of metal and rubber as an excuse, and it's bullshit."

There were no words that I could spit at him, nothing that I could hide behind, because he knew, and I knew he was right. But there were no words falling off my tongue to tell him that. They were stuck down my throat, in my stomach, somewhere hidden and coated in sticky, thorny pride.

Levi nodded slowly because, damn him, he saw it.

"I hate you right now," I whispered unevenly, tears burning hot in my throat and nose and eyes.

"You don't hate me." He matched my tone. "You may not like me right now, but you don't hate me, Jocelyn Abernathy. It scares the hell out of you that your wheelchair doesn't bother me, that I don't care that you're the prickliest woman I've ever met in my life, and that I'm not running off because your legs don't work the way you want them to."

One tear fell over the edge of my lashes, and he swept it away with his thumb. There was no lingering this time, nothing romantic in the way he touched my cheek.

I cursed my stupid pride. My stubbornness. Because there was this tiny spark, this sliver of light that made me want to throw my arms around his neck and kiss him again, but I couldn't. I *couldn't*.

He didn't mean it.

He couldn't mean it.

That he'd been in front of me this entire time, and never said a word, never hinted, I just couldn't force my head to move past that. Not with him sitting in front me saying everything that I should want to hear, but everything that terrified me the most.

"I—" I started but stopped again, shaking my head. "I can't do this right now."

Levi didn't move for a few seconds, searching my face with those bright golden eyes. Then he nodded slowly.

"Of all the times I imagined this date," he said sadly, "I never imagined it would end with you crying before I could even take you out to dinner. I should've done this better. Handled it better."

He stood fast, and I exhaled a rough breath, a hand coming up to my chest. Yup, my heart was still there.

"Call me when you're ready to talk, okay?" he asked.

I nodded.

Then he leaned down and pressed a quick kiss to the top of my head, which had me tightening the hand on my chest. Before he left, he opened the slider for Nero, who bounded over to me and burrowed his head on my lap.

I risked a glance at Levi, and on his face was a sad little smile.

"I told you that you look beautiful, right?" he said.

Another tear slid down my cheek unchecked, and I nodded. He was turning to go when I found my voice again, just enough to give him something. Something other than my fears.

"I promise I'll call soon," I told him.

He paused with his hand on the door, and I saw his shoulders relax.

When the door closed behind him, I wrapped my arms around my dog's neck, unleashed my sobs, and soaked his fur down to the skin because nobody was there to see it.

CHAPTER 18

JOCELYN

"Joss, honey, how long has it been since you've done ...
well ... anything to your hair?"

The frosting spatula didn't so much as waver while I
spread lemon buttercream over the four-layer raspberry cake as I
turned it on the lazy Susan.

"Are you trying to tell me something, Joy?"

She cleared her throat, and I kept my eyes straight ahead.

Oh, I'd been a real peach the past four days. When I did talk, it
came out like a snarl. Because if I tried to sound pleasant, or like I was
okay, I'd probably lose my shit.

"No, no," she hurried to say, "just curious. If it's a new trend, I
always like to know. Maybe ... maybe unkempt is the new thing, you
know? If anyone can pull it off, it's you. You look really wild. Kinda
like you were raised by wolves or ..."

Now I lifted my eyes to her. Her skin was pale.

"Wolves?"

Joy's face fell. "N-no! I just ..." She licked her lips, darting her eyes
around the kitchen like someone might rescue her. Mikey held his
hands up and ran back out to the register. One of the other part-
timers watched us like we were the Real Housewives of Green Valley.

163

I almost offered to make her popcorn. "I just want to make sure you're okay," Joy finished softly.

Carefully, I set the spatula down and took a deep breath. Four days was the longest I'd ever gone without talking to Levi in five years. Even when he was in the middle of midterms or finals or anything, we texted every single day and saw each other at least four days a week.

For five years.

And now I'd thrown myself, quite voluntarily, into the middle of Levi detox. Withdrawals were not fun. Symptoms ranged from snappish answers, scrolling through text history searching for clues that I'd missed, eating massive amounts of ice cream and then hating myself, to pulling up his contact info, only to set my phone down again.

And baking. Lots and lots of baking. The freezer at home was full of banana bread and zucchini bread and about seventeen kinds of cookies.

Looking in the mirror was even less fun than all those things. "Hot mess" did not even begin to cover the way I looked. I hadn't been sleeping well as my appetite pretty firmly trained onto the sugar part of the food pyramid. Thank goodness my mom was in the midst of a busy week at the hospital because it meant I didn't have to lie to her about what my frickin' problem was.

Heaven forbid we have the kind of relationship where I could confide in her.

The woman I *did* have that relationship with was the mother of the man who kissed the hell out of me. The thought of facing her, of facing his entire family, was daunting for the first time ever. I'd never had to worry about what they thought of me because their acceptance was so instant, so genuine. Did they know? Had he confided in them all these years? It was a toss-up whether I wanted that to be the case or not.

Worrying about it, whether they knew about his feelings, would only serve to drive me insane. If Mrs. B knew, it would only take one look, and I'd have my answer.

"I'm fine, Joy," I told her, giving the cake my full attention again.

The pale yellow buttercream smelled bright and tangy, and it made my mouth water as I spread the crumb coat.

Jennifer walked through the back door, giving us a sunny smile. "How's it going, ladies?"

Joy gave her a quick shake of the head, then jerked her chin in my direction.

Proceed with caution. Approach at your own risk.

I rolled my eyes. "Everything's good. We need more buttermilk, though. We only have one carton left."

"Really? I thought there were two full ones in there." She opened up the massive fridge next to her and cocked her head to the side. "Huh. How much pound cake did you guys sell this morning? Or was it the scones?"

"Mikey spilled one," Joy explained.

Jennifer looked over her shoulder. "Oh. What happened?"

I pursed my lips and absolutely refused to answer. Joy cleared her throat and nudged my shoulder.

With a sigh, I set down the spatula again and briefly met Jennifer's eyes. "I may have ... scared him. And he dropped it."

Her forehead wrinkled. "How'd you scare him?"

The embarrassment had my cheeks burning as she took in the state of my hair with wide eyes.

"He didn't know I was behind him. He backed up into me, and I, umm, I yelled at him. Just a little bit. I'm sorry, Jennifer," I said on a rush. "I'm having a crappy week, which is no excuse. I already apologized to him, and I helped him clean it up."

She rolled her lips between her teeth, seemingly trying not to smile at the crazy looking woman who was clearly in a delicate mental state.

"Okay," she said after a second. "We'll get more buttermilk."

When she came up behind me and laid a gentle hand on my shoulder, I felt my chin wobble, so I clenched my teeth tight and breathed through that bullshit. No crying. There was no crying in the bakery.

"Whatever it is, Jocelyn," she said quietly, "it'll be all right. I promise."

What would happen if I just opened my mouth and let the words tumble out? If I tried to explain to them how off-kilter everything was now that I knew? How precarious it made me feel?

On two wheels, I was steady. Very little made me feel like I would fall or stumble. I knew now that I treated my chair like a security blanket. I was the proverbial little kid who held it with a death grip and refused to admit that anything else might replace it.

Walking was scary because I wasn't good at it. No matter the way I felt when I stood up straight and saw the world from a different height, it was still scary as hell because one wrong foot placement and kaboom, down I'd go. Changing the way I viewed Levi was scary in the same sense because it held such big, big consequences.

The thought of dating Levi—let me repeat that out loud because even the words paired together felt really freaking weird, *dating LEVI* —was just as precarious to me as trying to take off at a dead run.

So many things could go wrong, so many things could mess me up or mess him up in the future, and at the end, the thought of not having him in my life at all was simply *awful*.

But the other side of the cookie was just as impossible to ignore. I couldn't pretend I didn't know. I couldn't pretend I didn't know what it was like to be kissed. Not just by anyone. Lips and tongues, hands and fingers weren't interchangeable, I had to imagine, so what was even bigger was that I knew what it felt like to be kissed by Levi. Those moments in his arms were the closest I'd felt to flying in my entire life.

Joy shifted to the side and seemed to be watching my face very carefully. "Do you ... do you want to talk about it?"

Jennifer squeezed my shoulder when my head dropped down to my chest. "I'll be back in my office if you guys need me, okay?"

I nodded, and Joy smiled as our boss—our really, really great boss —gave us some privacy. While I started the lazy Susan again, smoothing out the rest of the crumb coat before I'd lay the thin sheet of fondant on top, I took a deep breath.

Joy, the person I'd written off as silly and about as substantial as a good meringue, stood next to me, patient as a saint.

"I kissed Levi." It seemed like the most logical place to start. "Or he kissed me. I don't really remember who initiated it."

"Oh." She exhaled meaningfully.

"Yeah."

She twisted her lips to the side when I didn't say anything else. "Was it like, bad? Or weird?"

My eyes fell shut so I could remember for the millionth time how his firm, soft lips felt moving over mine. How surprisingly slick his tongue was but not in a bad way. How the scrape of his teeth along my bottom lip was the thing that snapped me violently out of the moment because it made my breasts tingle and my thighs press together desperately.

"Not bad." I glanced at her. "Definitely not weird."

"Was it good?" she asked, eyes sly and cheeks pink.

If her cheeks were pink, then mine must have turned fuchsia. Joy giggled.

"So"—she waved a hand at my hair and face—"why is allll this happening?"

I smiled a bit, amazed how one little curl of my lips and the shift of my muscles on my face could feel so good after such a shitty week. Sometimes you didn't realize how little you'd smiled until it finally happened again.

I set the spatula down and spun the lazy Susan once more to make sure everything looked even. Then I snagged a clean spoon and scooped it through the buttercream. Rolling it over my tongue, I thought about what to say without unloading five years of history onto an unsuspecting Joy.

"He's been, I don't know, wanting this to happen between us. For a long time."

"That's so roman—"

"Do not even say it," I interrupted. "You can think it all day long, but don't say it to my face right now."

She frowned. "Why not? I can think it's romantic without it changing your opinion."

Shit. "Well if you're going to be logical about it," I mumbled. My tongue swiped the last of the frosting off the spoon, and I leaned over to toss it into the sink. "It doesn't feel romantic because it feels like our friendship has been a lie."

Joy hummed, reaching forward for a spoon of her own to dip in the bowl. "That's delicious, by the way."

"Thanks."

She ate the small bite of frosting slowly before speaking again. "A lie sounds malicious, doesn't it? Purposely deceitful. I don't know Levi well. I knew him in high school, everyone did, but he's nice. He was nice to everyone." She shrugged. "If someone asked me what kind of friend he'd be, I'd never think words like deceitful or malicious."

"No, he's neither." I missed him. Talking about him, even for a minute, made me miss him so damn much. "So maybe it's a lie by omission, but he's had this thing in his head for years, and I didn't know. And that thing, about me and us and some future relationship he was hoping for, wasn't something I was aware of. Not even a little. It feels like someone's had me on a stage this whole time, only I didn't realize it. Was he dissecting things I said or did, or I don't know."

Joy picked up the cake off the turntable and walked it to the large fridge for me.

"Thanks," I told her. I could've done it, but trying to set it on my lap without it tipping sounded like a bit too much responsibility for me in my current unkempt state. I couldn't even manage to brush my hair, for crying out loud.

"So if Levi had told you, say ... three years ago, that he wanted to date you. What would you have said?"

I looked down at my lap. "I probably would've laughed at him. Not like, in a bitchy way, but it was just so far off my radar at that point still."

She nodded. "And he probably knew that."

"Probably," I hedged.

"What about two years ago? Or one? Is it the same thing?" She held my gaze even though my eyes were narrowing as her point sank in. "Clearly, your friendship is more important than anything else he might have felt or might have wanted for him to wait for you to have dating on your radar. If he'd pushed at the wrong time?"

"I would've run," I whispered. Joy's mouth popped open, and I rolled my eyes. "Figuratively speaking."

She laid her hand on my shoulder. "I think it's okay if you're not ready to see the romance of it. And maybe you never will. But if kissing him was good enough that your face matched the raspberry coulis you made yesterday, then you just might need a few days to get used to the idea."

I nodded, shifting uncomfortably in my chair. "Thank you, Joy. I don't—I don't have many people to talk to. He was kind of it, you know?"

Her face transformed into a beaming smile. "Well, now you have two people."

I laughed under my breath. "I guess I do."

CHAPTER 19

LEVI

I never thought I'd be as thankful for my big brother as I was after the past five days. There was no way for me to know that the day after I left Jocelyn's, ready to punch my fist through a wall, that I'd get a call from the Washington Wolves organization, saying they wanted to fly me out to Seattle for the next round of interviews.

It was the first time in five years that she wasn't the first person I called with the news. The first time in five years I'd flown across the country without her knowing. I spent three days in Seattle, trying not to gape at Pike's Place Market, the mountains stretched behind the sound, and the smells and sights and all the people.

As soon as my mom's car cleared the outskirts of Knoxville, the roads and the views all seemed changed somehow, just from three days of seeing something new.

"So you liked Seattle?" she asked.

"I loved it," I told her honestly. "The sights and the food, the culture, all of it. Hunter made me try seafood I've never even heard of, but it's so fresh. Like they snatched it from the ocean straight to your plate."

"That's wonderful." Her voice, because I knew it so well, sounded a little strained.

"They haven't offered me the job yet," I said gently.

She smacked my leg. "I'm just asking some questions. Now what about the team? The buildings and stuff? You'd like it there if they did?"

I sank my head back and stared out the windshield. "Mom, it was … it would be a dream come true."

"Yeah?"

"Yeah." I shook my head, thinking back on what I saw and the people I met—the athletes I'd followed for years. "I know the people who work there get used to seeing each other, the players, the coaches, just walking the halls like normal people, but I think my mouth hung open from the moment I walked in until the moment I walked out."

"That's wonderful, honey." She clucked her tongue. "And I'm sure you didn't gape like a fish the entire time."

I laughed. "Not the whole time."

"What was the best part of the interview?"

"Oh, man." I rubbed my palms over the tops of my thighs and grinned. I couldn't help myself. "We were in the training room. He was asking me about some of my favorite cases in school and in walks Jared Conway."

"No." She gasped. "Did you tell him you had his Vols jersey all through high school? Wore it every Saturday?"

"Hell no, I didn't tell him," I answered. "I acted like a professional and tried not to shit myself that my favorite player from Tennessee had just limped through the damn door."

"So what happened?"

I shrugged. "He asked me to assess Jared and tell him what to do."

Her smile was so full of pride, it looked like she might burst wide open. I still wanted to grab my phone, scream my story to Joss, and hear her freak the hell out that I'd met one of my football idols.

"And did you?"

"Yeah." I laughed. "Got him up on a table, and we did some

stretches, I checked out his quad. There were no tears or sprains, so I showed him what I'd do, we talked for a few minutes, and then he was just ... gone."

"You'll give your dad a heart attack when you tell him that story."

"I promise to wait until he's sitting down."

"And your brother? How's he doing? How was Samantha? Did she ... was she welcoming?"

I smiled at her not-so-subtle dig at my sister-in-law, who'd been an adequate hostess though not by southern standards. Adequate in the way that I have a roof over my head, a place to sleep, and a bathroom to use. Any whispered statements she made to my brother about the hassle of having a guest underfoot weren't meant for me to hear, but I'd heard them nonetheless.

"Hunter seemed good," I told her. "Quiet, but you know him, he always is."

She cut me a side-eye, not at all missing the fact that I didn't answer her about Samantha.

"Levi William Buchanan, don't think I'm slow just because I'm getting old. I asked you a question."

"What do you want me to say? She's wasn't all that friendly, and I'm still just as confused about why he married her as I was the day he did it?"

Her face got sad for the first time since she met me at the airport curb. "I don't know, honey. It makes me hurt for my son. When you have kids, you'll understand. From the time they start walking, and even before that, all you want is for them to be happy and healthy and loved. Who they choose to spend their life with is such a big part of that."

"Funny, I didn't think we got to do much choosing, thanks to the Buchanan curse."

Did I sound bitter? Maybe. But five days of silence would do that to a guy. And I wasn't pissed at Joss, not really. I knew her well enough to know that facing something that scared the shit out of her would pull out the stubborn in her faster than just about anything.

"Oh Levi, the curse doesn't mean you don't get a choice," she chided gently.

I looked over at her. "I don't feel like I have one right now."

"Uncle Glenn married the wrong one," she said. "He and your aunt, I know you don't know her because she moved as soon as they got divorced, but they were never suited. It's why your cousins think we're crazy for believing in all this. But you do have a choice, son."

She was quiet for a second, waiting for a semi to pass so she could make the last turn toward Green Valley. The stretch of road ahead of us was empty. The Smoky Mountains and a town where I knew everyone were in front of us. At our backs, with one turn of the car, I could no longer see the possible future that I'd spend days pondering.

Choices. I'd had plenty of choices about a lot of things in my life. But how I felt about Joss didn't seem like one of them. A choice sounded like you could turn it on or off.

"So, if Uncle Glenn made a choice, and you're saying it was wrong, what about Hunter?"

My mom chose her words carefully when she did respond next, and it wasn't what I expected. "Do you think Samantha is the one?"

"I assumed so. I guess I never thought about it."

She smiled and gave me a quick look. "Now, it's not my story to tell, but your brother loved someone before he met Samantha at college."

"Do I know her? Does she still live in Green Valley?"

"Not my story to tell," she repeated.

My eyebrows popped up briefly. "I guess I shouldn't be too surprised. She's ... well, she doesn't seem like the one for him."

She shrugged. "He's there, though, and that's all that matters right now."

"Hunter told me he's getting in late the night before the wedding. Promised he wouldn't miss it."

"That's what I was told too, last time we talked." She shook her head. "And he's got to go back the day after."

"Quick trip," I commented even though he'd already given me an explanation—something about work.

174

Mom gave me a knowing look. "We all make choices."

"And he made his," I muttered.

"He did. Whether it was a good one or not is another matter entirely. But ... but you could too, if you really wanted to."

Taking in the weight of her words and the possible outcomes made my head spin. I didn't want to choose anything that didn't include Joss, but there was no way for me to bring up the possibility of moving to Seattle unless she was in. All in.

"You mean Seattle, right?" Because I couldn't imagine my mom encouraging me to stay in Green Valley and be with someone other than Joss. They already loved her like a daughter.

"Partially. You loved it, right?"

I nodded. "It almost surprised me how much, you know? It's so different than home, and I've never felt the itch to move away, but"—I swallowed and hedged over my words for a minute, like I wasn't sure I was ready to say them out loud—"but I think going there forced me to admit how stuck I've been."

She kept her eyes on the road. Conspicuously so. "Stuck how?"

"Maybe stuck isn't even the right word. It's more like ... complacent, you know? I chose a master's program where I could commute from home. I graduated six weeks ago, and even though I know I won't be able to find the kind of job I need in Green Valley, I'm not out trying to find my place because I don't ... I don't want to leave her. If it wasn't for Hunter, it's not like I would've been looking at jobs in Washington."

That was the simple truth of it. I didn't want to leave her. If Joss never felt the way I did, I'd probably love her for the rest of my life, even if someone else settled into a corner of my heart that I'd managed to keep free. And I still couldn't imagine leaving her.

"Honey, you have so much life ahead of you. Everything feels big and important and life-changing, every single decision. But the truth is, you've got so many options, things that you'd be happy doing, jobs you'd love, and towns and cities that would feel like home. If you feel stuck right now, like you're not pushing yourself forward, I think that's okay." She reached over the console and patted my hand. "As long as you don't stay there once you realize it."

"Is that your way of telling me to get off my ass and get a job, even if it's not in Washington?"

"Yes."

I smiled, shaking my head a little bit.

"And she'll come around," she continued quietly.

I closed my eyes even though my sunglasses covered them. "You think so? You know how stubborn she is."

"I sure do. That's why she's good for you."

"I don't know, Mom. I think I scare her more than anything else could."

Her smile was soft. "And that's why *you're* good for her. She needs that. Her momma doesn't push her, never has. Jocelyn has all this fire in her. It's one of the things I love most about that girl, but sometimes she uses it as a weapon rather than a way to burn off the stuff that holds her back."

I was quiet because I didn't know what to say next. It helped that my family knew her so well and loved her all the more for it.

"Well," my mom said quietly as Green Valley came into view, "I hope you hear from them soon about the job."

"Me too." One less unknown in my life would be great.

"And you're home just in time to help set up for the rehearsal dinner tomorrow night. Aren't you glad? Sylvia wants lots of twinkle lights strung up in that big oak in her parents' backyard to look like a tent or something. I told her you'd help Connor."

I sighed heavily. "Not even home for three hours and I'm already signed up for forced labor."

The car pulled up to a red light, and she turned to me with a tight smile. Her hand lifted to pat my face, then she smacked a little harder than necessary.

"Ow," I muttered.

"I raised sons with good, helpful attitudes. You remember that, young man. I'm the one making your supper tonight."

"Yes, ma'am."

While I laughed, I still fought the impulse to pull out my phone and text Joss. My desire to want her to know the things I thought were funny, the things that were exciting, and the things I wanted to share with her were unconscious. And I didn't think that would ever go away.

CHAPTER 20

JOCELYN

*J*oy, as it turned out, was a closet makeup artist. She spent hours watching YouTube videos and practicing techniques she'd never worn out of the house because she felt it helped her be a better cake decorator. That made sense too because she did shit on some wedding cakes that brought a tear to the eye of even the greatest cynic.

Which was how I ended up with a face full of makeup that somehow didn't look like I had a face full of makeup, but the version of me in the mirror was—in my mind—so much more beautiful than I looked every day.

It was me, but it wasn't.

She did something to my eyes that made the blue bluer and the shape bigger. My cheekbones were highlighted and the perfect shade of peachy shimmery pink. My lashes were thick and black but not spidery or gross. I'd asked for her to leave my lips alone because I felt like a clown when I wore lipstick, so with a grimace, she allowed me to slick on some tinted ChapStick.

It was only because of her secret superhero skills that I felt even remotely prepared to put on the dress that I'd bought weeks ago for Connor and Sylvia's wedding.

The fact that I had a dress in my closet at all was one thing. That it was long made it even stranger. The lines were simple, the color one solid line of bluish purple—summer lavender, the girl at the shop in Maryville told me. With a halter that hooked behind my neck with a thin string, I could show off my arms, clearly my best trait. The daring part, the part that made my tummy flip, was that my back was completely exposed. The dress tied around the back, wrapping around my waist in a way that sitting, or standing, it looked flattering.

"I don't think I can do this," I whispered to Nero before I left the house.

Like an asshole, he didn't answer and simply cocked his head and twitched his ears.

"You're right. I'm being a chicken." My fingers played with the clasp on the small purse I'd borrowed from the back of my mom's closet. It was probably outdated, something she'd used in college, but I'd forked over enough for a dress I'd only wear once, so I was not about to add a purse into my budget too. "It'll be fine. It's not like he'll kick me out or something, right?"

Nero sniffed, shaking his head. I laughed.

"Thanks, bub." I scratched under his chin, which made him groan happily. "Have a good night while I'm gone, okay?" I sighed. "Honestly, I don't know how late I'll be."

That kinda depended on Levi. And my ability not to screw this up.

I took one last look in the mirror over the entryway table and managed one heaving breath to get my lady balls firmly in place.

Wheeling out to my car, I carefully, so very carefully lifted my chair into the back. Walking in a long, flowing dress felt far more terrifying than it should have. Each step was an accomplishment. When I was sitting in the driver's seat, I realized that I'd been holding the air in my lungs for too long because my head felt a little dizzy.

Or maybe that wasn't oxygen deprivation, I thought as I started driving toward Sylvia's parents' house. Maybe it was sheer, hanging-off-a-cliff-face nerves. By going into that wedding alone, I was about to let go. Let my hands fall off the edge and hope to God he'd catch me.

I'd arrived early enough that finding a close parking spot wouldn't be a problem, and off to the side of their three-acre spread, I saw the wedding party posing for the photographer.

Levi was easy to spot as he was a head taller than his brother, wearing dark navy pants, a crisp white shirt, and a fitted gray vest that molded to his broad chest. I couldn't help my smile. I'd missed him this week.

I saw him look in the direction of my car, but from this distance, it was impossible to know whether he'd actually seen me. When the photographer moved them to a different spot, in the back corner of the yard with the tall weeping willow behind them, I took my moment to get out of the car while I wouldn't be a distraction to him.

Normally, a backyard wedding would fall on my list of top ten things I'd dread attending because of simple wheelchair issues, but because I'd snagged a parking spot on concrete, and Sylvia's parents' yard was one long stretch of even, neatly manicured grass, it wasn't as daunting as it could have been.

I stood and exhaled, pulling my skirt down and checking to make sure it wasn't wrapped funny around my ankles or anything before I took my first step to get my chair.

Levi's parents beat me to it. I heard Mr. B clear his throat, and before I could move, I found them both beaming at me. Mrs. B was already wiping underneath her eyes.

"Oh my gosh, you are not crying already," I chastised her.

With a watery laugh, she gathered me in her arms and hugged me tightly. One of my hands was still on the door handle, but I held her with my free arm.

"Sweetheart, you are as pretty as a picture." She stepped back. "Look at you in *a dress.*"

"Right?" I laughed. "It feels as weird as it looks, trust me."

Mr. B was smiling at us. "Nothing weird about it, Joss. You look beautiful," he said in that gruff voice of his. "Let me grab your chair for you."

"Thanks, Mr. B."

Mrs. B rubbed my back and smiled softly at me, her eyes an

obvious mixture of sadness and hope. "We've missed you, sweetie. You better not be gone too much longer. House feels empty without you."

I narrowed my eyes at her. "How much did he tell you?"

Mr. B brought my chair over and locked it for me, before hooking a hand in his wife's elbow. "You're not meddling, are you?"

She sniffed. "I'd never."

He caught my eye and winked. When he bussed a kiss on her cheek, I couldn't help but sigh. In his starched shirt and gray bowtie, his dark gold hair—lightly peppered with gray—and beard freshly trimmed, he looked so handsome. Levi might get his personality from his mom, but his looks were all from his dad.

"You look very dapper today, Mr. B," I told him as I sat in my chair.

He grimaced, tugging on his tie, but his cheeks flushed a soft pink at my compliment. "No one told me I'd have to wear one of these."

Mrs. B clucked her tongue and swatted his hand away. "Leave it alone. I've already had to fix it once."

The look in his eye when he looked at his wife made me melt. No other way to say it. Even after five years of watching them together, the way they loved each other still made me feel gooey. Those were the parents I'd wished for growing up.

"Can we help you find a seat, sweetie?" Mrs. B asked.

I smiled. "No, I'm sure you guys have stuff to do."

She waved that off. "Nonsense. Besides, we need to make sure you're up by the family."

"What?" I shook my head. "No, no, that's okay. I wouldn't want to intrude."

My protests were summarily ignored when she looked at her husband. "Why don't you have Grady move that chair at the end. That way she'll have the best view, and I can have someone next to me to hold my hand when I'm blubbering mess."

Again, he winked at me and went off to do his wife's bidding.

I gave her a flustered look. "I don't think I knew y'all were this stubborn when I first met you."

"We hide it well, sweetie," she answered sagely.

"Do we ever," a dry voice said from behind me.

Mrs. B smiled as I turned and saw Grace, Levi's cousin from California, approaching us. She was a beautiful as I remembered, vaguely reminding me of a lioness in the tilt of her green eyes, the way her hips swung as she walked, and the tawny color of her hair.

"You look lovely, honey," Mrs. B said, giving her niece a peck on the cheek. "I like those boots."

Grace kicked one heel out behind her, and I laughed because the chunky black combat boots might have seemed like an odd choice paired with her flirty red dress, but damn, it worked on her.

She pinned her eyes on me. "Jocelyn, right? We met a few years ago."

I nodded. "Good to see you again, Grace."

Grace threaded her arm through Mrs. B's. "Now tell me, ladies, how is one supposed to conduct themselves at a proper Southern wedding? Because I'll be thoroughly disappointed if I don't have the opportunity to drink moonshine straight from the jug at some point."

Mrs. B laughed. "Oh, I'm sure Levi and your brother will have something for you."

I rolled my eyes. "I don't know. The last time Levi touched moonshine, he puked for three hours straight."

Grace grinned. "What a pansy."

"Oh, you say that now," I said. "Wait till you've been drinking it for two hours, then tell me how you feel."

They both laughed. Grace glanced around the yard with a tiny smile on her face.

"You know, Grady has it in his head we need to move here. He thinks we should 'get in touch with our Southern roots.'"

"I think that would be wonderful," Mrs. B exclaimed. "We'd love to have y'all here. And you already know Joss. She's practically part of the family."

Grace winked at me. "So I've heard."

She had a dimple in the same spot as Levi, and I knew from pictures that her twin brother did as well.

Damn those Buchanan genes.

Mrs. B glanced behind me, her smile growing. "Grace, sweetie, let's go find Memaw."

"Now?"

Mrs. B's eyes turned flinty, and I gave her a strange look. "Yup, right now."

"Okaaaay." Grace shrugged at me and let her aunt lead her away.

I let out a deep breath when they all but disappeared. No one had parked next to me yet, so I turned my chair slightly to the side so I could look at the fairy-tale setup in Sylvia's parents' backyard. Lights were strung from one center point underneath the sprawling oak tree that served as the centerpiece. It was like a tent of lights, swooping out to the side. Chairs were lined up with bales of hay along the sides for extra seating. To the side of where the ceremony would take place were mismatched tables of varying lengths. Some had benches, and some had high backed seats. Jars full of white and pink flowers decorated the different surfaces.

It was perfect.

And staring at it was the only reason I didn't hear him approach until he crouched next to me. When his hand landed on my shoulder, I pinched my eyes shut tight. The skin of his palm was so warm, so rough and familiar that my belly flip-flopped dangerously.

"Hi," he said.

I opened my eyes and turned my head.

He was so close. He wasn't close enough.

"Hi," I said back. "Your mom saw you coming, didn't she?"

His lips lifted in a crooked, unrepentant grin. "I slipped her a twenty as soon as I saw your car pull up to keep you occupied until I was done with pictures."

I tipped my head back and laughed. Any tension I'd been carrying was gone. *Poof.* Just like that.

"There she is," he said under his breath, almost to himself. If we hadn't been so close, I might not have heard him.

Tentatively, I lifted my hand and cupped the side of his face. He closed his eyes and leaned into the touch. "Was I gone?" I asked.

Levi opened his eyes when I stroked my thumb along the side of

184

his mouth. He turned and pressed a kiss into my palm. It made my fingers curl up instinctively.

"Not gone," he answered. "Just hiding from sight for a little bit."

I nodded. "Sounds right. I'm sorry it took me so long."

Immediately, he shook his head. "No apologies, okay?"

"Okay."

His eyes zeroed in on my mouth, and he sighed heavily. "I wish we weren't in view of half the damn town right now."

I chuckled. "Patience is a virtue, Levi Buchanan."

"And a virtue never hurt you," we finished together.

He groaned, leaning his forehead forward until it touched mine. "I rue the day my mom told you that one. It was the bane of my existence growing up."

Someone called his name, and he sagged.

"Duty calls," I said.

As he stood, he dropped a soft kiss onto my shoulder. I shivered. His eyes glowed gold when I did.

"You'll sit with me at dinner?" he asked.

I nodded.

"And you'll dance with me after?"

I narrowed my eyes. "We'll see."

Levi grinned, leaning back down so he could whisper in my ear. His lips brushed the edge of my earlobe, and I had to knit my fingers together and clench, like, everything. "You are stunning, by the way. It's like trying to look at the sun."

Even though I rolled my eyes, I felt myself go warm and melty. "You'll have to work on your lines, mister."

He winked as he backed up, then notched two fingers to his temple and gave me a salute as he walked away. "I look forward to it."

The stupid dopey grin on my face didn't disappear as I pushed my chair down the gentle slope of the grass toward the chairs. Levi's parents were waiting at the edge for me, talking to a few people.

Gentle bluegrass music started up in the background, the plucking strains of a banjo and fiddle giving a soft, romantic atmosphere. Mrs. B laid a hand on my shoulder and squeezed gently as I stopped next to her. Yeah, she saw everything, I realized when she dabbed under her eyes again.

"Twenty bucks, huh?" I muttered in her direction. "I would've paid you forty for a heads-up, you know."

She laughed under her breath, leaning down to wrap an arm around my shoulder. "Oh, sweetie, I love you so much."

"Love you too," I said after I swallowed around the emotions gripping my throat with a tight fist. "I'm going to find my seat, okay?"

The usher, one of Sylvia's cousins, showed me to the freaking front row, and I cursed under my breath when I pulled my wheelchair into the empty spot right on the inside of the aisle, where they'd moved a chair out of the way for me. The seats filled up while the music slipped seamlessly from song to song.

I tipped my head to the side to see who was playing, and I grinned when I realized Cletus was on the banjo. Joy would've had a heart attack if she saw him right now, cleaned to a spit shine and as dressed up as I'd ever seen him. A couple of others joined him. One was definitely his brother, judging by the build and the beard, and their sister, Ashley, sat on a bale of hay next to them, swaying gently to the music with a mic in her lap.

Connor seated both sets of parents, and Mrs. B slid her arm around my shoulder the moment she sat down. The groomsmen filed in behind Connor, and I caught my first glimpse of the elusive oldest Buchanan brother. He was taller than his brothers and had darker hair like their mom but with a more serious face. Where Levi grinned at me as soon as he took his place at the front, Hunter gave me a curious once-over, then scanned the people sitting in the chairs. Grady, Grace's twin, stood on the other side of Hunter, just as handsome as his sister was beautiful.

Seriously, *what* was in their DNA? It should be bottled and sold on the black market.

"Where's Hunter's wife?" I whispered to Mrs. B.

She sniffed. "Didn't come."

"Oh," I answered knowingly.

"Mm-hmm. Isn't right," she mumbled. "But it is what it is. Today will be beautiful, and that's all that matters."

"It will." I patted her hand.

And it was.

When Ashley and her brother started a sweet, lilting harmony, Cletus providing a soft background on his banjo, the audience stood, as did I. I locked my chair and held hands with Mrs. B as the bride started her journey. Sylvia was radiant on her father's arm as they walked down the flower-lined aisle. Her eyes shone with happy tears, and when I caught sight of Connor's face, I almost lost it completely. He hid nothing. His smile was wide, and when Levi slapped him on the back, he wiped at the tears that spilled over his cheeks.

Even Hunter cracked a tiny smile behind his dark beard.

The pastor's message was brief and heartfelt, talking about the selfless love that should be the foundation of marriage. The two clasped their hands and couldn't break their eyes away from each other. Mrs. B quietly cried, leaning her head into her husband's shoulder when they said their simple vows, making promises to love and cherish. Sylvia gave a watery laugh when Connor promised never to finish the last of the coffee.

Everyone cheered when he wrapped her in his arms for a passionate kiss. Levi's eyes glowed happily in his handsome face when he looked over at me, and I was sniffing into a balled-up tissue from his mom.

People began to file out both sides of the rows of chairs, and I told Mr. and Mrs. B to go ahead so I could wait for the crowd to dissipate a little bit. As people milled around, chatting happily, I saw Levi's tall frame weave toward me.

He set his hands on the armrests and leaned down to kiss my forehead. "You were crying," he accused with a sly grin.

"I was not."

With a cocked eyebrow, he looked at the tissue that I still held with a death grip. "Really?"

"Shut up." I sighed. "It was a really beautiful ceremony."

"It was." He hooked a thumb over his shoulder toward where we'd be eating dinner. "Do you want to stay in your chair for the meal?"

"As opposed to what? You gonna make me stand?"

Levi growled under his breath, "You make me insane, Sonic."

I laughed. "Normally, I'd say my chair, but ..."

"What?"

I scrunched up my nose. "I don't want to be sitting lower than everyone in the pictures."

"That would be awful," he said seriously.

The band continued to play softly in the background, but it was a tune I'd never heard before.

"I think we should dance now," he told me.

"Why now? Everyone will stare."

Levi looked over his shoulder. "Nah, they're all too busy gabbing. No one will even notice us over here."

Staring hard at everyone, I knew he was probably right. Not one single set of eyes was on us as far as I could tell. They were looking at photos of Connor and Sylvia, taking pictures, and milling around the tables full of different teas, lemonade, and appetizers to tide them over until the dinner started.

I took a deep breath and locked my chair, pulling up my dress so that I could set my feet safely on the even ground. Levi held his hand out, and I took it, standing as gracefully as I could manage.

His smile was wide, and I couldn't help but match it.

"I like your dress," he said as he slid his hand around to the bared skin of my back.

Leaning my weight into him, I curled one hand into his as he pressed it again his chest. My other arm went around his shoulders, where I could feel parts of him that I'd never felt before. The soft hair where it met the hot skin of his neck.

We swayed gently to the music, and I breathed easier when I realized this wasn't hard at all. He led with his body first, so I knew when to shift one foot to the side, then the other as we made a slow turn.

His cheek was pressed against the top of my head, and occasionally, he'd press his nose into my curls and inhale audibly.

I smiled into his shoulder. Levi's thumb brushed up my spine, tracing each bump under my skin before he moved to the next one.

"I missed you this week," he said quietly.

I closed my eyes and wrapped my arm more tightly around his shoulder. Ashley sang quietly in the background, and I pressed the words into my heart before I tried to answer.

And if I love but once in this cruel, weary world, well, I'm glad I loved once with you.

"I missed you too," I told him once I could lift my head and meet his eyes. "You don't seem surprised it took me this long."

"Because I know you," he answered as if it was the simplest thing in the whole world.

"I don't ..." I started, then exhaled slowly when the words weren't coming in the way I wanted them to. "I had to make sure this was about you and me. Not just that I was ready for more with anyone. Does that make sense?"

His eyes searched my face. "I think so."

"It was like, if I just wanted a boyfriend, but the person could be interchangeable, then I'd never want to risk your friendship in my life. I wanted to be able to look at you, look you in the eye and know that you're what I want. No substitutes."

Levi gathered me even closer, placing a feather-light kiss on the curve of my neck. I barely had to move my feet now because he was holding me so tightly that he practically had all my weight in his arms. I smiled, burying my head into the side of his neck. We were wrapped around each other, and I never wanted the moment to end. And it wasn't because I was standing or dancing on my feet; it was because of him. Because of us together. That was what felt right.

He pulled back and smiled softly at me.

"I'm going to kiss you if you keep saying stuff like that to me," he warned with a playful glint in his eye.

"What kind of punishment is that?"

Levi laughed, and his mouth fitted seamlessly over mine. I sighed into his mouth when his tongue swept over the seam of my lips. My arm was clutched so tightly around his neck, his arm the same way around my waist that my feet came off the ground completely. My heart was somewhere off in the clouds. Maybe we were too, as he kissed me deeply.

A whistle pierced the air, and I pulled back. Then I heard another and the sound of Connor whooping happily.

"Atta boy, Levi," he yelled through cupped hands.

"Oh my gosh," I groaned, burying my face into Levi's chest.

His whole frame shook with laughter. "I guess people were watching after all."

I pinched his side. "Ya think?"

He dropped a hard, fast kiss onto my lips and then scooped me up in his arms.

"What are you doing?" I hissed.

"We're going to dinner," he said calmly, walking us through the crowd of people. Some people smiled, some clapped, and some whistled. "Come on, Sonic. If they're watching, let's give them something good."

I wrapped my arms around his neck. My face was probably the same bright pink as the bridesmaid's dresses.

"It is too late to back out of this whole thing?" I asked grumpily.

"Yup," he replied.

"That's what I was afraid of."

But even as I said it, I smiled into his shoulder. Because the funny thing was, I didn't feel so afraid anymore.

CHAPTER 21

LEVI

I'd underestimated one aspect of the friendship line between Joss and me being obliterated. I had to figure out how the hell to keep my hands off her at any given moment.

She swatted at me approximately eighteen times at the wedding reception, especially when my memaw came over to talk to us. Not the appropriate time, in her mind, to see what her skin felt like just underneath the fabric of her dress where it cupped her waist.

But even though she smacked my hands a few times, she was the one who dug her hands in my hair and tried to swallow my tongue in the cab of my truck when I took her home that night. If you ever wondered how easy it was to maneuver a hot make-out session on a bench seat, paraplegic or not, I could tell you that it was pretty easy.

Still, as I sat across from her at the steakhouse (our attempt at recreating the first date that never happened) and imagined how our days would play out now, I had to remind myself that Joss was not only a virgin, but she was inexperienced in just about every way possible when it came to men.

She made a face at me when the server asked her if she'd like some wine. "No, thanks. Just a sweet tea for me, thanks."

"Of course," he said, looking at me.

"Same," I said with a smile. One of my rules, from the day I met her, was that if I'd had a single drink, I'd never get behind the wheel of a car that would be carrying Joss anywhere. Even if a drunk driver hadn't caused her paralysis, I'd heard enough stories. There wasn't a drink in the world worth having if I was driving.

"I'm so hungry, I could eat an entire side of beef right now," she said as soon as he left the table.

I grinned at her. "That so?"

"At the very least."

Instead of looking at the menu, I looked at her while her eyes tracked up and down each column of neatly typed letters.

Ripe summer blueberries blue.

Except for this time, I said it out loud without meaning to. She glanced up, forehead wrinkled in confusion. "What about blueberries?" She looked down again. "Where are blueberries?"

I swiped a hand over my mouth and felt the flush cover my cheeks. "Ahh, nothing."

"What?" She narrowed her eyes. "You look weird. Tell me."

"It's nothing."

"Levi."

Sinking back in my chair, I sighed heavily. "Fine. It's just ... a weird thing I've done, and as soon as I say it out loud, you'll think I'm creepy."

Her grin made my heart turn over slowly. It was the kind of heart turn that was born from anticipation. Because now I could watch that grin unfold and see how it changed the shape of her lips.

"Tell me," she insisted. Joss set her chin in her hand and stared expectantly across the dimly lit table. She'd tried to tame her hair for our date, but it still sprung out of whatever knot she'd attempted to pin it back into.

I shook my head because it was too easy to sit there and pick apart all the separate things that I noticed, the things that I loved and wanted and had spent years trying not to stare at.

"Your eyes," I said. She blinked, straightening in her seat. I scratched the side of my face. "The first time we talked, I was trying to think of what kind of blue they were, and it just ... became this thing in my head. Trying to come up with something I could compare it to."

Her face went soft. "Really?"

"If you make fun of me right now, you're buying your own steak."

Joss leaned forward and wove her fingers through mine. "Tell me what you came up with. Just one or two more."

"No way."

Her delighted laugh made me feel a little bit less embarrassed. A little.

"Oh, come on," she teased. "I can tell Joy, and she'll think it's *so romantic.*"

But I saw the look in those blue eyes. She wasn't asking for Joy. She was asking for herself. Again, I had to remind myself that this was all new for Joss, not just because it was with me. She'd never had a boyfriend, given that she had been too young to date when she got sick.

I flipped her hand over and traced the lines on her palm and the length of each of her long, graceful fingers.

"The morning glories climbing up the sides of Mom's porch." I turned her hand over and reverently followed the path between each knuckle. "The tiles lining the pool we swam in." I rubbed the tip of my finger over the smooth bed of her nails, which she'd painted a delicate pink, and gave her a wry smile. "And there were a few bird comparisons thrown in there too."

She was quiet when I risked a glance at her face. I felt like an animal pinned to a display box.

"Creepy, right?" I said on an uncomfortable laugh.

Joss untangled her fingers from mine and slid her hand up my forearm. Gripping my shirt in her fist, she tugged me across the table with surprising strength. She lifted her chin and planted a hot, hard kiss on my lips. I was half standing, my hands braced on the neatly pressed tablecloth when she turned her head and slipped her tongue against mine in one devastating, slick slide. A few people around us were staring when I sat back down.

She looked satisfied.

I probably did too.

"So romantic," she whispered seriously.

"Are we ready to order?" our server asked when he approached the table. His cheeks were flaming, so he saw our little show.

Joss grinned at me, and I grinned back.

"We're going to need another few minutes," I told him, my eyes not leaving hers.

* * *

"So how does this work?" she asked me a couple of hours later. I held the door to my place open and went in after her.

"How does what work?" I walked around, flipping on the lamp next to the couch and the small light over the sink in the kitchen area.

She gestured to the couch. "Do I take my normal spot? Do we have new spots? Do I still get first dibs on viewing options? Because I wasn't done with Marie Kondo yet, no matter what you think of her."

I pointed a finger at her. "New rule. No cleaning shows on date night."

Joss laughed, locking her chair and shifting over to the couch. Her normal spot. My normal spot was on the other side. The throw pillow went under her side, and she punched it a few times until she got it exactly the way she wanted it.

I stood watching her, my hands propped on my hips.

She froze. "What?"

"*That's* not how it's gonna work."

Her eyebrow cocked up. "No?"

Slowly, I shook my head. The shift in my thoughts must have been written on my face, seeing her on my couch and knowing that I could touch her, that she could touch me. Joss' smile curved up, and she slowly turned onto her back, her legs with the knees bent slightly and resting against the back of the couch.

I flopped onto the couch in my normal spot, and she gave me a strange look.

"See?" I told her. "Too far away. It won't work."

"You're right," she answered seriously. "It won't."

I turned, sitting up on my knees as I faced her. My hands curled up the backs of her calves, and even though I couldn't feel her skin under the black leggings she wore, I could feel the heat of her. I shifted her to the side, just a few inches, and she adjusted her head on the pillow as I crept over her so I could wedge between the couch and her body.

"Am I supposed to face the TV?" she asked, clearly not worried about the TV in the slightest since she was now nose to nose with me.

"Nope."

"Okay," she whispered, her hands wandering along the front of my chest and shoulders.

My hands slid up the strong line of her back, and she arched into my touch. Lifting her head slightly to gauge the position of our legs, she used her hand to lift her top leg so I could fit my knee between.

"Don't tell me this doesn't spark some serious joy," I whispered, brushing my lips with hers.

She laughed. Unable not to, I pressed my hips into hers, and the sharp inhale from her mouth killed the laughter in an instant.

I was so hard it hurt, and she felt it. Her eyes widened, her mouth falling open into a small, surprised O. I tilted my chin down and licked slowly along the line of her bottom lip.

Her mouth followed mine, but I didn't deepen the kiss.

"Do you have any idea how sexy you are to me?" I told her.

The way she exhaled shakily against my lips had me closing my eyes. Slow, I reminded myself, *take it slow, Levi.*

That was when she attacked me.

Joss wrapped her arms around my neck and slanted her mouth over mine. I groaned at her unleashed enthusiasm because what she lacked in practice, holy shit, she made up for in fervor. Her fingers tangled in my hair, and she pulled at the strands. I licked into her mouth, and she pressed her chest against me. One of my hands slid down her back, my hand cupping her bottom, and she whimpered softly.

Her fingers started plucking at the buttons on my shirt, and I reached up to help her.

Together, we managed to rip open about five or six, and when she slid her hand over my chest, I pulled my chin back and hissed in a breath through clenched teeth.

"Your skin is so hot," she whispered, biting at my chin. I could barely manage a chuckle because *she'd* tipped over the gasoline can, struck the match, and dropped it with a simple flick of her wrist.

I leaned up, turning us slightly so I was over her. Joss dropped her head and pushed her nose into my neck, inhaling deeply.

"And you smell so good," she moaned. "Why do you smell so good?"

"Uhh," I stammered, my mind flustered from the feel of her, the smell of her, the way she arched her chest up into me. "I-I don't know."

I rolled my hips, and our lips fused again with tongue and teeth, and my hands tightened on her hips. Her fingers dug into my chest, pricking the surface of my skin with the fingernails painted soft pink. The same thought rolled over and over in my head.

This is what I've waited for.

This.

This.

This.

Her mouth was sweet and soft, and she tasted like the mint she stole from the glove compartment of my truck. The bright burst of fresh on her tongue had my head spinning when I sucked it into my mouth. The sound that left her when I did that caused me to pull away, and I had to lock it into my brain so that I'd never forget it. The sound was surprise and delight and want.

All the things I was feeling too.

My hands itched to test the soft, warm weight of her breasts and see what the skin on her stomach felt like under my lips. My mouth watered thinking about the slope of her shoulder and the curve of her ribs down to her waist.

The ticks on the clock disappeared, and the only sound was lips and breaths and whispered names as we discovered each other even though we didn't push past boundaries. It was a luxury to kiss her over and over and over. To learn what she liked and have her learn what I liked too.

Joss liked it when I sucked on her tongue.

I had to stop myself from mauling her when she tugged on my earlobe with her delicate teeth.

"We should slow down," I heard myself say. Oh my *gosh*, I was an idiot.

"Nooooo," she moaned immediately, snapping her hands onto my ass to lock me into place. I laughed into her shoulder before licking the softness of her skin. "No, no, it's so good, Levi. We're okay. We won't go too far, I promise."

"How can you promise that?" I asked breathlessly because I sure as shit struggled to believe it when she raked her fingernails up my back under my wrinkled, twisted shirt.

She blinked, running a hand over her flushed face as she thought. "I … umm, we'll keep pants on." Her smile was brilliant. "Yes, we'll keep pants on. Nothing too important can happen when you're wearing pants. New rule."

There it was again. That slow roll of the organ pumping all the blood through my body. It took everything in me not to tell her right there that I was in head over heels in love with her. That if it were up to me, I'd never leave her. That we'd be together forever. That for me, *she* was forever.

I pressed my forehead to hers. "My sexy, sexy little hedgehog, we're in no rush, okay?"

She blew a raspberry between her lips. "Speak for yourself, Buchanan. You know how long I've been waiting for someone else to help me out down there? I can feel everything, I promise. I've got twenty-one years of waiting for some assistance, mister."

Because I knew she could handle it, I wrapped my arms around her and gave her all my weight while my frame shook with laughter.

Joss must have sensed how serious I was because she hugged me too, pressing a kiss into my cheek. She sighed dramatically. "Fine, but tomorrow, I'll make you pay for this little display of chivalry."

I lifted my head. "Yeah? How?"

Her eyes, sapphire set in an antique ring blue, twinkled dangerously.

CHAPTER 22

JOCELYN

"*R*eady?"

From behind the weight bench, Levi watched me enter through the door with narrowed eyes. His eyes tracked up and down my perfectly normal workout attire. My promised retribution must have been written all through my sly grin because he set his hands on his hips, clearly waiting for something.

"What?" I asked. "Are we working out or not? I've got some new exercises you can help me with."

That loosened his tightly held frame a bit. "Yeah? Did *PT boy* give you those ideas?"

Well hello, jealousy. I shrugged. "I didn't see him this week."

"Good."

I snorted. "Levi, you had your hands on my ass last night; how jealous can you possibly be?"

With three long strides that had my tummy flipping, he was right in front of me, leaning down to plant a hard kiss on my upturned lips. "I'm not jealous," he said against my mouth.

"Okay." I nipped at his lower lip, which made him growl.

Levi stood. "I await your instructions."

"Grab that exercise band. The black one."

He plucked it off the wall behind him while I locked my chair and slid onto the floor by the yellow pad.

"Do you still need to stretch?" he asked.

I blinked innocently up at him. "Everything but my legs. I figured you could help me."

His throat worked on a swallow. "'Kay."

Some might have called me crazy or said I clearly had a few screws loose, but this was the most fun I'd had in years. The ability to be with him like this had a giddy, bubbly sort of happiness threatening to explode out of my skin.

I laid on the mat as Levi kneeled between my legs. Placing his hands on my knee and ankle, he picked up my right and pressed it back into my chest.

"Good?" he asked, eyes never leaving mine.

I smiled. "You can push ... harder."

His cheeks flushed, his lips stayed in a firm line, but his eyes sparked hot as he pressed his chest against my leg, pushing it farther toward my chest.

After a few pulses, complete with delicious, heavy eye contact, I swear, if he so much as brushed his fingers between my legs, I would've exploded. He pulled back, carefully set down my right and switched to the left, this time not waiting for me to ask for more.

Levi braced my shin in the middle of his chest, then set his hands on either side of me, pressing down.

Inhaling a sharp breath through my nose, I closed my eyes. The stretch of muscle along the back of my leg hurt, hurt so good, but it was him too. So much *him*.

Rocking himself forward, he pulsed the other leg too until we both knew I was adequately stretched.

Sweat popped along the back of my neck even though I'd barely moved, just from the things racing through my head at our position.

Sliding into relationship mode with Levi was like breathing, much to my delight. Which was good because I wanted to slide us even further past whatever arbitrary line he'd erected. I wanted to have sex. But not just any sex. I wanted to have sex with my best friend turned first boyfriend, who looked at me like he wanted to rip my clothes off with his teeth.

I wanted sweat-slicked skin and tight muscles and his hardness in my hands. I wanted arching bodies and hands against my skin. And I wanted him so badly that I'd been jittery all night, all morning. Fine, fine, he was trying to be respectful, blah, blah, blah, but being friends for five years gave us a bit of a leg up in the dating world if you asked me.

And respect was excellent. It was. I wanted to respect the *hell* out of his strong, muscled body. The one he'd honed out of hard work and determination. I wanted to respect that body so badly.

Hence my well-crafted plan for today. I'd spent a little time on YouTube last night, looking up leg exercises that would:

1- Benefit me physically.

2- Drive him out of his fucking mind.

The sports bra that I'd dug out of the back of my dresser drawer was my ringer for goal number two. Today, she'd be my shining star because showing skin when trying to seduce your best friend turned first boyfriend was always helpful. Two years ago, I'd bought it on impulse and had only worn it under baggy T-shirts.

"Legs feel better?" he asked, standing up from the mat as I pulled myself to a sitting position.

"Mm-hmm." My fingers played with the hem of my T-shirt, and I had to take a few deep breaths to bust through a sudden flurry of nerves. Playing the seductress had never once been at the top of my to-do list.

"You'll need the band around your waist," I told him. "Then loop around mine too."

Levi nodded, and I saw him switch into trainer mode. "Glutes?"

"Yeah. You'll be stationary, and I'll do my reps going forward."

"So"—he paused, staring hard at the yellow mat—"you'll be ..."

"On my hands and knees in front of you." Oh, look at me, I said it with a straight face.

His hazel eyes narrowed again, but he didn't say anything.

Just do the damn thing, I yelled in my head. So I channeled my inner stripper and pulled my T-shirt off as gracefully as I could manage. As it cleared my head, I arched my back just a touch, and I heard a supremely gratifying inhale come from Levi.

Not making eye contact, I tossed the shirt over by my chair and then propped my hands behind me.

"Ready?" I asked him.

If I thought his eyes sparked hot before, I was terribly mistaken.

By the way he stared at the contraption of thin straps crisscrossing my chest and the glorious amount of cleavage shown in the deep V, it was no spark.

He'd just set me on fire with one look.

"You are an evil, evil woman," he said in a low voice.

Attempting a super casual shrug of my shoulders, I sighed. "It's hot in here."

"Is it now?"

He'd barely moved his eyes away from my bra, and honestly, I couldn't blame him. It made my tits look absolutely fantastic. I'd never thought of them as *tits* in my entire life, but when I'd stared at myself in the mirror before coming here, it felt like the perfect time to add it into my vocabulary.

"Ready?" he asked when I didn't say anything.

I had to fight to keep a pout off my face because I was expecting him to descend on me like a ravenous animal by this point, but apparently, I'd underestimated his willpower.

Which shouldn't have surprised me, in retrospect. He'd hid his feelings for five years. Clearly, he had a lock on his ... urges. What an asshole. I wanted those urges unleashed. Unleashed on my entire freaking body.

"So we're still pretending we're going to do the exercises?"

"Who's pretending?" he said, staring straight-faced and unblinking. Like I could see clear through him, I knew the wheels and cogs were turning in that brain of his. Trying to process how serious I was.

"Come here," I pleaded.

He didn't.

It was my turn to narrow my eyes.

"Did I mention I'm not wearing underwear?"

Levi swiped a hand over his mouth, letting out a small, strained laugh. "You are determined to kill me, aren't you?"

I answered him as seriously as I could. "If by kill you, you mean have sex with you, then yes."

Tipping his chin up to the ceiling, he took a few chest-expanding deep breaths. "Joss." He laughed quietly.

"Levi. Great, we know each other's names."

With a growl, he dropped to his knees and prowled over me, moving one leg to the side until I had no choice but to lay back on the mat. Halle-freaking-lujah. I slid my hands up his back and felt the tension he held in all those muscles.

Even though he was over me, he didn't kiss me. Levi propped his elbows on either side of my head, caging me in so I couldn't really go anywhere, which was fine by me. I lifted my chin to find his mouth, but he evaded me.

"I had plans, you know," he said, looking deep into my eyes. His thumb tangled lightly with the hair next to his hand.

"Yeah?"

I shifted my hips, bringing us closer, and his eyes closed. Levi, my best friend turned first boyfriend, was hard. And big. There was one moment when I had the same thought that probably every virgin had.

Holy shit, how's this gonna work?

"Joss." He sounded like he was in a great deal of pain, and based on what I felt tight against my core, he probably was. "I am not making love to you for the first time on this ugly yellow mat."

I smiled a little, using my fingertip to trace the edge of his lips. I really, really liked his lips. "Okay."

He dropped his forehead to mine, then kissed the tip of my nose. Next to my eye. The corner of my jaw. With each tiny kiss, I got all melty. My whole body went warm and soft.

"I had plans," he repeated. "They were romantic and sweet. I want it to be perfect for you."

"Were rose petals involved?"

He laughed, finally kissing me on the mouth. We stayed there for a couple of seconds, and my arms went tight around his neck while I enjoyed the feel of his lips against mine.

I pulled back and cupped the side of his face. "Do you know what I need for my first time? The best thing that could possibly be in any plan that your brain could come up with?" I traced my finger over his forehead, where a few worry lines had popped up. "Just you. That's it. Just you and me, Levi. It could be anywhere, and as long it's you and me, it'll be exactly what I need."

His eyes searched mine, weighing the sincerity of my words. The moment he saw what he needed to see, a switch flipped in his brain.

"Hold tight," he told me quietly.

One of his big hands cupped my bottom as I tightened my grip on his neck. With an ease born of incredible strength, Levi held me to him and stood. I squealed when it made my head spin, and he laughed into my neck.

"Good?" he asked as he boosted me higher on his chest. My legs dangled on either side of his slim hips while his arms braced underneath my thighs and ass.

"Good." I kissed him. I kissed him deeply because even though we weren't moving now, my head was still spinning just a little bit. Our tongues tangled, his head turned, and I felt his fingers dig into my skin where he held me so tightly.

Levi broke the kiss and walked us out of the gym. He paused just as he cleared the door into the garage. "Do you want your chair? I guess I got presumptuous."

I grinned. "Presume away. I'm perfectly fine with a little manhandling today."

"Good to know," he murmured against my lips.

As he walked us to his apartment, my body tucked into him, I knew that Levi would never view anything that was about to happen as manhandling, though, and neither would I.

I pressed my face into his neck and breathed him in. This was the person who made me feel the safest, the strongest, who made me feel the best just exactly as I was.

He kicked the door shut behind us, the harsh clap of sound tightening the skin around my bones. It wasn't bright in his place, only brief pockets of the sun coming through the edges of the curtains. As he tipped me back onto his bed, I liked what those slices of light did to his body.

"Take off your shirt," I told him. "I want to see."

Levi lifted his chin in the direction of my sports bra. "Just remember, now that I know this kind of payback is on the table, you're not the only one who can use it."

"I do not think this is your style," I answered seriously. "The straps would do nothing for you."

Even though he grinned, I felt the joke dry up like sawdust in my throat when I yanked his shirt off, exposing row upon row of twisted, roped lines of tight muscle under his skin.

I ran my hand over his stomach, and his chest heaved. My fingers tucked into the edge of his gym shorts and boxer briefs, and against my pinky, the thick line of his hardness jumped.

Before he pulled those off, he offered me his hand, and I sat up.

"Lift your arms," he said. I complied, falling just a little bit further because he actually had to stop to think about how I'd get this strappy bullshit sports bra off on my own. We laughed together when he had to tug it roughly over my head, but his laughter died as soon as I dropped my arms. Even though I wanted to and felt the undeniable urge to, I didn't cover my breasts with my arm.

I laid back, and he followed, licking up the line of my stomach, then stopping to press a kiss on the center of my chest. He breathed there for a second. He cupped the weight of one breast in his hand, and I squirmed, wanting more of ... something.

When his thumb circled around the edge of my nipple, followed by his mouth closing over me, I got it.

Sighing his name, I clutched him to me. His mouth increased its suction, and I gasped. Hot, bright white, I felt it down my back, which arched up off the mattress. He moved to the other side, but I gripped his face with both hands and dragged his mouth up to mine for a searching, seeking kiss.

Levi pressed against me, rolling his hips with a groan.

As we traded wet kisses, my hand slid down his chest and under his shorts so I could feel him, feel how heavy and hard he was with my fingers curled around him. He hissed out a breath through clenched teeth when I moved my hand experimentally.

"Is this," I whispered, "is this okay?"

His laugh was strained. "Yeah, yeah."

I rolled my thumb, and he made a sound like he was dying. Watching his face tighten with pleasure when I did was my new favorite thing in the entire freaking world. *I* did that to him with one tiny swipe of one tiny finger.

"You can," he started, then wrapped his strong fingers around mine, moving my hand faster, tightening my grip harder than I would have dared. "Yes, just like that. Shit, Joss, that feels so good."

He dropped his mouth to my chest again, this time working his tongue and teeth against my skin, and my rhythm faltered.

When his forehead pressed to my shoulder, and his breathing picked up, he stilled my hand with his. "Wait, stop, I don't want ... I want to be right there with you, okay?"

My nod was shaky and fast. "Right, okay. Let's do that then please."

His smile was brilliant, and the look in his eyes softened when he gazed at me. There was affection there and undeniable, bright, unwavering love.

"Oh, my beautiful girl, there's no rush right now. Trust me."

"Speak for yourself," I mumbled when he sat up and tucked his hands into the waistband of my leggings, dragging them slowly down my hips. His entire body froze when they cleared just a few inches, and there was nothing underneath but skin.

I grinned up at him.

"You were serious," he said.

Biting my lower lip, I nodded.

Levi sucked in a breath, then pulled them carefully off one leg, then the other. Tears pricked my eyes at how perfect he was being, how he knew exactly what to do and didn't hesitate, or question, or make me feel uncomfortable. Not only because of my legs but because of the two people here, one of us was new at this whole sex thing.

But the newness for both of us was in the uncovering of our bodies, the unveiling of skin so that we could touch and taste it. I pushed his shorts down and tracked the V bracketing his hips with my fingers as I stared unabashedly at him. He leaned down and kissed the tops of each of my thighs and spread his hand over the middle of my stomach, only turning his fingers toward my core when he kissed me deeply again, claiming my mouth, claiming everything.

He worked his hand between my legs, and my body started trembling after only a few touches from his finger. I clapped a hand over my mouth as I felt a terrifying, mounting pressure climb. He pulled my hand down and whispered against mouth. "Don't hide those sounds. Give them to me, give all of them to me."

His fingers pressed down again, and I cried out as my body separated in a blinding, overwhelming pulse of light that split my skin wide open.

It was bigger, bigger, so much bigger than anything I'd felt alone.

"Holy shit," I breathed as I sagged back onto the bed. He kissed me, moving between my legs and leaning up so he could grab a foil wrapper from his nightstand. I couldn't stop kissing his shoulders, his chest, his chin, his lips. He laughed under his breath while he tried to focus on his task.

"Joss," he groaned when he was finally done. He clutched my hands and pressed them down on the bed. My frantic movements still had him smiling when I couldn't stop myself from trying to catch his mouth again. "It might hurt, just a little."

"I trust you," I whispered against his mouth.

He lined himself up against me, and I whimpered at just that one meeting point of him and me, a fraction of what waited.

His eyes snagged mine as I breathed through the delicious aftershocks. I pulled in a breath and slid my hands away from his and down his back. Levi pushed his hips forward, inch by inch, his forehead pinched tight with concentration, and I held my breath through the sharp pop of pain. He felt it, and I saw his shoulders start to shake as he held himself still.

"I'm fine," I breathed. "Please, Levi, it's good. It's so good."

We kissed softly as he pushed the rest of the way forward. When he was fully inside me, I wrapped my arms around his neck and wound my fingers through his hair.

"You feel," he whispered, pulling back and pushing forward again, "you feel incredible, Joss. You're so perfect."

His hips picked up speed, then the pace would lessen, and beads of sweat coated my forehead at the slow, slow build of pressure in my core. We stayed wrapped tight like that, his arms clutching me tight as his back curved up over me with each movement. I never wanted to leave. Never wanted it to end.

His muscles bunched under my hands as I moved them greedily over his damp skin.

As he moved faster, my body tensed tight at the surprising build of another explosion that simmered dangerously under the surface, waiting, waiting, waiting for something to release it.

With three words, he pulled the pin.

"I love you," he breathed against my mouth.

Boom.

It was sharp and hot and excruciating and perfect.

I cried out again, and he thrust forward with a loud groan, sinking slowly against me as he tried to catch his breath.

Tightly, so tightly, I held him to me, two tears rolling down my temples into my hair.

He loved me. I was loved by him.

Maybe it hadn't been according to his plan, but it was perfect.

CHAPTER 23

LEVI

"*D*id you want more corn?" I asked Joss.

That was what came out of my mouth, at least. Across the table on my parents' deck, my eyes were saying something completely different. I might have been holding out the plate of bright yellow corn on the cob, but she smirked because she could read between the lines just fine.

"Not at the moment, thank you," she answered politely. Her eyes bugged out in warning.

I sighed quietly, and my mom cleared her throat.

My dad winked at me, giving me a nod because I guess I wasn't very good at being subtle. But after four days of being able to do whatever I wanted with Joss—and we'd done that whatever every single day—I was feeling a touch out of control.

Any moment of privacy was urgent, almost frantic, especially after our first time. Joss unleashed was my new favorite kind of Joss. A close second was the way she laid her head on my chest and stroked her fingers idly over my chest and stomach when we lay in bed, talking about our days in the same way we used to.

"Joss, I'm going to need to pick your brain," my mom said.

"What about?"

"Well, I signed up to bring a dessert to the Fourth of July party at the community center, and I feel like I bring the same tired thing every year."

"Lemon ice cream cake," Joss and I said in unison, then grinned at each other when my mom rolled her eyes.

"See? I need something new."

"What's wrong with it?" Joss asked. "Everyone loves it. Remember last year, you caught Jackson James trying to take four pieces."

"I like your cake, honey," my dad said, patting his stomach.

My mom eyed it. "I know you do. I'm going to stop making so many sweets at home if you keep needing me to let out your pants."

He mumbled something into a glass of water. I couldn't hear him, but Joss covered her mouth and laughed. My dad winked at her.

Contentment spread warm and sweet in my veins. Everything was the same, but it wasn't. It was better.

As I stared at Joss across the table, the light growing dusky and blue around us as we talked and laughed through the meal, I knew I'd marry her tomorrow if she'd say yes. Only a handful of days earlier, I told my mom that I'd been stuck.

But that was the wrong word, I could see now.

Waiting and stuck weren't the same thing. Stuck implied no choice. No action. No forethought or planning.

But waiting, that fit better in my head. I'd been waiting for Joss as sure as the Earth spun around the sun. And waiting was just fine when you held firm to the belief that it was the right course of action.

She was right for me. I was right for her.

And I think she felt it too, when I caught her sending a small smile my way.

During our first time, I told her I loved her because I did. And I wanted her to know it when we shared something so big and precious together. She hadn't said it back, but strangely, I was okay with that. Joss loved me, of that I had no doubt. She'd loved me for years.

But to make the switch to *in love*, I'd give her time because time was what I had in my years of waiting.

My mom stood from the table, patting Nero's head when he

popped up from his spot next to Joss' chair on the deck. "You little beggar." Grabbing a half-finished roll from her plate, she slipped it to him. "Y'all done with your plates?"

"Let me help," Joss said, taking her empty plate and setting it in her lap. I handed her mine, and she stacked it on top of hers, then grabbed my mom and dad's.

"Thanks, sweetie. I'll get the glasses." My mom eyed me. "And then my youngest son and the light of my life will grab the rest."

I saluted. "Come on, old man, you going to be the only one not helping?"

"Oh, I best stay out here and make sure Nero doesn't feel lonely."

My mom rolled her eyes, Joss laughed, and I shook my head while I gathered the silverware and balled-up napkins.

The dog to which he referred trotted into the house behind Joss' chair. I gave Dad a look, but he'd already leaned his head back and closed his eyes. His hands rested over his stomach as he sighed contentedly.

Once the kitchen was cleaned up, my mom went back out onto the deck to wake my snoring dad.

Bracing my hands on the back of Joss' chair, I tipped her backward so I could smack a kiss on her lips. "You coming to my place for a while?"

"He says as if it's not forty feet from here," she teased.

I tugged one of her curls, and she yelped. "Yes, but that forty feet is very important for noise purposes. Plus, it has a lock."

Her eyes, dusk on a summer night blue, sparkled up at me. "That it does."

"Is that a yes?"

She pushed her hands on the wheels, so I had no choice to let her up, and she spun to face me. "I can't. I've got an early shift at the bakery."

"How early?" I murmured, leaning down to taste her lips slowly. My hands cupped her neck when she tilted her chin up to deepen the kiss.

"Very early. I told Jennifer I'd do breads, so they need to be fresh and ready to go when we open. My alarm is set for four."

"That's horrifying."

She laughed. "I'm preemptively tired, trust me."

"So," I said slowly, "no ..." I waggled my eyebrows.

"S-E-X?" she spelled. "That's correct. Plus, if you can't say it, you shouldn't be doing it, Buchanan."

"I'll remember that the next time you tell me to shut up and take off my pants."

Joss sighed. "Well, it's not my fault, really. You were sitting there, looking all handsome and giving me sex eyes."

I chuckled and followed her out to the garage. After I put her chair into the back of her car, I leaned into the open driver's door, and we spent a few minutes kissing, her hands digging into my hair the way she loved to. I brushed a thumb over her breast, felt the skin tighten to a point under her thin tank top.

Joss growled, pulling back with a warning look. "You're terrible. I'm going to be cursing your name when my alarm goes off if you keep this up."

"And wouldn't it be worth every second?"

"Probably," she answered glumly.

I was still grinning when she pulled back and started her car.

"See you tomorrow?" I asked after I closed her door. She lifted her chin for one more kiss through the open window, which I happily gave her.

"I'll call you when I'm done," she promised.

Watching her drive away, I felt that same slow roll of contentment. My waiting for her was over, and nights like this could easily be my future, even if living in the converted garage apartment in my parents' driveway now had a shorter shelf life. Saving up my money was smart, and I felt no shame about where I laid my head. But our future would need more than this. Jobs and homes and things like that.

Just as that thought crossed my mind, I felt the vibration from my cell phone tucked into my front pocket.

I pulled it out, mouth falling open when I recognized a Seattle area code. It was just after five there.

"This is Levi," I answered, staring hard at Joss' car as it turned out of view.

"Hey, it's Brian Castello with the Washington Wolves."

I almost laughed. As if I'd forget where he worked. "Hey, Brian, good to hear from you."

"Did I catch you at a good time?"

I'd begun pacing the driveway the second he said his name.

"Ah, yeah. All the time in the world."

"Great. I won't beat around the bush." I held my breath as he paused. "I'm calling because I'd like to offer you the assistant trainer position if you're still interested."

My heart stopped. My feet froze on the concrete. If I tried hard enough, I could still see the red glow of taillights.

"You still there?" he asked.

"Sorry, yes, I'm just … wow." I laid a hand on my forehead and tried to settle my suddenly racing brain. "I can't believe it. I figured you'd want someone with more experience," I admitted. "Which is probably really stupid to admit out loud, now that I'm saying it."

He laughed. "I like you, Levi. And you had a good rapport with the players you met. That's important in this job. To like you is to respect you, to respect you has them taking better care of their bodies."

"Right."

"Should we talk some specifics?" he asked, and I could still hear a smile in his voice.

I closed my eyes and shot up a desperate prayer. "Yeah, let's."

CHAPTER 24

LEVI

*M*y phone rang as I drove to Donner Bakery to pick up Joss from work. She didn't know I was coming, which was probably why she called me. I pulled my truck into a secluded turnoff so I could answer safely and swiped my thumb along the screen.

"Hey."

"I got out early," she said in a happy voice. "Where are you?"

"Driving to you, actually." I tipped my head back and let it rest on the seat. "Thought I'd pick you up."

"Oh. Well, where are you now?"

Lifting my head, I looked around. "Uhh, I'm at the turnoff just past Bandit Lake. The one with the big pine that fell over."

"Don't move. I'll be there in ten." And she hung up.

Great. Ten more minutes to sit and obsess about what I was going to say to her.

Oh hey, I forgot to tell you this little thing that happened, and now I'd really like you to relocate across the country with me because I love you and can't imagine not being with you, but if you said no, I just might turn down the dream job of all dream jobs in order to stay with you. How was your day?

The conversation played out a few ways, all but one scenario

215

ending with celebratory sex that I'd been offered a job as an assistant trainer with a professional sports team. Her reaction ranged from screaming fury that I hadn't told her right away, excitement about the opportunity itself, sadness about a life away from Green Valley, to her shutting me out completely and dumping my ass because of it.

I covered my face with my hands and groaned, dropping my head forward so I could rest it on the steering wheel of my truck. The salary Brian mentioned made my head spin, and the benefits were incredible. It would be hard work, and the season would be insane, but I knew, without a shadow of a doubt, I'd love every second of it. I'd love living there too. And I could see her there, surrounded by all the exciting things we'd be able to explore together.

She could finish her degree, and still be able to pursue anything she wanted to with more opportunities than Green Valley would ever be able to offer her.

I'd worked out all these things in my head for when she inevitably started listing off why it wouldn't work or why she couldn't do it.

"So this crazy thing happened," I practiced quietly. That was always how I started it. That was how I'd start it as soon as she got here.

The sound of her car pulling up next to my truck had me lifting my head. She motioned that she was going to come to me, and I nodded, unlocking the passenger door. I leaned over to open the door as she stood out of her car. Through the open door, I gaped at the bright blue summer dress she was wearing as it floated around her knees when she took her first step to my truck.

Because she was concentrating on her foot placement, reaching her hand out to grab the door, she didn't notice the dumbfounded expression on my face.

"Hi," she said breathlessly, smiling over at me as she pulled herself up using the handle on the ceiling of the truck. She positioned one leg up on the bench and faced me after yanking the door shut.

"You're wearing a dress."

"And you are quite observant," she said seriously. "Come here."

Sliding toward her on the seat bench, I greedily took her mouth as soon as she slipped her hands into my hair.

"I missed you," she said, brushing her lips against mine. She grabbed one of my hands and pushed it up on her thigh. My fingers dug into her flesh as she kissed me again, tilting her head to the side.

Her hair smelled like oranges and vanilla and cinnamon, and she tasted like sugar.

My need ignited instantly.

In the back of my head, I wondered if this would ever cool or dampen between us if left unattended. If we followed where it led, would we ever burn out?

I wrapped my hands around her ass and lifted her into my lap, her knees settling on either side of my hips.

"You read my mind." She gasped when she felt me hard underneath her.

"Yeah?" My hands ran up and down her thighs, coming around to dip beneath her underwear and the firm flesh underneath.

"Last night, when I was home and in bed, all I could think about was how I missed feeling you," she whispered against my ear. "Feeling you over me, your hands on me."

"Joss," I groaned. "It's broad daylight outside."

But even as I said it, my hands ran up her back underneath her dress, came over her bra and dipped my thumbs inside so I could feel the warm skin underneath. Her hands tugged at my belt buckle, her lips never left mine, my argument ignored. Then she leaned back and produced a condom from her purse.

"I want to have truck sex," she announced, then cocked an eyebrow. "Don't you?"

"Quite badly."

She smiled at my serious answer.

Normally, I wouldn't have questioned the mechanics of it, because Joss knew her body, knew what she was capable of, but I pulled back.

"Will this ... position work okay?"

Her grin was sly. "Perfectly." She glanced down at the bench, even as her hands wrapped around me. I hissed in a breath as she protected us both with swift movements. "Move us over like, six inches that way."

"Only six?" I muttered, which made her toss her head back and laugh.

Once I'd done what she asked, I sucked at her neck, pulling the strap of her dress down so I could trace my tongue over the edge of her delicate lace bra.

I felt Joss' weight lift up slightly, and I raised my head. Her hand was gripping the handle, the muscle on her bicep curling out. I chuckled, tracing the definition I could see there when she lowered back down, pressing her center tight against me.

"So strong," I murmured. "So beautiful."

"All those chin-ups are about to come in handy, big guy."

And they did.

It was all steady, small movements, a graceful, rolling ride that had me cursing under my breath. Joss didn't take her dress off, and I kept my jeans barely shoved past the edge of my ass. My hands gripped her waist, but she lifted herself up with one hand, sliding back down onto me so, so slowly.

"Pull up again," I told her through gritted teeth.

She did, and I saw the way the skin on her hands turned white as she gripped the handle. When I was almost free of her body, I stilled her progress with a tight hand on her hips. She held still, her chest heaving, eyes lit brightly in her flushed face.

"I love you," I told her.

I snapped my hips up, and she threw her head back with a cry.

It didn't take long after that for either of us.

Joss whimpered my name when she exploded, and I wrapped her in my arms as we came down from the peak.

"Truck sex is awesome," I breathed, burying my head in the mass of her hair.

Her frame shook with laughter. "Agreed."

"When I decided to pick you up from work, this is not what I envisioned."

Joss lifted her head and pecked my lips. "What did you envision? Just being a nice boyfriend?"

Apprehension squeezed my stomach into a block of ice. "Oh, umm, just something I wanted to talk to you about. Something, uhh, something pretty crazy happened."

She tilted her head and gave me a sweet smile. "What is it?"

For some reason, having her still on my lap like this, felt wrong. "Here, let me grab you a tissue or something."

I lifted her off my lap, and she hissed in a quick breath when I set her on the bench next to me. Her cheeks were red when I grabbed a package of Kleenex from the glove compartment. I lifted off the seat and fastened my pants.

Her eyes looked up at me expectantly when I didn't start speaking, but I didn't say anything until she'd finished, and her dress was smoothed down over her lap. I laid my hand on her thigh and took a deep breath.

"Something crazy happened ..." she prompted.

"Yeah." My hands curled so easily around her thigh, the skin warm and soft. It was easier to focus on that than her face when I said this, trying to keep what I'd practiced straight in my head. "I got a job offer."

"What?" she gasped. "Where? Levi! That's great! What's the job?"

"Well, it's a favor my brother called in. I never, ever thought they'd even want more than a first interview."

Her eyes were bright with pride and excitement, her mouth spread in a wide smile. "Of course they did. You're amazing."

"It's an assistant trainer position for a football team."

"Oh my gosh," she breathed, slapping my shoulder. "It's exactly what you wanted. For who? High school? College?"

I held my breath. "Pro, actually."

"What?" she screeched. I saw her mentally rifle through teams, her smile drop just a little. "Nashville?"

I shook my head, and her smile dropped just a little bit more. Her face lost some of its color.

"The Washington Wolves."

She blinked. Her mouth popped open. I took my hand from her thigh and wrapped my fingers around hers.

"Th-that's in Seattle," she said when she finally spoke. Her chest rose and fell rapidly. "Seattle. Holy shit."

"I know. It's insane to me too." I tightened my fingers even though she hadn't tried to pull away. "He called me last night after you left."

"Did you," she swallowed, "did you take it?"

Her eyes were wide as she looked at me, and I saw the fear in them. The shock.

"I told him I'd call him back today or tomorrow with my final decision."

"T-today or tomorrow?"

Shifting closer to her on the bench, I carefully took her face in my hands. "Come with me."

"What?" she whispered, face going sheet white.

"Come with me to Washington." I kissed her, but her lips only barely nudged mine in return. "I never, ever thought they'd offer me this job, Joss, and yes, it's a huge shock, but I only want to go there if I can go with you."

She pulled her face back, eyes searching mine. "You'd give it up? Are you crazy?"

"I'm crazy about you," I clarified. "I couldn't move across the country from you, not now, not after this."

Joss raised a shaking hand to her mouth and stared out the windshield. "What the hell is it about this truck?" she said, almost to herself.

"What do you mean?"

She laughed under her breath and shook her head. "You kiss me for the first time and then tell clueless me that you've wanted to be more than friends for the entire time you've known me."

I closed my eyes.

"We have sex, and now you've got this whole future planned across the country that clueless me had no idea about."

"Hang on, I don't have a whole future planned there." When she wouldn't meet my eyes, I felt a quick stab of panic. "I want to plan that future together. And if your heart is here, if Green Valley is the only place you can imagine yourself, then I'll beat the pavement as long as I need to in order to stay right here with you."

Her breathing got faster and faster as I spoke. "Great, so I can be the dream crusher. Always a role I've wanted for myself."

"There will be other jobs, Joss," I said, and my voice was sharp enough that she finally gave those eyes back to me. But the shuttered emotion I saw there had my chest squeezing tight. "You are the dream I've had longer than any work I might do."

"You can say that after a couple of weeks," she said quietly.

"It's not about the length of time, and you know it."

Her face turned away, but she didn't argue.

"When did you go?" she asked.

I inhaled slowly. "They flew me out a couple of days after ... after you asked for time to think."

She nodded, turning her chin back toward me. "You are asking a lot of me, no matter what I say. You know that, right?"

"I know." I took her hands again, and she let me. "I know."

"Did you like Seattle?" Her tentative voice was so unlike her. She was scared of my answer, and I could hear it, plain as day.

"Will you look at me?"

"Just answer the question, Levi." She sniffed quietly.

I lifted our hands and kissed her fingers, breathing in the scent of her skin.

"I loved it," I told her, my lips brushing against her knuckles.

"And you could see yourself living there?"

"Without you? Not happily," I answered immediately.

Her face turned to mine. There was a shine in her eyes, but she wasn't crying. "That's not what I asked."

"I feel like I'm being baited here, Sonic."

"Really? Because I'm the one who's always tossed into these conversations right before everything changes. You feel like you're being baited, Levi, when you've known about this for weeks and didn't tell me." Her voice rose, and her eyes flashed. She pulled her fingers from mine.

I had two worst-case scenarios, and this was one of them. I bit down on every defense I could've conjured and let her unload. It was better than her leaving, shutting down.

"You had how many interviews? Two? Three?" she guessed. "I'm your best friend, and you didn't tell me shit. And all of a sudden, I get one or two days to either decide to uproot my life or tell you to give up an amazing opportunity. How the hell do you expect me to react to that? We've been dating for like, five minutes, Levi."

"Don't," I interjected. "Don't diminish it because you're pissed at me. One I'm fine with, and the other I'll call bullshit every time."

"Great," she said back, straightening her legs and unlocking the door. "I have school. I have a job."

"You can get another bakery job," I told her.

"Don't diminish it because you're pissed at me," she repeated my words dangerously. Her hand yanked on the door handle.

"You're actually leaving?"

Her eyes flashed hot as she paused in the open door. "Yeah, because sometimes other people get to decide when big things get talked about, Levi."

"That's not what I'm doing."

"Bullshit." She grabbed the handle and slid off the seat.

"Give me a break, Joss. How are we ever supposed to discuss things if you bolt every single time it makes you uncomfortable? This is what a relationship is, working on things together."

"Working on things?" she scoffed. "That's not what this is. This isn't our first fight over something like Christmases with families or who made dinner last or why you forgot my birthday. This is me, once again, being the person in the really shitty position. I either give Levi the thing that will make him happiest, or I break his heart."

I dropped my head to my chest and struggled to breathe evenly.

"You can't even deny it."

"I'm not trying to," I told her. "But you're not being fair either. I got the call last night, and this is the first I'm seeing you, so here we are, ready to discuss it, like normal, rational adults in a relationship."

She narrowed her eyes, framed in the open doorway, gripping the seat as she leaned toward me. "Except I'm deciding that I'm not ready to discuss it right now. You can't spring this shit on me and expect that I'll be ready to make a massive life decision in the course of five frickin' minutes."

Joss turned her back to me.

I got out of the truck, slammed my door, and marched around, good and pissed now. "Great, so now I can wait a week or two until you've deemed the topic safe? 'Sorry about that, Brian, I couldn't answer you about the job because my girlfriend shut down on me.'"

She glared, still holding the truck door where she stood. "You're such an asshole when you don't get your way." She paused and tapped her chin. "Oh wait, you always get your way. Everything gets dropped in your stupid, golden boy lap."

I laughed under my breath. "Lashing out unnecessarily. Mature choice, Joss."

"I'm twenty-one fucking years old," she yelled, head tilted back as her words echoed off the trees. "I *get* to be immature sometimes. Now get out of my way."

"We are not done talking about this," I said, even as I did what she asked. She took two even steps to her car, yanking open the door after her other arm was braced on the roof, all without so much as looking at me again.

"Right now?" she said, lifting her chin stubbornly. "Yeah, we are."

CHAPTER 25

JOCELYN

There was a crack in the concrete in front of the bakery. I never noticed it until I pushed over it the next morning. For a second, I stopped and stared down at that crack. An imperfection that escaped my notice. Not because it would hurt me, or make it hard for me to get where I needed to go, but it was there all the same.

Someone might trip over it. Stub their toe. Stumble a little on their way in to buy a banana cake for their grandma's birthday party.

I found myself noticing those types of imperfections everywhere for the next twenty-four hours. All over town.

Daisy's Nut House needed to replace one of the lights on their sign. It flickered a little bit.

A member of the Iron Wraiths rode his bike down the middle of the road, whistling and hooting at me. I flipped him my middle finger when he passed in the thundering rumble.

I guess I had blinders on, too, in my own way.

Go about my day. Do what I needed to do.

Not focus on the bad because it was too easy to feel like your head was submerged under murky water. I'd learned that lesson too many years ago. Allowing the bad, the inadequacies, the defects to take center stage was an invitation to a life of misery.

But over those short hours, I made sure to look for the good stuff too.

A neighbor who I never talked to fixing the way our mailbox leaned to the side. He waved as I pulled my car down the long driveway. I lifted my hand in return.

Joy scooping change out of her apron when one of the little kids who came in after school didn't have quite enough for a treat and slipping it into the cash register when she thought no one was looking.

Cletus fixing the big mixer before Jennifer came in without her asking.

Good people doing good things for the people who lived and worked with them.

Every little thing I saw, good or bad, felt like an item added to a list. Two columns written in indelible black ink.

If your heart is here, Levi had said, *if Green Valley is the only place you can imagine yourself, then I'll beat the pavement as long as I need to in order to stay right here with you.*

It was the scariest possible thing he could have ever said to me. Because as I drove home, bubbling and full to the brim with righteous indignation, I'd desperately tried to ignore the realization that I'd never thought about it.

How dare he, I'd thought.

I'm always catching up.

Can't I ever just feel things in my own time?

That's not fair, came right on the heels of that one. If I didn't own up to the fact that Levi never pushed me to cross a line until I'd indicated that the line might be flexible and flimsy, then I probably wasn't deserving of the love that he'd held on to for so long.

When I approached hour twenty-five, my phone silent and my heart heavy, I pulled into the driveway and saw my mom's car. When I had something to discuss, something to work through and untangle, she was never the person I went to. She never had been, even before I got sick.

I let myself in quietly, in case she was still asleep, but when Nero came running to me from the kitchen, I knew she was up.

"Hey, bub," I whispered as he attacked me with pink tongue and waggling butt. The effusive greeting made me laugh, and I instructed him to drop his paws from my lap, which he did immediately.

"In here," my mom called. "I'm just making some eggs if you're hungry."

"I'm okay, thanks."

She was in blue scrubs with her dark hair twisted into a low knot. She told me once that I looked like my father, and it wasn't hard to imagine because there was nothing familiar in her face, nothing I could match to mine. Her face was tired, her movements slow.

"Long night?"

Over her shoulder, she nodded, then looked back at the eggs she was scrambling on the stovetop. "Lots of babies last night. If it wasn't a full moon, I'd wonder what was going on."

"You're up early."

It was midday, a time she would normally be sound asleep.

"I took some overtime. Figured the extra money wouldn't hurt."

I was quiet, watching her move the spatula around the pan. Nero nudged my hand, and I scratched his head.

"What's wrong?" she asked without looking at me. "Was it work?"

I shook my head. "No, work was fine. I like it there."

Mom didn't say anything for a second, sliding her eggs from the pan onto a waiting plate. "Is it Levi?"

My head snapped up. "How did you know?"

"Oh honey, you've been floating around here on a cloud. Plus, that boy has looked at you like you hung the moon for years; you're the only one who didn't see it."

Great. Another thing that I could add to the list.

What Was Joss Wearing Blinders To: #47

"He got a job offer."

"That's great. Something he wants?"

I smiled sadly. "With his degree? It's like hitting the jackpot."

Her eyes searched my face briefly, then focused on her food. Between her fingers, she twirled the fork before digging it into the eggs. "So why the face?" she asked after she swallowed her first bite.

"It's in Seattle."

"Ohhh."

"Yeah."

"When does he leave?" she asked carefully.

I dragged my finger along the top of Nero's muzzle when he laid his head on my leg. "He needs to give them an answer today or tomorrow."

My mom nodded.

"He asked me to come with him," I said once I screwed up enough courage to get the words out. I couldn't look at her face, almost afraid of what I'd see there. "But ... that's crazy. I can't just, you know, move with him."

The sound of her fork sliding across the plate was the only thing punctuating the silence. I had to grit my teeth from yelling something insane like, can't you just be a mom and tell me what the hell I'm supposed to do! For once!

Raising a self-sufficient child, wheelchair or not, was great and all, but sometimes you just wanted your parent to tell you which direction would benefit you most.

"Can't you?" she asked quietly.

When I lifted my eyes, she was watching me.

"Don't get me wrong," she continued, holding up her hands at whatever she saw in my face. "I'd miss you, Jocelyn, I would. I know I'm not the best mom. I raised you the way my momma raised me. To do things myself, pick myself up by the bootstraps, and not rely on anyone to fix what was wrong." She blinked rapidly. "Maybe that wasn't right, but I can't undo it now."

"I don't think you did anything wrong," I told her. "It's not like you abandoned me or anything. I know I'm fine to take care of myself, and that's important, especially for me. Plus, I wasn't alone. I had ... Levi."

She smiled. "I'd wager you still do."

"He said he'd give up the job and stay here if that's what I wanted, if this is where my heart is."

Mom whistled. "Goodness."

"Yeah."

She stood slowly, then picked up her chair and set it down in front of me. "I'm going to say something to you that your grandma said to me when I was around eighteen."

My chest rose and fell rapidly because she didn't talk about Grandma much. Nero whined, pushing his nose into me when he felt the pitch and roll of my emotions.

"When you left Green Valley?" I whispered.

She nodded. "I can tell you right now that your heart isn't in this town, Joss."

I sucked in a breath. "And that means I have to pick up my life and move across the country?"

"Course not," she said easily. "I think you like it here, just as I did. I think if you stayed, you'd be just fine, just as I would've been. But if your heart was here, you'd know the names of everyone you passed on the street. You'd feel like your insides were splintering apart at the thought of leaving every imperfect, wonderful little part of this town." My mom looked down and sighed heavily, shaking her head as she did. "That's what your grandma said to me. Because she did know every name and every story of every person in this town. And I didn't because I wanted something else in my life."

My nose burned as I watched her impart more advice than she'd given me in over five years. The thought of leaving Green Valley caused no splinters. No splitting. No heartache. I viewed it with a strange sort of detachment, like the idea was simply too big to contemplate, but not because I couldn't imagine myself elsewhere.

It was the differences.

Little to big. Mountains and backroads and country to city and ocean and boats and wealth. But when I set those things aside, the thought of leaving Green Valley caused me no pain.

My mom took my hand and gripped it tight in hers. Her eyes were straight on mine when she asked, "What makes your heart break when you try to imagine life without it? Is it this town? Or something else?"

She knew the answer. So did I.

I dashed a hand at my cheek to stem an errant tear and looked away.

Imagining a life without Levi made my heart crack.

That was the splinter, the knife down the middle, the inconceivable thing that made my brain reject the very notion.

I sucked in a watery breath. "Oh my gosh, I'm in love with that stubborn ass, aren't I?"

My mom smiled and set my hand down. "I reckon so."

"So now what?" I sighed.

"Honey"—she laughed—"now *you* get to figure out what comes next. Maybe this job offer is hitting the jackpot for him, but you just had a whole different part of the world open up to you too, you know? What comes next is whatever you want, and that's the biggest, scariest, most beautiful part of living."

CHAPTER 26

LEVI

*A*nother text came through as I left Piggly Wiggly.

Mom: Can you stop at Daisy's and get a dozen of those maple Long Johns your dad likes?

"Seriously?" I whispered. Throwing the truck in reverse, I turned away toward Daisy's Nut House. I pulled into the first open spot and tapped out a reply. This was the fourth errand I'd run for her today, each one more random than the last.

Me: I thought you said Dad needed to stop eating so many sweets.

Mom: I know you're not sassing me about something I asked you to do. It's for the office tomorrow, NOT that I need to explain myself to you.

Sighing, I heaved my body out of the truck and jogged into the diner. It was busy, which it always was at this time of day, and by the time I got back into the truck with a box of fresh Long Johns, I was beyond ready to get home and flop face forward into bed.

Funny how last week, I thought a week of silence from Joss felt like forever. Now, two days seemed like two months.

Brian was fine with me taking a couple of days, reassuring me that he knew what a big move this was, and that I needed to make sure it was the right fit for me too.

That I knew.

I'd known it from the moment I walked through the doors and into the practice facility on the outskirts of Seattle. The fit was more than perfect. But signing the dotted line and pressing my foot down on the gas pedal without more clarity from the person who held my heart in her incredibly stubborn hands was a bit more complicated.

"You just need to keep busy is all," my mom had said earlier that morning when I finished working out, unleashing my frustrations on the heavy bag bolted to the ceiling in the corner. "I've got an errand you can run. It'll keep you from moping."

One errand turned to two, then three, then four. If I got another text from her, I'd toss my phone into a lake. Mainly because she'd been dead wrong. Staying busy didn't help. Nothing helped. I was ready to crawl out of my skin.

I wanted to shake her. Kiss her. Make love to her. Fold her in my arms and promise her that we could do this. That it would be as amazing for her as it would be for me. But it was easy for me to say, the one with the job offer and a sure thing waiting at the end of a very long trip.

My truck rumbled slowly through town, my hands turning the wheel by rote.

I'd driven these streets my entire life and recognized almost every person I passed. People who I went to high school with now walked down the sidewalk with their spouses, maybe a kid or two.

My phone rang as I took a right toward my parents' house and I groaned.

But when I picked up, it was Connor.

"Hey," I said with a smile. "How was the honeymoon?"

He sighed contentedly. "So good that I won't tell you shit about it."

I laughed. "Did you even leave the room?"

"Oh, once or twice," he drawled. His voice turned serious. "Hey, we were gonna stop by and say hi to Mom and Dad now that we're back. You around?"

"I'll be back in about five minutes. I'm out running some errands for Mom."

"All right. See you later."

He hung up, and I tossed my phone onto the bench next to me.

But when I pulled in, I didn't see his car or Sylvia's.

What I did see had my heart racing.

In the middle of the driveway, with her arms crossed and two bags on the ground next to her, was Jocelyn.

It wasn't the stubborn set of her mouth that had me pausing before I got out of the truck. It wasn't even the bags next to her. It was the look in her eyes—my favorite coffee mug blue, the one I used every day because its color came closer to hers than anything I'd ever been able to find—was brimming with a challenge. On fire with it.

Try to get rid of me. I dare you.

I was smiling as I opened the door, and it had her lips curling back at me.

"Beautiful afternoon," I said, leaning up against the ticking, clicking hood of the truck as I faced her.

"It is."

I found myself staring at her lips, which widened even farther at my pointed study.

"What are you doing here, Joss?" I asked, lifting my eyes to hers.

"I'm picking you up."

One eyebrow lifted slowly. "That so? Where are we going?"

Casually, she lowered her hands into her lap. "We're going to the airport."

That had me straightening and walking toward her. "We're, what now?"

"Lord save us from a master's grad." She sighed, rolling her eyes. "Airport. Planes. Flying."

I gave her a long look.

Now her nerves showed just a touch in the quick swallow. The slight flush to her high cheekbones. The rapid blink of her long lashes. "We're going to look at apartments in Washington. After you sign your contract."

"Joss," I said, crouching in front of her and gripping her hands with mine. But I'd be a fool to deny that excitement had my skin buzzing like a split open wire. "I could've handled that about a million times better. I don't blame you for being upset."

"Shut up," she whispered, bringing our hands to her mouth so she could kiss our intertwined fingers, just as I had a couple of days ago. "Yeah, you should've told me right away. You could've brought up it up a different way. Coulda woulda shoulda doesn't matter right now. It's done. We're both stubborn, and I'll probably always freak out over things that surprise me, just like you'll probably have neat little names to the way you feel long before I do. I will definitely drive you insane from time to time."

"Oh, that's a guarantee, Sonic."

She laughed. "I want to go with you. I want to do this together."

"You're sure?" I whispered, sliding my hand around the back of her neck.

Joss nodded. "Someone will think it's crazy. Think we're too young, or we haven't been together long enough, but that doesn't matter either."

"No?" I was so impossibly in love with her. "What does matter?"

Her fist clutched at my shirt and pulled me in so that her forehead rested on mine. "What matters is that it's you and me. It always has been. Five days, five weeks, five months or years, the time doesn't matter. The only thing that matters is that you love me"—she paused, pulling back so that I could see her eyes—"and that I'm just as in love with you."

I wrapped my arms around her, lifting her easily from her chair as we sank back together onto the ground. She sat on my haunches, her arms tight around my neck. My mouth found hers, and the kiss that was waiting was sweet and full of promise. Her tongue touched mine as her fingers dug into my hair.

We stayed there, lips brushing softly, her nose grazing mine and the curls escaping from her ponytail tickling the side of my face.

I pulled back and smiled. "Did you really pack my bag?"

"I did. Do you know how many boxer briefs you have?"

"I hate doing laundry."

She laughed. "So do I. Heaven help us."

I glanced back at the bags—one for her and one for me. "So this wasn't just for show?"

"Nope." Joss tilted her head to the house. "The errands your mom sent you on were to give me enough time to pull this off. She booked the tickets while I packed."

"Nice work," I muttered, trying to ignore the warm, aching spot in the middle of my chest at the fact she'd done all this. That she was in this with me. That she was mine. "When do we have to leave for the airport?"

She lifted her arm to look at her watch. "In about fifteen minutes. I'll need extra time to get through security."

I slid my hands up her back, tilted my head to the sky, and whooped loudly. "We're going to Seattle!"

Joss was laughing when I kissed her deeply.

"You're excited now," she said. "Just wait until the apartment hunt begins."

I held still while she braced her hands on her chair and lifted herself up into it. "Why's that?"

"Are you kidding?" She lifted her bag into her lap and handed me mine. "You'll need space for a big dog and a place with big doors for me. I'm a high maintenance roommate."

My hands gripped her armrests as she tilted her chin up for another kiss. "You're forgetting a really, really big bed," I whispered.

"I love you," she told me, eyes sparkling and mouth stretched in a smile.

"Because I want a big bed for us?" I teased.

Joss shook her head. "Because of all of it. Just ... because you're you."

We kissed slowly. I might have been a man cursed, but when she took my hand, nothing else mattered.

EPILOGUE

JOCELYN

Two months later

"*I* swear, if you don't move these boxes out of here today, I'm kicking you out."

His heavy sigh was loud from the bathroom attached to our bedroom. "The romance is dead already, huh?"

When I snickered loudly, Nero lifted his head from where he was curled up on Levi's side of the bed. I folded the sweater in my lap and added it to the pile of laundry. "It will be if you don't move them."

Levi popped his head out of the doorway, his toothbrush stuck in the side of his mouth. "I'll move the boxes, but Sonic, you're stuck with me."

My lips curved up because this was about the fifteenth time he'd made comments like that in the past couple of weeks since we'd made the long drive to Washington.

Not-so-subtle remarks about our future, the certainty of us being together. He wasn't making them because he thought I needed the reassurance. I was all in, happier than I ever could have imagined, even among the chaos and stress that came with a cross-country move.

"Eh," I said flippantly. "Maybe I'll find some swoony Seattle hipster who knows his recycling rules and would *never* let boxes fill up the second bedroom because he knows they could be used to make some fancy hipster paper or something."

Levi attacked from behind, burying his mouth in the side of my neck and blowing raspberries into my skin while I laughed helplessly. His arms wrapped around me as the tickles turned into sweet kisses onto the curve of my shoulder. My hands gripped his forearms, holding his sexy, frustrating, non-box moving ass in place.

When he sucked the lobe of my ear into his mouth, my nails dug into his skin. I felt his lips curve up into a smile when they did.

"No hipsters for you, Miss Abernathy," he whispered, pecking a kiss on my upturned lips before he sat in front of me on the edge of the bed and took my hands in his.

"You know, I had no clue that underneath your easygoing façade was a chest-beating, possessive Neanderthal just waiting to be unleashed." My words were meant to tease, but sometimes, I couldn't help but marvel at how sure, how certain he was. We were so young even though, by Green Valley standards, we should've been married already at this age. In Seattle, though, we had a decade to go before anyone expected us to be settled and popping out babies.

His eyes searched mine, his mouth opening and closing a couple of times before he spoke.

"There's something I never told you," he said, his fingers twining through mine. "And it might sound a little ... crazy."

"Oh gosh, now what?" I eyed him. "Is it some weird, disgusting quirk you've hidden all these years? Because we signed a twelve-month lease, and I really don't want to move again if you're about to tell me something about you is a deal breaker."

Our house—a small two-bedroom bungalow on the south side of Bellevue—was perfect for us. All on one floor, wide doorways, a covered patio large enough for Nero to be able to go outdoors, and a kitchen that I could maneuver easily in. After our first trip to Seattle, we'd both decided that downtown life wasn't for us even though we loved to explore it on the weekends. If he was about to tell me something freaky, I'd really, honestly kick his ass out and keep the house for myself because I loved it.

"I don't think it's deal breaker status," he murmured, still smiling at me. Ugh, we were disgusting. All he had to do was *smile* in my general direction, and I wanted him to do naughty things to me. "Do you remember me telling you about when my parents met?"

Insert my confused blinking. "Uhh, I think so? They were super young, right?"

Levi nodded. "Fifteen. My dad told us the story a hundred times growing up. Just like we heard the story about how his dad met his mom. And how my great-grandpa met my great-grandma and the same for their parents."

"Levi," I said on a laugh, "what are you talking about?"

He let out a slow breath. "I used to think their stories were crazy, that it wasn't true, that the men in our family were ... cursed in love."

My eyes narrowed. "What now?"

"Not cursed in a bad way," he rushed to add. "But, it's like, every man in the Buchanan family falls in love once, and it's fast, and once they meet her, they know. And there's no going back, no one else could ever come close."

As he said it, eyes serious and glowing and intense in a way I'd never seen, I felt my cheeks get hot. But still, I laughed under my breath. "You can't be serious."

"Trust me, until the day I saw you, I thought the entire thing was just some wacky Southern family story."

I licked my lips. "And what happened the day you met me?"

Levi smiled again, and I felt that smile in my heart.

"My world shifted," he answered, leaning forward to give me a soft kiss. "I don't know how else to explain it. Before then, I would've bet a million dollars that love at first sight wasn't real, couldn't be real."

I sat back, staring into his face. "Levi, you're seriously telling me that the day you saw me, not even the day we talked, you fell in love with me. That some weird family legend had us ... like, fated or something?"

He shrugged one shoulder. "I don't know what terms to use, Sonic.

Fate or destiny or a curse, all I know is that once I met you, there'd never be anyone else. Not ever."

"That's why you asked me out even though we'd barely spoken," I said, my brain furiously trying to replay that day in the community center more than five years earlier. It wasn't cemented in my memory, not like it was for him, I had to assume. For me, it was the day I met my best friend, and some snippets of it were clear, and some were fuzzy. I rubbed a hand over my heart, that organ currently flopping around in my chest like a gasping fish.

"Are you freaked out?" His thumb traced the knuckles of the hand he was still holding.

I was shaking my head before I'd really processed my answer. "No. Not freaked out."

With a laugh, he cupped my face and pressed a sweet, sweet, lingering kiss on my lips. "Good. Because I kinda like living with you."

"I love you," I told him, my mouth brushing against his as I spoke the words. "I'm really glad that your wacky family curse exists."

He laughed. "Me too, Sonic. Me too."

We kissed again when I abruptly pulled back. "Dude, you're going to be late. What are you doing?"

"*Dude*," he repeated, "I've got plenty of time."

Our house was about thirty minutes north of the Wolves training facility, and he was supposed to be at work in forty-five minutes.

"You're not even dressed, Levi."

He rolled his eyes but stood from the bed, dropping a kiss on my head as he did. "It'll take me four minutes to get ready."

"Men," I muttered. "You don't even know how easy you have it."

Levi was still laughing as he grabbed some athletic pants and his black Washington pullover. His phone buzzed from the top of our dresser, and I turned my chair so I could grab it for him.

Grady: Tell me that moving to Green Valley is a good idea because I think I'm trying to talk myself out of it.

. . .

With a grin, I handed him the phone, watching his smile broaden as he read his cousin's text.

"So obviously Grady hasn't been *cursed* yet," I said.

Levi typed out a response before looking up at me. "Not yet, but they were raised by their mom out in California, so I don't think they ever actually thought it was true. She and my uncle Glenn had a nasty divorce when I was little; I don't even remember them being married because they met at college out west. Kinda makes it hard to believe in love at first sight if your parents are the example, you know?"

I nodded. "Are he and Grace really moving to Green Valley?"

Levi shrugged. "I don't know. I told him they should. Uncle Glenn would love having them around more and so would my parents. And I think it would be good for both of them. Grace hates her job in LA, and Grady's whatever the hell tech job he does is going to send him to an early grave. I told him he should start a new business in Green Valley. Guided hikes and camping trips and stuff, bring in companies to do employee retreats and morale building stuff. He could make a killing if he found the right partner."

"I think they should too," I said, thinking about my conversation with Grace at the wedding. "Besides, that town could use some new Buchanan blood now that you're gone."

"I suppose it could."

"And," I added, "maybe the Buchanan curse only works in Green Valley. They might move there and find their person right away."

Levi froze, glancing over at me with a speculative gleam in his eye. "Why, Miss Abernathy, I think you may have just figured out something that no one in our entire family ever has."

I snagged the front of his shirt and dragged him down for a kiss. "That's because I'm a freaking genius."

"My humble little hedgehog," he said against my mouth.

"You're going to be late." I shoved at his chest.

"Love you," he called out as he left the room.

I didn't respond, waiting until he paused at the end of the hallway to look over his shoulder at me.

"Don't you have something you want to say to me, Joss?"

"Move the boxes, Levi, then I will."

"Stubborn, crazy-ass woman," he muttered.

"And I love you too," I shouted right before he left.

When he passed the bedroom window on the way to his truck, I caught the wide smile on his face.

If figuring out what I wanted was the biggest, scariest, most beautiful part of living, then I was in for the biggest, scariest, most beautiful life, because this, *exactly this*, was what I wanted.

The End

ACKNOWLEDGMENTS

I feel like I need to start with thanking Penny Reid, first and foremost. The mastermind and evil genius behind Smartypants Romance, and who introduced this group of authors to each other and gave us an opportunity that we'll never forget. Some I knew before, most I didn't, and it's been such a mind-blowing experience. (M.E. Carter, Jiffy Kate and Ellie Kay, especially, who dealt with the most, in regard to my rambling messages and random questions.)

Besides Penny (and Fiona Fischer!), the biggest, hugest, longest cyber hug is reserved for Brittany Sisk. THANK YOU, Brittany, for making sure Joss was realistic. For making sure that she made sense for someone who sees the world from the same vantage point. Your sense of humor and candor about the reality of your life absolutely influenced Joss, and I could not be more grateful that you were willing to read for me and give me such wonderful, honest, and helpful feedback.

To my husband, my boys and my mom, who helped me basically disappear for 22 days to finish this draft.

To Kathryn Andrews, for being such a good friend, and being such a valued set of eyes on this book.

To Caitlin Terpstra, for always being willing to read for me.

To Fiona and Staci, even though you didn't read this one for me, you still talked me through a LOT and encouraged me to take this chance.

To my Lord and Savior, for everything.

For more information on Transverse Myelitis, please visit myelitis.org

ABOUT THE AUTHOR

Karla Sorensen has been an avid reader her entire life, preferring stories with a happily-ever-after over just about any other kind. And considering she has an entire line item in her budget for books, she realized it might just be cheaper to write her own stories. She still keeps her toes in the world of health care marketing, where she made her living pre-babies. Now she stays home, writing and mommy-ing full time (this translates to almost every day being a 'pajama day' at the Sorensen household...don't judge). She lives in West Michigan with her husband, two exceptionally adorable sons, and big, shaggy rescue dog.

Website: http://www.karlasorensen.com/
Facebook: http://www.facebook.com/karlasorensenbooks
Goodreads: https://www.goodreads.com/author/show/13563232.Karla_Sorensen
Twitter: http://www.twitter.com/ksorensenbooks
Instagram: https://www.instagram.com/karla_sorensen/

Find Smartypants Romance online:
Website: www.smartypantsromance.com
Facebook: www.facebook.com/smartypantsromance/
Goodreads: www.goodreads.com/smartypantsromance
Twitter: @smartypantsrom
Instagram: @smartypantsromance
Newsletter: https://smartypantsromance.com/newsletter/

Made in the USA
San Bernardino, CA
22 January 2020